The ragazzi

The ragazzi

by Pier Paolo Pasolini

Translated from the Italian
by Emile Capouya

CARCANET

FIRST PUBLISHED IN ITALY IN 1955 AS
Ragazzi di Vita

Published in 1986 by
CARCANET PRESS LIMITED
208–212 Corn Exchange, Manchester M4 3BQ, UK
and 108 East 31st Street, New York, NY 10016, USA

British Library Cataloguing in Publication Data
    Pasolini, Pier Paolo
        The Ragazzi.——2nd ed.
        I. Title   II. Ragazzi di Vita, *English*
        853'.914[F]   PQ4835.A48

        ISBN 0-85635-605-0
        ISBN 0-85635-691-3 (p)

The publisher acknowledges financial assistance from
the Arts Council of Great Britain.

Printed in England by SRP Ltd, Exeter

Contents

1 The Ferrobedò 7

2 Riccetto 32

3 Night in the Villa Borghese 65

4 The ragazzi 88

5 The Warm Nights 116

6 Swimming in the Aniene 159

7 In the City 187

8 The Old Hag 232

1 · The Ferrobedò

Below Mazzini's monument . . .
—*Popular song*

It was a very hot July day. Riccetto, who was going to make his first Communion and be confirmed, had been up by five o'clock, but as he went down by the Via Donna Olimpia in his gray long pants and his white shirt, rather than a first communicant or a little soldier of Jesus, he looked like a kid roaming around down by the Tiber, trying to make a pickup. In a troop of boys like himself, all in white shirts, he went down toward the church of the Divina Provvidenza, where at nine o'clock Don Pizzuto gave him Holy Communion and at eleven the Bishop confirmed him. But Riccetto was in a hurry to take off. From Monteverde down to the Trastevere station, all that you could hear was a steady drone of motor vehicles. You could hear the horns, and the motors revving up on their way uphill and around the curves, filling with their deafening rumble the outskirts of the city, already burning under the morning sun. As soon as the Bishop's short sermon was over, Don Pizzuto and two or three young priests led the boys to the playground to have their pictures taken. The Bishop walked among them, blessing the parents kneeling in his path. Riccetto felt a gnawing in his insides and decided to skip the whole thing. He went out through the empty church, but at the door he ran into his godfather, who said, "Hey, where you going?" "Going home," called Riccetto, "I'm hungry." "Come to my house, you little bastard," his godfather yelled after him, "we're having lunch." But Riccetto took no notice of him, running away along the asphalt pavement that was simmering in the heat. All Rome was one droning rumble. Only up on the heights was there silence, but the atmosphere there was as charged as a land mine. Riccetto changed his clothes.

It's a short way from Monteverde Vecchio to the Granatieri. You go by the Prato, and cut in among the buildings under construction around the Viale dei Quattro Venti: garbage piles, unfinished houses already in ruins, great muddy excavations, slopes heaped with junk. The Via Abate Ugone was just down the way. The crowd streamed up from the quiet asphalt streets of Monteverde Vecchio toward the Grattacieli.* Now you could even make out the trucks in endless columns, with half-tracks, motorcycles, and armored cars among them. Riccetto plunged into the crowd heading for the warehouses.

Over there the Ferrobedò was like an immense courtyard, a walled-in field sunk in a valley, as big as a town square or a cattle market. Gateways were set into the rectangular wall. On one side were the rows of wooden dwellings, on the other the warehouses. Riccetto traveled the length of the Ferrobedò with the yelling crowd and stopped in front of one of the houses. But there were four Germans who kept them from going in. Beside the door was an overturned table. Riccetto shouldered it and ran toward the gateway. Just outside he bumped into a boy who said, "What you doing?" "I'm taking it home, what

---

* Literally, "skyscrapers."—*Trans.*

do you think?" said Riccetto. "Come on with me, stupid, we can get better stuff than that."

"Coming," said Riccetto. He dropped the table, and someone passing by picked it up.

He went back into the Ferrobedò with the boy and made his way toward the warehouses. There he picked up a coil of hemp rope. Then the boy said, "Come here and get these nails." So, with the rope and nails and other stuff, Riccetto made five round trips to Donna Olimpia. The midafternoon sun was cracking the paving stones, but the Ferrobedò was still full of people competing with the trucks running by Trastevere, Porta Portese, Matatoio, and San Paolo, making the scorching air ring with deafening noise. Returning from the fifth trip, Riccetto and the boy saw a horse and cart by the wall, right between two small buildings. They sidled over to see if there was any way they could pull the job off. Then Riccetto found a cache of arms in one of the buildings and slung a submachine gun over his shoulder and stuck two pistols in his belt. Armed to the teeth, he got up on the horse's back.

But a German came and chased them away.

While Riccetto was carting coils of rope from the warehouses to Donna Olimpia, Marcello was with the other boys, among the buildings in Buon Pastore. The pond swarmed with kids, ducking themselves and yelling. In the dirty field surrounding the pond other kids were playing with a football.

Agnolo asked, "Where's Riccetto?"

"He went to his first Communion," Marcello shouted.

"The shitheel!" said Agnolo.

"He's probably having lunch with his godfather," Marcello added.

They still hadn't heard the news up there by the pond in

Buon Pastore. The sun beat down in silence on the Madonna del Riposo, the Casaletto, and beyond it, Primavalle. On their way back from swimming they passed by the Prato, where there was a German camp.

They started to reconnoiter, but a motorcycle and sidecar came by, and the German in the sidecar yelled at the boys: "Rausch! Contaminated area!" The military hospital was close by. "What the hell do we care?" yelled Marcello. Meanwhile the motorcycle had slowed down. The German jumped out of the sidecar and gave Marcello a slap that sent him spinning. With his mouth swelling up, Marcello twisted away like a snake, and stampeding down the slope with the others, he made a vulgar noise at the German. Running away, laughing and yelling, they finally came to the barracks. There they met some other boys. "What you been doing?" said the others, who were dirty and messy.

"Why?" asked Agnolo. "What's there to do?"

"If you want to see something, go on up to the Ferrobedò."

So they rushed off, and when they got there they trooped noisily into the workshop. "Let's take the engine apart!" yelled Agnolo. But Marcello left the workshop and found himself right where everything was happening, in front of the oil sump. He was just about to fall in, and drown like an Indian in quicksand, when a yell stopped him in his tracks. "Hey, Marcè! Look out! Hey, Marcè!" It was that little bastard Riccetto, with some friends. So he went off with them. They entered a warehouse and grabbed cans of grease, drive-belts for lathes and bundles of steel rods. Marcello carried home a hundred pounds of iron and dumped it in the alleyway where his mother wouldn't notice it right away. He hadn't been home since morning. His mother cuffed him. "Where have you been, you good-for-nothing?" she yelled. "I was only in swimming," answered Marcello, a bit round-shouldered and skinny as a

grasshopper, trying to fend off her slaps. Then his big brother
came home and saw the loot in the alleyway. "You little jerk,"
he yelled. "He stole this stuff, the little bastard." So Marcello
went back to the Ferrobedò with his brother, and this time
they carried off auto tires from a wagon. Evening was falling
and the sun was hotter than ever. The Ferrobedò was still as
crowded as a carnival; you couldn't move at all. Every once
in a while someone would yell, "Run! Run! Here come the
Germans!" so that the others would run away and he could
steal everything himself.

The next day Riccetto and Marcello, who were beginning to
enjoy the whole thing, went down to the general market, which
was closed. A big crowd was milling around and there were
some Germans, walking up and down and shooting into the
air. But even more than the Germans, it was the Italian
African Police who were keeping people out and in general
breaking balls. The crowd kept growing anyway, pushing
against the gratings, screaming, howling, cursing. Then the
attack began in earnest, and even those stinking Italian cops
decided to give it up as a bad job. The streets around the
market were black with people and the market itself empty as
a graveyard, under a sun that beat down mercilessly. When
the gratings went, the market filled up in a second.

There wasn't a thing in the market proper, not even a
cabbage stalk. The crowd began to swirl around the warehouses,
under the sheds, among the stalls; they couldn't resign themselves to going away empty-handed. At last a group of kids
found a storeroom that seemed to be full of goods. Through
the grating you could see piles of auto tires and inner tubes,
oilcloth, tarpaulins, and, on the shelves, molds for pressing
cheese. The word went out immediately. Five or six hundred
people swarmed in after the first few. The door was kicked in
and the crowd poured into the storeroom, jammed together.

Riccetto and Marcello were right in the middle. They were sucked in by the human tide and went through the doorway almost without touching their feet to the ground. They went down by a spiral staircase; the people in back pushed forward, and some women, half-suffocated, began to scream. The spiral stair overflowed with people. The thin iron handrail gave, then broke, and a woman fell through screaming and pitched headfirst against a step. The crowd outside kept pushing forward. "She's dead!" a man inside the storeroom yelled. Panic-stricken women began to shriek, "She's dead!" No one could get in or out. Marcello kept on moving down the stairs. At the bottom, he hopped over the woman's body, charged into the storeroom, and began to fill a basket with inner tubes; so did the other boys, who were picking up anything that wasn't nailed down. Riccetto had disappeared; he must have managed to get out. The crowd had thinned. Marcello stepped over the dead woman again and ran toward home.

At the Ponte Bianco there were some militiamen. They stopped him and took the stuff away. But he wouldn't leave. He stood to one side with his empty basket, feeling terrible. In a little while Riccetto came up to the Ponte Bianco from the Caciara.

"Well?"

"They took the inner tubes off me, they robbed them off me," said Marcello, looking black.

"What do those bastards think they're doing? Why don't they mind their own fucking business?" yelled Riccetto.

There were no houses by the Ponte Bianco, only a huge construction lot at the end of which, right where the Viale dei Quattro Venti passed through a ravine as deep as a stream-bed, Monteverde's limestone hill rose up. Riccetto and Marcello sat down in the nearby sunbeaten field, all black and bare, to watch the Italian African Police giving people a hard time.

Then after a while a group of boys carrying sacks full of cheese reached the Ponte Bianco. The Italian African Police threatened to stop them, but the boys faced up to them and started to argue, and they looked so mean that the police thought it better to give it up as a bad job. They let the boys keep their stuff, and they even returned the stuff they had robbed off Marcello and the others, who had come back looking ready for trouble. Running and skipping, and figuring up the profits, Riccetto and Marcello started for Donna Olimpia, and the others went their own ways too. The only thing left at the Ponte Bianco, besides the Italian African Police, was the smell of garbage stewing in the sun.

At the foot of the Monte di Splendore was an area of beaten earth, a plateau, six or eight feet above the level of the surrounding ground, which cut off the view of Monteverde and the Ferrobedò, and, on the horizon, the line traced by the sea. There, one Saturday when the younger boys were tired of playing, some older boys began to kick a soccer ball around near the gate. They formed a circle and passed the ball around, giving it nice quick taps with the insides of their feet to make it sail along close to the ground, not trying to score. In a little while they were all soaked with sweat, but they didn't want to take off their good jackets, or their blue woolen sweaters with black or yellow stripes, because of the casual, joking way they had started playing. And since the younger boys who stood around watching might have thought they were showing off, playing in the hot sun all dressed up like that, they laughed and clowned around, but in a way that didn't encourage anyone else to join in.

Passing and blocking the shots, they kidded one another. "Jesus, you're half-dead today, Alvo," cried a dark boy whose hair was slicked down with brilliantine. "Those women'll get you in the end," he added, returning the ball. "Fuck you," answered Alvaro, a youth with a bony, pushed-in face, and a big head that would make a louse die of old age before it could finish the round trip. He tried to pull a fast one, using his heel on the ball, but he didn't connect right and he drove it a long way, over toward Riccetto and the other younger boys who were sprawled on the dusty grass.

Agnolo, the redhead, got up and, taking his time, sent the ball back. "You don't want to strain your milk," Rocco yelled to Alvaro. "We're going to have to sweat tonight."

"They're going after some pipe," Agnolo said to the others. At that moment the three o'clock whistle blew at the Ferrobedò and at the other distant factories, down by Testaccio, the Porto, and San Paolo. Riccetto and Marcello stood up and without saying a word to anyone went down along the Via Ozanam, and slouched along half-dead under the burning July sun toward the Ponte Bianco, where they could hitch a ride on the number 13 or the number 28. They had gone into business with their Ferrobedò stock, and had kept it up when the Americans came, but now they were back to picking up butts. It's true that Riccetto had worked at a job for a while: he had been taken on as helper at a truck service station in Monteverde Nuovo. But then he had stolen five hundred lire from the boss and the guy had fired him. So now he did nothing all afternoon, hanging around Donna Olimpia on the Monte di Casadio, that little yellow hummock in the sun, playing with the other boys, or bothering the women who came to spread out their wash on the shriveled grass later in the day. Or else they went and played ball in the empty space between the Grattacieli and the Monte di Splendore, hundreds of boys playing in the back lots invaded by the sun, in the dried-up fields around the Via Ozanam or the Via Donna Olimpia, or in front of the Franceschi elementary-school buildings, filled with hooky-players and dropouts.

The Ponte Garibaldi, when Riccetto and Marcello got there and started climbing down the pilings, was empty under the African sun; but among the pilings under the bridge the stream was alive with bathers. Riccetto and Marcello stopped for a while, the only ones on the bridge, and with their chins on the ruined iron railing, they stood and watched the river men taking the sun in their boats, or playing cards, or shuttling across the stream. Then, after arguing a little over the best way to go, they hitched a ride again on the half-empty old trolley that creaked and rumbled its way toward San Paolo. At the Ostia station they jumped down and fooled around among the tables in the station bar, around the newsstand, the waiting-room benches, and the railed passage in front of the ticket office, looking for butts. But they were already sick of the whole thing. The heat made it hard to breathe; it would have been murder if it hadn't been for the bit of breeze that was coming from the sea. "Hey, Riccè," said Marcello in a rage, "why can't *we* go swimming?" Twisting his mouth and shrugging his shoulders, Riccetto said, "Let's go."

Behind the Parco Paolino and the golden façade of San Paolo, the Tiber flowed past a levee covered with posters. The river bank on this side was empty—no buildings, no boats, no bathers—but over on the right it bristled with cranes, masts, and chimneys; there was an enormous gas tank outlined against the sky, and then all Monteverde on the horizon, rising above the smelly, sunburned terraces with their old houses looking like little boxes drowning in the sunlight. At the boys' feet were the pilings of a bridge that had never been completed, and the dirty water was making whirlpools around them. The bank near San Paolo was all reeds and brush. Riccetto and Marcello ran down to the first piling, and were right at the water. But the place where they went to bathe was nearer the sea, a quarter of a mile downstream, where the Tiber began a long curve.

Riccetto was naked, lying on his back in the weeds with his hands clasped beneath his head, looking up at the sky.

"You ever been to Ostia?" he asked Marcello suddenly. "Hell, yes," answered Marcello, "didn't you know I was born there?" "Hell, no," said Riccetto, looking at him speculatively, "you never said nothing about it." "So what?" said the other. "Were you ever out at sea in a boat?" Riccetto asked curiously. "Sure," said Marcello slyly. "Whereabouts?" asked Riccetto. "Jesus, Riccè, you ask a lot of questions," Marcello said, quite pleased with himself. "Who the hell remembers? I wasn't even three years old then." "Yeah, you've been out in a boat about as much as I have, fathead," said Riccetto sarcastically. "What a pain," Marcello promptly replied. "We went out every day in my uncle's sailboat." "Fuck you," said Riccetto, making a noise with his mouth. "Hey, salvage!" he said, watching the water. "Hey, salvage!" The current was carrying some wreckage, a broken chest and a chamber pot. Riccetto and Marcello moved to the water's edge, which was black with oil. "Jesus, I'd like to have a ride in a boat," Riccetto said, sounding discouraged, as he watched the chest pursue its destiny, bobbing up and down among the garbage. "Don't you know you can rent boats at Ciriola's?" asked Marcello. "Yeah, and who'll give us the money?" Riccetto said dejectedly. "Why don't we go after pipe ourselves, what the hell?" asked Marcello, all excited at the idea. "Agnoletto's already got hold of a wrench." "Hey," said Riccetto, "I'm with you."

They stayed till late in the afternoon, stretched out with their heads resting on their dusty, sweaty pants, but at last they found the energy to get up and leave. All around them were bushes and dry reeds, but under the water there were only pebbles and gravel. They played at skipping stones across the water, and even after they had made up their minds to leave they kept it up, still half-naked, throwing the pebbles high into the air, toward the opposite shore, or at the swallows skimming over the surface of the river.

Then they started throwing whole handfuls of gravel, yelling and laughing: the pebbles fell everywhere among the bushes. Suddenly they heard a shout, as if someone were calling to them. They turned, and a short distance away through the already darkening air they saw a Negro kneeling in the grass. Riccetto and Marcello understood right away, and started to leave; but as soon as they were a little way off they each picked up a handful of gravel and threw it toward the bushes.

With her breasts half out of her dress, the whore got up in a spitting rage and started to scream at them.

"Ah, shut up!" yelled Riccetto, making a megaphone with his hands. "Your ass is sucking wind, you dirty no-good bitch!" But at that moment the Negro sprang to his feet like a wild man, and holding up his pants with one hand and brandishing a knife in the other, began to run after them. Riccetto and Marcello ran out from among the bushes, shouting for help, toward the high bank and the path that led over it. When they got to the top they dared to look back for a moment, and they saw the Negro down below, waving the knife in the air and yelling. Riccetto and Marcello went on running, and looking at each other, they laughed and laughed. Riccetto finally threw himself down on the dusty ground and rolled over and over. He laughed at Marcello and shouted, "Jesus! It felt like you was paralyzed, didn't it, Marcè?"

They had been running along the Tiber, in the direction of the façade of San Paolo, still glowing faintly in the sun. They went on down toward the Parco Paolino, full of workmen scattered among the young trees and soldiers on passes from the barracks. They went past the Basilica and turned into a dark, empty street where a blind man was begging, sitting with his back against the wall and his legs stretched out before him on the sidewalk.

Riccetto and Marcello sat down near him on the edge of the sidewalk to get over their panting, and the old man, hearing their movements, began his complaint. His legs were thick, and between them he held his cap, which was full of coins. Riccetto nudged Marcello with his elbow and nodded toward the blind man. "Hey, relax," Marcello whispered. When his breathing had quieted down, Riccetto nudged Marcello again, looking annoyed and gesturing with his hand as if to say, "Well, how about it?" Marcello shrugged, meaning, "You're in this all by yourself, friend," and Riccetto, turning red with anger, gave him a pitying look. Finally he said in a low voice, "Wait for me over there." Marcello got up and crossed the street to wait for him among the small trees on the other side. After Marcello had gone, Riccetto waited a moment to make sure that no one was coming, moved near the blind man, grabbed the handful of coins in the cap, and ran off. When they were safely away, they stopped to count the coins under a street lamp: It came to nearly five hundred lire.

The next day the Monache convent and the other buildings in the Via Garibaldi had no water.

Riccetto and Marcello had bumped into Agnolo in front of the Giorgio Franceschi elementary-school buildings in Donna Olimpia. Agnolo and some other boys were kicking a ball around with no light other than the moon's. They asked him to go get the wrench, and he didn't wait to be asked twice. Then all three went down toward Trastevere by the Via di San Pancrazio, looking for a quiet spot. They found one in the Via Manara, deserted at that hour, where they could start in on a manhole cover without anyone coming to bother them. They didn't get scared even when a window opened above them and an old woman, half-asleep but all made-up, started to yell, "What's going on down there?" Riccetto raised his head for a moment and called, "It's nothing, lady. We just come to see about a broken water main." By that time they were finished with the job; they took up the manhole cover by either side, Agnolo and Riccetto got under it, and they went off very quietly to a tumbledown building below the Gianicolo that had once been a gymnasium. It was dark there, but the practical Agnolo found a sledgehammer in a corner, and with that they pounded the cover to pieces.

Now they had to find a buyer, but in this case too Agnolo knew the right answer. They turned into the Vicolo dei Cinque, deserted except for a few drunks. Under the junkman's window, Agnolo cupped his hands around his mouth and called, "Hey, Antò!" The junkman came to the window, then came down and let them into his shop, where he weighed the metal and gave them 2700 lire for the seventy kilos. Now that they were at it, they felt like finishing the job. Agnolo ran to the gymnasium to get a hatchet, and they all went off toward the Gianicolo stair. There they lifted up a sewer manhole cover and went down among the pipes. With the hatchet handle they beat in a pipe to stop the flow of water, and then they cut it, removing sixteen or eighteen feet of pipe. They took it to the gymnasium, pounded it to pieces, put it all in a sack, and took it to the junkman, who paid them 150 lire a kilo. Toward midnight, with their pockets full of money, they strolled happily up to the Grattacieli. There Alvaro, Rocco, and the other older boys were playing cards, curled up or sprawled silently on the first landing of the stairway at Rocco's house, which faced one of the many inside courts. Agnolo had to go by there on his way home, and Riccetto and Marcello were keeping him company. So they stopped to play cards with the older boys. In a little over half an hour, they had lost all their money. By good luck, they still had the five hundred lire stolen from the blind man in case they wanted to go for a boat ride down at Ciriola's; Riccetto had it all in his shoe.

"Here comes the kindergarten," said one of the boys on the bathing barge, watching them come down the burning-hot pavement. Riccetto couldn't resist the temptation to jump up and balance himself on the handrail. But he jumped down again to catch up with the others, who had already crossed the short gangplank to the bathhouse afloat on the Tiber and who were each forking over fifty lire to Orazio's wife. Giggetto didn't act pleased to see them. "Over there," he said, and pointed out a single locker for all three. The boys hesitated. "What are you waiting for?" Giggetto burst out, thrusting his arm toward them with the hand held wide open to emphasize how unbecoming their conduct was. "What, am I supposed to take your clothes off for you?"

"Up yours," Agnolo muttered. He pulled his shirt over his head without waiting any longer. Giggetto went right on: "Little ball-breakers. You can all go screw. You and whoever sent you." Humiliated, the three little ball-breakers took their clothes off, and then stood around naked with their clothes in their hands. "Well?" roared Giggetto, coming out from behind the counter. "How about it?" The boys didn't know the drill. Giggetto snatched the clothes out of their hands, tossed them into the locker, and locked it. His little boy watched the three novices with a grin. The other boys hanging around, some naked, some in sagging bathing-trunks, some combing their hair in front of the mirror, some singing, looked around out of the corners of their eyes as if to say, "Get a load of me, will you?" As soon as the boys had gotten into their ragged oversized trunks, they dashed out of the locker room and gathered by the iron railing of the barge. But they were chased away from there immediately. Orazio himself issued from the centrally located bar, with his paralyzed leg and his blood-red face. "Damn you," he yelled, "how many times do I have to tell you you can't stay here, breaking the goddamn railing?" They took off, passing by the showers, followed by Orazio's music, for he went on yelling for ten minutes, sitting in his cane chair. Inside the bar, some of the older boys were playing cards, others were sitting and smoking with their feet up on the rickety tables. At the other end of the little gangplank that stretched from the barge to the shore, Agnolo's puppy was waiting for them, joyous, his tongue lolling out. The sight cheered up the three criminals, and they started to run along the retaining wall, with the dog after them. They stopped for a moment at the diving board, and then they ran on again toward the Ponte Sisto.

It was still very early, no more than one-thirty, and Rome was burning in the sun.

From the Cupolone beyond the Ponte Sisto, to the Isola Tiberina beyond the Ponte Garibaldi, the air was as taut as a drumhead. Silently, between banks that stank like a urinal in the sun, the Tiber flowed as yellow as if it were casting up all the garbage it was freighted with. The first bathers to get there, after two o'clock or so, when the six or seven employees who had been hanging around the barge left, were the fuzzy-heads from the Piazza Giudia. Then came the group from Trastevere, down across the Ponte Sisto, long lines of them, half-naked, yelling and laughing, always on the lookout for a chance to play a joke on somebody. Outside Ciriola's, the dirty little beach filled up, and so did the locker room, the bar, and the deck inside. It was an ant heap. A score of boys clustered around the diving board. Now the first headers, jackknives, and swan dives began. The diving board was no more than five feet high, and even the six-year-olds took plunges off it. Somebody passing by on the Ponte Sisto stopped to watch them. On top of the retaining wall, astride the railing overhung by plane trees, some young boys who were too broke to use the bathhouse watched the bathers. Others lay stretched out on the sand, or on the meager patch of withered grass at the foot of the levee.

Getting to his feet, a dark, hairy little kid yelled to the boys hanging around, "Last one in's a rotten egg!" But nobody paid any attention except Nicchiola, who took off, with his curved and twisted back, and threw himself into the yellow water, his legs and arms spread out, his rear wriggling. The others, clucking their tongues pityingly at the little dark kid, said, "Well, how about it?" and then, moving lazily, got up and moved off like a flock of sheep, up toward the patch of sand beneath the railing by the bathhouse, to watch Monnezza, his feet in the burning sand and his face all red from the strain, lifting the fifty-kilo weight in the midst of an army of boys. Only Riccetto, Marcello, Agnolo, and a few others, and the dog, who was the youngest of all, were left at the diving board. "Well?" said Agnolo to the other two, threateningly. "Fuck you," said Riccetto, "you in a hurry or something?" "Fuck you too," said Agnolo, "what did we come here for?" "What do you say we go in?" said Riccetto, and he walked to the end of the diving board to look at the water..

The dog followed him. Riccetto turned round. "You coming in too?" he asked gaily and affectionately. "You coming in too?" The dog looked at him and wagged its tail.

"You want to dive in, huh?" said Riccetto. He grabbed the dog's fur and pulled it toward the end of the board, but the dog drew back. "You're scared," said Riccetto. "O.k., I won't make you dive in." The dog looked at him, trembling all over.

"What's the matter?" Riccetto asked protectingly, bending down. "What's the matter, you ugly vicious bloodhound?" He patted the dog, scratched its neck, put his hand in its mouth, pulled it along. "Ugly brute," he said affectionately. But the dog, feeling itself pulled forward, was still a little frightened, and it jumped back.

"No, no," said Riccetto, "I won't throw you into the river." Agnolo yelled sarcastically, "You diving, Riccè?" "I got to take a leak first," Riccetto answered, and he ran to piss at the foot of the levee. The dog came after him and watched him, its eyes shining and its tail wagging.

Agnolo took a running jump into the water. "Jesus!" yelled Marcello, seeing him fall lopsided and land belly-first. "Christ!" yelled Agnolo, coming up in the middle of the river. "What a belly-whopper!" "I'll show you how!" yelled Riccetto, and he dived into the water. "How did I do?" he called to Marcello when he came up again. "You had your legs spread," said Marcello. "Got to try it again," said Riccetto, scrambling up the bank.

At that moment, the noisy boys who were hanging around watching Monnezza lift weights came in a body toward the diving board. They came along wearing self-satisfied grins, spitting, the younger boys jumping around them or scuffling and rolling along the gangway. There were more than fifty of them, and all together they invaded the little plot of dirty grass around the board. First Monnezza dived, blond as straw and covered with red freckles, doing a swan dive with all the airs and graces. After him came Remo, Wise Guy, Tar Baby, Fats, Pallante, and even the smallest boys, for they wouldn't back down at all. On the contrary, Ercoletto, from the Vicolo dei Cinque, was probably the best diver of the group; he took his dive running nimbly along the board on his toes with his arms outspread, as if he were dancing. Riccetto and the others moved off a little way, sulking, and sat down on the parched grass to look on in silence. They were like bits of bread tossed onto an ant hill, and they became impatient at being left out, and at having to listen to the pack in full cry. The boys were everywhere, their shanks filthy with mud, their bathing trunks sticking to their bodies, sarcastic looks on their faces, watching and cursing. Mean-faced and bald as an egg, Fats took off, and sliding along the bank at the water's edge, gave a ferocious laugh as he fell in, yelling, "Hey, fuck you!" Remo, on the bank, shaking his head, muttered happily, "Jesus, that's the way!" Then Shorty, over by the footpath, grunted as his head stopped a handful of mud. He turned around in a fury, yelling, "Who the fuck—" But he couldn't find out who had thrown it because everyone was facing the river and laughing. Then he caught another handful with his head. "Fuck you!" he yelled. He started to grab Remo. "What do you want?" Remo asked, looking hurt. "Fuck you and your old man too!" In a minute, hundreds of gobs of mud were whizzing through the air. Someone up to his knees in the stuff was throwing handfuls against the cornice, making a rain of mud fall all around. Others were sitting down to one side, looking innocent, and throwing a handful of mud once in a while when no one was looking, making the missiles hiss like a whiplash. "Fuck the whole bunch of you!" yelled Remo, in the center of the battlefield, pressing his hand to his eye in fury, and he ran to throw himself into the water to get rid of the mud plastered over his eyelids. Seeing him jump in, Monnezza went in after him, yelling, "Last one in's a rotten egg!" And he jumped, curling up and turning over in the air, striking the water loudly with back, knees, and elbows all at once. "Up yours!" laughed Wise Guy, wrinkling up his forehead. He took a running jump and landed like Monnezza. "Pallante!" he yelled. "Who's going to make me?" said Pallante. "Hey, coward," Monnezza and Wise Guy yelled from the water.

"Ah, fuck those guys," Riccetto was muttering to himself. "What the hell are we supposed to be doing anyway?" said Agnolo fiercely. The only one of the three who knew how to row was Marcello. It was up to him to commence operations. They moved off to sit on a pile of rotting skiffs. "Hey, Marcè," said Agnolo, "we'll wait for you, go ahead." Marcello got up and began to wander toward Guaione, who was doing a bit of work on the barge with his knife, half-drunk. "How much is it for a boat?" he asked point-blank. "A hundred fifty," said Guaione without raising his eyes. "You got a boat now?" asked Marcello. "When it comes back. It's out now." "Will it be long?" Marcello asked after a while. "Christ," Guaione said, lifting his bleary drunkard's eyes, "how the fuck do I know? When it comes back." Then he glanced down the river toward the Ponte Sisto. "There it is," he said. "Pay now or later?" "Better now." "I'll go get the money," cried Marcello. But he hadn't thought about Giggetto. He was a great bathing attendant for the older boys, but if they were looking for someone to drown all the little kids, Giggetto would be ready to sign up for the job. Marcello hung around for a while, trying to get his attention, but Giggetto ignored him. He went back to the pile of boats, disconcerted. "How the fuck am I supposed to get the money?" he asked. "Go to Giggetto, you dope." "I been to him," Marcello explained, "but he won't pay no attention to me." "What an idiot!" Agnolo burst out in a rage. "Look," said Marcello, pushing out his open hand in the same gesture that Giggetto had made earlier, "why don't you go?" "Why don't you both square off and fight?" said Riccetto. "I'll give that idiot all the fight he wants," said Agnolo. "I told you already, why the hell don't *you* try, you son of a bitch?"

Agnolo went off to confront Giggetto, and in fact he came right back with the hundred and fifty and a lighted cigarette. They went to the railing to wait for the boat, and as soon as it touched its berth and the other boys came ashore, the three jumped in. It was the first time that Riccetto and Agnolo had ever been in a boat.

At first the boat wouldn't budge. The more Marcello rowed, the more it stayed where it was. Then, little by little, it began to pull away from the barge, ranging this way and that as if it were drunk. "You little fuck-up!" Agnolo yelled with all the lung power he had, "you can row, can you?" The boat acted as if it had gone crazy, and wandered aimlessly back and forth, now toward the Ponte Sisto, now toward the Ponte Garibaldi. But the current carried it to the left, toward the Ponte Garibaldi, even if it happened that the bow was pointing the other way, and Guaione, appearing at the railing on the barge, began to yell something to them, the cords standing out on his neck. "What a dope," Agnolo kept shouting to Marcello. "They're going to be fishing us out at Fiumicino." "Will you get off my back?" said Marcello, struggling with the oars, which either waved around in the air or plunged into the water up to the handles. "Why don't you try it? Go ahead." "I don't come from Ostia," Agnolo yelled. Meanwhile Ciriola's was retreating, rising and falling behind the stern of the boat. Under the green of the plane trees, the whole length of the levee was coming into view, all the way from the Ponte Sisto to the Ponte Garibaldi, and the boys scattered along the bank, some at the seesaw, some at the diving board, some on the barge, grew smaller and smaller, and now you could no longer hear their voices.

The Tiber carried the boat toward the Ponte Garibaldi like one of the wooden crates or one of the carcasses floating along in the current; and below the Ponte Garibaldi the water foamed and swirled among the shoals and rocks of the Isola Tiberina. Guaione had realized what was happening, and he kept yelling in his hoarse bargeman's voice. Now the boat had reached the shallows where the little boys who didn't know how to swim ducked and splashed behind a paling of boards. In answer to Guaione's cries, Orazio and some other loafers came out of the main shed to observe the scene. So then Orazio began waving his arms; the older boys were all laughing. Riccetto was looking at Marcello with his eyebrows raised and his arms folded on his chest. "Can't you get this tub to go anywhere?" he asked. But Marcello was beginning to catch on. Now the boat was pointing more or less steadily toward the opposite shore, and the oars were managing to get a grip on the water. "Let's go that way," said Agnoletto. "What the hell do you think I'm doing?" Marcello answered in disgust, running sweat like a fountain.

While the bank near Ciriola's was in full sunlight, the shore here was in soft gray shadow. On the black rocks, covered with two inches of grease, little bushes and green brambles were growing, and here and there in a quiet eddy the water bore nearly motionless scraps of garbage. At last they were alongside the bank, scraping the rocks, and since there was hardly any current, Marcello managed to turn the boat upstream toward the Ponte Sisto. But the port oar kept striking the rocks and Marcello was kept busy trying to see that it didn't splinter or go skittering off along the water. "Let's go out in the middle. What is this, anyway?" Riccetto said, not paying the least attention to Marcello's efforts. He liked to be out in the middle of the river, where he could feel himself surrounded by all that water, and it enraged him that by lifting his eyes a bit he could see, a stone's throw away, the Ponte Sisto and its gray reflection in the turbid water, and then the Gianicolo, and the dome of St. Peter's, fat and white as a

cloud. Little by little, they floated down toward the Ponte
Sisto; there, around the right-hand piling, the river broadened
and slowed, deep, green, and filthy. Since at that point there
was no danger of being carried off by the current, Agnolo
wanted to try his hand at rowing, but he had no luck. The
oars smote the air, or else caught crabs, filling the bottom of
the boat with water. "Aw, fuck you!" shouted Riccetto indig-
nantly, while Marcello, dead tired, stretched out on the bottom
in two inches of tepid water. Seeing Agnolo, who was killing
himself and getting nowhere fast, two boys who had come
down to fish with a cane pole on the steps by Fontanone began
to make fun of him and laugh. Panting, Agnolo yelled,
"What's it to you?" The boys shut up for a moment. Then
they said, "Who taught you how to row? Can't you see, even
the walls are laughing."

"Who taught me how to row?" said Agnolo. "My prick."

"Shove it up your ass," they returned promptly.

"Up yours," yelled Agnolo, red as a pepper.

"Oh, you jerk!" cried the boys.

"Sons of bitches!" yelled Agnolo.

Meanwhile he kept straining away at the oars, but the boat
didn't move an inch. On the other piling, to the left, were
some other sons of bitches. They were stretched along the
joints in the stones like lizards taking the sun half asleep. The
boys' yelling stirred them up. They got to their feet, covered
with white dust, and moved to the edge of the piling nearest
the boat. "Oh, boatman," one of them called, "wait for us."
"What does he want?" asked Riccetto unsuspectingly. Another boy clambered halfway down to the water's edge on
the rings let into the stone, and dived in with a yell. The
others jumped from wherever they were, and they all began
to swim across the river. In a few minutes they had reached
the boat, their hair in their eyes, their faces looking mean,

and their hands stretched out to grasp the gunwales. "What do you want?" asked Marcello. "Want to get into the boat. Why, don't you want us to?" They were all big, and the others had to keep quiet. They climbed in, and without losing any time, one of them said to Agnolo, "Let's have them," and took the oars. "Let's go on the other side of the bridge," he said, looking Agnolo right in the eye as if to say, "Is that O.k. with you?" "Let's go on the other side of the bridge," said Agnolo. The boy started to row with all his strength, but downstream from the piling the current was strong, and the boat was heavily loaded. It took more than fifteen minutes to go those few feet.

> "*Borgo antico,*
> *gray-roofed under a dull sky,*
> *I sing of thee . . .*"

caroled the four big boys from the Vicolo del Bologna, lounging in the boat, as loud as they could so as to be heard by the people passing by on the Ponte Sisto and along the banks. The overloaded boat moved forward, sunk nearly to the gunwales.

Riccetto was still stretched out, paying no attention to the new arrivals, sulking in the water-soaked bottom of the boat, with his head barely showing above the gunwales. He was still pretending to be at sea, out of sight of the mainland. One of the group from Trastevere, who had the face of an old thief, cupped his hands into a megaphone, and standing up in the bow, yelled, "Here come the pirates!" The others went on singing at the tops of their lungs. At one point Riccetto turned on his elbow to look more closely at something that had caught his eye on the surface of the water near the bank, almost beneath the arches of the Ponte Sisto. He couldn't make out what it was. The water was trembling there, making little circles as if it were being splashed by a hand—and in fact in the very center was something that looked like a bit of black rag.

"What's that?" Riccetto asked, getting to his feet. They all looked in that direction at the almost motionless mirror of water under the last arch. "It's a swallow, for Christ's sake!" said Marcello. There were many swallows about, flying close to the retaining wall, under the arches of the bridge, and out on the river, grazing the water with their breasts. The current had sent the boat back a little, and you could see it was a swallow that was drowning. It beat its wings, and kicked. Riccetto was kneeling at the gunwale, leaning out of the boat. "Hey, you dope, don't you see you're going to capsize us?" said Agnolo. "Look at it," cried Riccetto, "it's drowning!" The Trastevere boy who was rowing kept his oars suspended over the water, and the current slowly drew the boat near to where the swallow was struggling. But after a while he lost patience and began to row again. "Hey, you, buddy, who told you to row?" said Riccetto, putting his hand on him. The boy clucked his tongue in disgust, and the biggest boy said, "What the fuck do you care?" Riccetto looked at the swallow, still struggling, its wings quivering spasmodically. Then without a word he jumped into the water and began to swim toward the bird. The others called after him and laughed, but the one at the oars kept on rowing away against the current. Riccetto moved downstream, carried swiftly by the current. They saw him grow smaller in the distance, swim up to the bird in the mirror of stagnant water, and try to catch hold of it. "Hey, Riccetto," yelled Marcello, with all the breath in his body, "why don't you catch it?" Riccetto must have heard him, because they could just make out his voice calling back, "He's pecking me!" "Fuck you!" yelled Marcello, laughing. Riccetto tried to grab the swallow, which escaped by beating its wings, and now both were being carried down toward the pilings by the cur-

rent, which at that point was strong and full of whirlpools.
"Hey, Riccetto!" his friends in the boat yelled at him, "give
it up!" But just then Riccetto managed to catch the bird, and
he began to swim with one arm toward the bank. "Hey, turn
around, come on," said Marcello to the boy who was rowing.
They turned. Riccetto was waiting for them, sitting on the
dirty grass by the water's edge, with the swallow in his hands.
"What good did that do anyway?" said Marcello. "It was
nice watching it drown." Riccetto didn't answer at once. "It's
soaking wet. Let's wait for it to dry out." It didn't take long
for it to dry out; five minutes later it was wheeling among its
companions above the Tiber, and Riccetto couldn't tell it
from the others.

2 · Riccetto

Summer of 1946. At the corner of the Via delle Zoccolette, the rain coming down, Riccetto sees a group of people and slowly drifts over toward them. In the middle of the huddle of thirteen or fourteen people, their umbrellas shining in the wet, was an open black umbrella much larger than the usual sort, on which three cards lay in a row, the ace of diamonds, the ace of hearts, and a six. A Neapolitan was dealing, and the bystanders were betting five hundred, a thousand, even two thousand lire on the cards. Riccetto stood there watching the game for half an hour. A gentleman who was playing doggedly lost on every bet, while some of the other players, also Neapolitans, were losing one and winning one. When that first crowd had had enough, it was already drawing on toward evening. Riccetto went up to the Neapolitan who was shuffling the cards and said, "Say, can I ask you something?"

"Yes," said the Neapolitan, sticking out his chin.

"You're from Naples, right?"

"Yes."

"You play that game in Naples?"

"Yes."

"How do you play it?"

"Well, it's hard, but you get on to it after a while."

"Will you show me how it goes?"

"Yes," said the Neapolitan, "but . . ."

He started to laugh like a man who's thinking out a plan and saying to himself, "Let's see, what am I going to tell this guy?" He wiped his face, which was dripping with water; it was a young face but all wrinkled, and he had thick, pendulous, pouting lips. He looked Riccetto in the eye. "I'll show you, sure," he said, since Riccetto made no move, "but you have to give me a little something for my trouble." "Of course," Riccetto answered seriously.

Meanwhile another crowd was gathering around the umbrella; the other Neapolitans were there too. "Just wait a while," the dealer said, winking, as he dealt out the cards again. Riccetto moved aside, and began to watch the game again. Two hours went by. The rain stopped, and it was almost dark. The Neapolitan finally made up his mind to quit, closed the umbrella, put the cards into his pocket, and looked meaningfully at his companions. There were two of them. One was light-haired and missing some teeth. The other was a stocky man in a three-quarter-length checked tweed coat who looked like a Jew. They listened good-humoredly to the first man, who told them he had some business to see to, and went off gaily with their stuff, even waving good-by to Riccetto.

"Let's go," said the Neapolitan. Riccetto was flush, so they caught the trolley, got off at the Ponte Bianco, and in a few minutes were in Donna Olimpia. Riccetto's mother, sitting in the middle of the single room that was her home—with four beds at the four corners of the walls, which weren't even walls but partitions—looked at the two of them and said, "Who's he?" "A friend of mine," said Riccetto with an authoritative air, not giving an inch. But since she hung around breaking balls, Riccetto looked into the next room, which belonged to Agnolo and his family, to see if the grown-ups were out of the way. It turned out that only two or three of the littlest boys were there, whining, their noses dripping. Riccetto and the Neapolitan went in and sat down on the bed that Agnolo and his little brothers slept in, with its blanket scorched by the iron. The Neapolitan began the lesson.

"There are five of us. One deals and the others stand around like they just happened to be passing by. Let's say I'm the dealer. I start the game, and the others come around the umbrella. People start coming up, and then one of the boys takes off so as to open up the crowd, and then one of the people steps into his place. First he doesn't know whether he wants to play or not. But one of our boys plays. He bets a thousand, two thousand, all according, depending on what he thinks best. While he's taking out his money, the man that's dealing, let's say it's me, well, I change his card, but when I change it I give him the good card, and the no-good card I put in the middle. So you don't know the game and you don't see that I changed the card, so you bet. But then I say, 'If you want to lose, I don't care,' and our boy goes on playing—win one, lose one, win one, lose one. 'O.k., let's see both cards at once.' Then our boy wins and the other loses. When the sucker's lost a couple, then our boy plays again, and let's say he bets a thousand. . . ." The Neapolitan continued for a while, explaining how the game went, and Riccetto listened to him chattering on and on and didn't understand a goddamn thing.

When the Neapolitan had finished, Riccetto said, "Look, I didn't get you. You'll have to tell me again, right from the beginning, if you don't mind." But just then Agnolo's mother came in. "Excuse us, Sora Celeste," said Riccetto, leaving hurriedly, with the Neapolitan behind him. "I just had to tell my friend here something." Sora Celeste, black and hairy as a bramble bush, didn't say a word, and the two boys ran down the stairs and went to sit on the Franceschi elementary-school steps. The Neapolitan began his explanation again, and he warmed up as he talked and got as red in the face as a plate of spaghetti. He got up, facing Riccetto—who kept saying yes —staring at him with a rather irritated expression, talking on and on, and he stared even more fixedly when he stopped talking for a moment, in order to lend greater emphasis to what he was saying, looking half-questioning, half-inspired, kneeling with his legs apart, his belly sticking out, and his hands raised and spread, like a goalie getting set for a high one.

Then with those big lips of his, looking like one of the starved ones who hang around the Porta Capuana, he made an explosive sound, as if the deep and dazzling thought that had crossed his mind must necessarily enlighten Riccetto also.

He was doing all that for five hundred lire. This time, too, Riccetto understood fuck-all. Meanwhile it was getting quite dark. The thousand lines and diagonals of the windows and balconies of the Grattacieli were lit up, radios were going full blast, and from the kitchens you could hear the clatter of dishes and women's voices yelling, arguing, or singing. In front of the stair where the two friends were sitting, there were lines of people moving along, going about their business, some of them coming home filthy from their jobs, some leaving their houses all dressed up to go for a walk with their friends.

"Let's go get a drink, what do you say?" Riccetto said expansively, like a man of the world, knowing his man and supposing reasonably enough that his teacher's throat must be dry. The Neapolitan seemed to get a new lease on life with that proposal, and, filled with enthusiasm, after responding to the offer of a drink with the casual, almost indifferent words,

"Let's go," he started talking again as if nothing had been explained, and as they walked toward Monteverde Nuovo, he made a big production out of it, showing Riccetto just how the dealer should act, in the center of the group around the open umbrella, or the man who bets, winning one and losing one, or the sucker, who's a dope but well-heeled and therefore respectable, standing among the players, deciding to play, and with a grand air betting a thousand, two thousand. . . . The Neapolitan—who incidentally came from Salerno—mimicked his expression and his gestures perfectly, and with a certain amount of deference, too.

They went to Monteverde Nuovo because Riccetto didn't want his business to be public property around Donna Olimpia, where everybody had nose trouble so bad it was sickening. "Spies always think you're spying on them," he said to the Neapolitan sententiously in order to justify that uphill walk, first along a street that was all rubble and broken pavement, and then by a path that led up through trodden fields toward the refugees' shantytown at the top. There too, and then in Monteverde Nuovo, everything was uproarious and gay, the bustle of Saturday night. The pair went into a little wine bar right on the market square where the trolley terminal was, a bit beyond Delle Terrazze. The bar had an arbor and a coarse lattice fenced it off from the street. It was already dark inside. They sat down on the broken-down benches and ordered a half-bottle of Frascati. They began to feel the wine after the first sips. The Neapolitan began his explanation for the fourth time; but Riccetto had had it by then, and didn't feel like listening any more. And even the Neapolitan was sick of saying the same thing over and over. While he talked, Riccetto watched him with a half-smile, partly resigned, partly sarcastic, as he got away from the subject little by little. Then, feeling better about the whole thing, they began to discuss other matters. They were two sports, and they had plenty to tell each other about life in Rome and in Naples, about the Italians and the Americans, each listening respectfully to the other and appearing to believe every word of it, but at the same time giving each other little underhand digs whenever they could, and at the back of their minds each thinking the other was an idiot, satisfied when he spoke himself and annoyed when it was his turn to listen.

But as he drank, the Neapolitan grew stranger and stranger. By the end of the second glass, his face looked as if it had been smoothed with sandpaper, and the features rubbed away: it looked like a piece of scorched meat, with its half-closed eyes lit with an intense light that came from God knows where, and thick lips that hung down and seemed stuck together. When he spoke it was as if he were complaining; his staring eyes laughed in spite of the serious, deeply felt words he was uttering. Now he spoke only in his own dialect. He sat bent forward, his shoulders hunched, pouring out sweat, his face pulpy and swollen, staring at Riccetto with eyes shining with brotherly love. "Listen," he said, "I'm going to make a confession to you." "What do you want to tell me?" asked Riccetto, who was feeling no pain himself.

But the Neapolitan smiled sadly, shaking his head, and was silent for a moment. Then he said, "It's something very serious. I want to tell you about it because you're my friend." Both of them were deeply moved by that declaration. The Neapolitan fell silent again, and Riccetto, grave and dignified, encouraged him to go on. "Tell me what you want to tell me, but only if you want to. I don't want to press you."

"I'll tell you," said the Neapolitan, "but you have to promise me one thing."

"What?" asked Riccetto promptly.

"Not to speak of it to anybody," he said solemnly, completely dizzy by now.

Riccetto realized what was up. He grew even more serious, stuck out his chest, and put his hand on it. "Word of honor," he said.

As if he had regained his courage—his eyes still laughing on their own account in their two slits—the Neapolitan began to tell his story. He said he had killed an old woman and her two old-maid daughters in the Via Chiaja, killed them with an iron bar and then burned the bodies. It took him a quarter of an hour to describe this feat, repeating things two or three times and making a grand mess of the story. Riccetto wasn't at all impressed, for he caught on right away that it was all just drunken maundering. But he listened attentively, giving the man lots of rope and making out that he believed him, so that he would have the right to tell his own stories next. And did he ever have them to tell, things that had happened to him in the two years after the Americans came!

In those two years, Riccetto had turned into a grade-A bastard. Maybe he wasn't quite like that kid he knew, to whom, one day when they were together at Delle Terrazze, somebody came up and said, "Hey, better get over to your house fast, your mother's very bad," and the next day when Riccetto asked him, "How's your mother?" he had grinned and said, "She's dead." "What?" said Riccetto. "She's dead, she's dead," he had assured Riccetto, amused at his surprise. Well, if Riccetto wasn't quite like that, he was well on the way. Already at his age he had known so many hundreds of people of every class and race that by now they were all the same to him. He was almost up to acting like the boy who lived near the Piazza Rotonda, who one day with a friend, when they'd been leaning on a mark to take a lousy couple of thousand lire off him and the friend had said, "Hey, we killed him," without bothering to take a look had answered, "So what?"

Riccetto had let himself drift with the current of memory, and while the Neapolitan was silent, stirred by his own confession, his face looking like a roasted dog's, Riccetto too began to talk. But he told the truth.

Since they had started in discussing the Americans, Riccetto took up the subject. "Listen to this," he said with an amused, worldly air. And he told a number of stories, each one saltier than the last, all from the time when the Americans were around, and in each story Riccetto always turned out to be the prize bastard.

The Neapolitan watched with a look of absorption, nodding his head, smiling a tired smile. Then all of a sudden he took a deep breath, and without changing his expression, still staring at Riccetto, he said, "I have to do penance!"—and on and on for another fifteen minutes, full of theatrical pride over his crime. Riccetto let him blow off steam, as was only fair, but he laughed as he watched. Then, when the Neapolitan began to slow down and stammer, he started up again himself.

"The Americans were all right. They got on my nerves a little, but I got some use out of them. But those fucking Polacks, they were bastards, out and out bastards. I remember one time I was in Toraccia, we had gone over to the Polack camp to see what we could pick up. We're walking along by the cellars there, we hear yelling, so we go over, and it's two whores arguing with these two Poles. They wanted their money. So just then one of the Poles comes out of a cellar, and we duck out of sight, and the other one is still in there with the two whores. I guess they thought the other guy went to get the money. But here he comes back with a big can of gas. Before going in he unscrews the top. Then he pours some into another can and calls his friend, the other Polack, and from the entrance to the cellar the two of them throw that gas on the two whores. Then the other guy lights a match and sets them on fire. We hear scream after scream, so we go over, and we see those two whores all on fire."

Then it was the Neapolitan's turn again, but by now he was so drunk he could hardly keep his eyes open. "What do you say we have another glass?" Riccetto said jokingly. Perhaps the other didn't even hear him; he just laughed a little. "Wheels going round and round?" Riccetto asked gaily, making propaganda for leaving. By now they were both tired of sitting and talking. Riccetto took the initiative. "Well, what do you say we go?" The Neapolitan giggled again, with his eyes lowered, and then he rose, swaying, and with long steps headed straight for the exit in the center of the latticework wall. It was already dark out; people had already eaten dinner, and had left their houses to be out in the cool air. Some young men were racing their motorcycles around the plaza, from Delle Terrazze, all lit up, across to the half-empty trolley shed. While Riccetto paid up, the Neapolitan conscientiously went through some fairly difficult maneuvers: he sneezed, blew his nose through thumb and forefinger, and pissed. Then they went over to the shed to get the trolley that was to take the Neapolitan back to Rome.

"Where do you live?" Riccetto asked while they were waiting. The Neapolitan treated him to a subtle, devilish smile, but kept silent. Riccetto returned to the charge. "What, you don't want to tell me?" he asked, looking a little hurt. The Neapolitan took his hand and pressed it between his own warm and swollen ones. "You're my friend," he began solemnly, and off he went again, with assurances of friendship, vows, declarations. Riccetto didn't get caught up in the other's enthusiasm because he was so hungry and sleepy that he could hardly stand up. It turned out that the Neapolitan's situation was like this: He and his friends had come to Rome just a few days ago, hoping to clean up. That's why the Neapolitan had been willing to go along with Riccetto for five hundred lire. If it hadn't been for that, do you think he'd have bothered, for Christ's sake? You could make millions with the card game, millions. But meanwhile he and his friends were sleeping in a cellar down by the Tiber, in Testaccio. Riccetto knew the place; he pricked up his ears. "But in that case," he said, seeing great possibilities, "you need somebody to give you a hand, show you the best spots. . . ."

The Neapolitan embraced him, then he put his finger along his nose, signing to Riccetto to say no more, it was all understood. He liked the gesture, and he did it again a couple of times. Then he took Riccetto's hand again and started in once more with his vows of friendship, topping it all with certain confused and majestic general principles that Riccetto—who had a much clearer notion and a much simpler scheme in his head—found it hard to follow. "Sure, sure," he said. One trolley had already gone by, and there went another one. Finally, when the third one came, the Neapolitan climbed aboard with five hundred lire in his pocket, and they made a date for the next day, repeating it two or three times, down by the Ponte Sublicio.

At last Riccetto had found himself a trade. Not like Marcello, who had taken up bartending, or like Agnolo, who worked with his brother as a painter. Something much better, something that put him out of that class, so that he could now think of himself as being on a par with Rocco and Alvaro, for example, who had gone on from stealing manhole covers to much more serious and responsible undertakings, with the result that they never had a lire in their pockets and their faces had a stingier look than before. Riccetto was now spending more time with them than with boys his own age, going on fourteen. Rocco and Alvaro would never think of going around with a kid who was always flush and not have a lira in their own pockets, or at the very most two, three hundred lire. To tell the absolute truth, a couple of times, maybe more than a couple of times, Rocco and Alvaro had been flat broke. But that was different! Just how different, Riccetto was to find out the Sunday he went to Ostia with them, flush as a prince.

The card game had gone very well in the beginning. Riccetto and the con men would set up on some good corner over by the Campo dei Fiori, or at the Ponte Vittorio Emanuele or the Prati, and then, when instead of the umbrella they had made themselves a little bench and instead of the cards they had three pieces of nicely planed wood and a rubber band, two of them without cards and one with a card slipped under the rubber band, they could even set up in the Piazza di Spagna or some other elegant place. They would call out invitations to the passers-by, and a fine crowd would gather, everybody well-heeled and ready to go. In appearance, Riccetto was only the boy-helper—the boy who sets up the bench—but in actual fact he had a more delicate job; he pulled down a thousand lire a day, sometimes even more. But one Saturday night around the first of June, when they had attracted a crowd in the Via dei Pettinari, all of a sudden the cops came, running down across the Ponte Sisto. Riccetto was the first to spot them, and he took off through the Via delle Zoccolette. A cop yelled at him, "Stop or I'll shoot!" Riccetto turned around and saw that the cop had his pistol in his hand all right, but he thought, "He doesn't want to kill me, I don't think," and went on running till he came to the Via Arenula and disappeared in the alleys by the Piazza Giudia. But the other three got pinched. They were taken to the police station, and the next day they were sent back to Naples on a travel pass, and so much for them. That same Sunday night, Riccetto went down to a cellar on the banks of the Tiber—it had been the wine cellar of a great house in centuries past—and threw away the collection of rags that had served the three unfortunates as a wardrobe, then went gaily to work pulling up the tiles covering the hole where the savings from a month's work were hidden away: fifty thousand lire.

So on that first Sunday in June, Riccetto was loaded and ready for action.

It was a fine morning, the sun beating down on the Grattacieli, which looked clean and fresh, shining through miles and miles of blue and spilling a golden shower everywhere, on the gleaming humps of the Monte di Splendore or of the Casadio, on the façades of the buildings, on the inner courtyards, the sidewalks. And amid that golden freshness, people in their holiday clothes swarmed about in the center of Donna Olimpia, by the house doors, around the newspaper stand. . . .

Riccetto had slipped out of the house, all spruced up and with his pistol pocket bulging pleasantly. All at once he saw Rocco and Alvaro surrounded by a bunch of young boys who were arguing and yelling in front of the entrance to the Case Nòve. The two were in their work clothes, for they still had to wash up, and they wore cloth breeches that were very wide in the hips and tight in the ankles, so that their legs moved inside them like flowers in a vase, and were crossed like those of soldiers in the pictures—and their two faces topped off the whole, looking like two exhibits in the criminological museum, preserved in oil. Riccetto went up to them, leaving behind the boys of his own age who were kicking around a ball that they had taken away from a little boy who was crying. On spotting Riccetto, Alvaro turned toward him his face of hammered and flattened bones that moved independently when he smiled, and said, casually, "It's a great life, huh?"

"Sure," said Riccetto, no less casually.

He was so self-confident and light-hearted that Alvaro looked at him more closely.

"What are you up to today?" asked Riccetto.

"Aah," said Alvaro, gaining time, with an expression that was partly weary and partly teasing and mysterious.

"What do you say we go to Ostia?" said Riccetto. "I'm loaded today."

"Yeah," said Alvaro, all the bones of his face doing dips and jumps, "you got two hundred lire."

Even Rocco was listening with interest now.

"Yeah, two hundred," said Riccetto, shaking the whole wad. "I got five thousand," he said after a moment. "Five thousand!" he said again, lowering his voice and cupping his hand around his mouth.

First Alvaro, then Rocco, imitating him, burst out laughing so hard that they had to sit down on the stairs and nearly rolled on the ground. Amused, Riccetto waited a while for them to get over it, and then with two fingers he took hold of the collar of Alvaro's shirt and said, "C'mere." All three went around the corner, and Riccetto showed them the fifty bills. The two buddies said, "Hey, you really got it!" and made a resigned gesture that meant, "That lucky bastard!"

"You want to go to Ostia?" asked Riccetto.

"O.k., let's go to Ostia," Rocco replied.

"We got to wash first, and change," said Alvaro.

"Go on, I'll wait for you," said Riccetto. The other two exchanged glances.

"Well," Alvaro finally said hesitantly, with his flat face settling into a satisfied grin, "Hey, Riccè, what do you say we get some snatch in Ostia?" Riccetto rose to the challenge at once.

"Sure, if you can find the head." "We'll find her," said Rocco, "we'll find her." "So we'll be back here in half an hour," said Alvaro. They went into the courtyard of the Case Nòve, but instead of going home, or going to scrape up the five hundred lire for the ticket and the dressing room, they went out through the smaller entrance on the right that opened on the Via Ozanam, and went into the tobacco shop, where there was a phone. They approached the phone as if on official business. Alvaro dialed, and Rocco, having fished up the fifteen lire, followed the progress of the call as a full partner in the operation.

"Hello," said Alvaro, "would you be good enough to call Nadia? Yes, Nadia—it's a friend of hers." The person who had answered the phone went to find Nadia, and meanwhile Alvaro looked at Rocco, who was leaning his shoulder against the peeling wall, concentrating.

"Hello," he said in businesslike tones, "is that you, Nadia? Listen, I got a deal for you. You got some time today? To go to Ostia. Yeah, Ostia. What? Sure. Hey, would I give you a bum steer? But it's all fixed up, all fixed up. We'll meet you at Marechiaro, got that? Marechiaro. Over where the dance floor is, right in front of it. Yeah, like last time. Three, three-fifteen. Fine. See you." He hung up the receiver, and, flushed with satisfaction, left the tobacco shop with Rocco.

Nadia was stretched out on the sand, motionless, her face full of hatred for the sun, the wind, the sea, and all those people who had come to the beach like an army of flies on a cleared table. Thousands of them, from Battistini to the Lido, from the Lido to Marechiaro, from Marechiaro to Principe, from Principe to l'Ondina, lying alongside dozens of bath-houses, some on their backs, some on their bellies—but those were mostly old people. As for the young ones, the males, wearing drooping drawers or else tight trunks that showed off what was underneath, and the females, those show-offs, in tight, tight swimming suits with their hair streaming—all of them were walking up and down ceaselessly, as if they had nervous tics. They were all calling to one another, yelling, shrieking, playing practical jokes, playing games, going in and out of the bathhouses, calling to the attendants. There was even a band of young boys from Trastevere, wearing Mexican hats and playing accordion, guitar, and maracas in front of the bathhouse; and their sambas blended with the rumbas on the Marechiaro loudspeaker, reverberating off the sea. Nadia was lying there amid all that racket, wearing a black bathing suit, and showing a lot of hair, black as the devil's, in sweaty coils under her arms, and the hair of her head was also coal-black, and her eyes were glaring murderously.

She was in her forties, a big woman, with firm breasts and thighs that looked like shining links of sausage, pumped up hard. She was in a rage because she was sick of that crowd of fresh-air fiends, and ocean bathing was not for her. She'd already done all the bathing she was going to do that morning in Mattonato, in Sor'Anita's bathtub. Riccetto, Alvaro, and Rocco had come along only ten minutes before, and she was already of a mind to go on about her business.

"What's eating your ass, Nadia?" asked Alvaro calmly, seeing that she was getting edgy. At these words, she blew up. "Let's get it over with! Let's do what we got to do, quick, and so long, sweetheart! What are we waiting for, do you mind telling me?"

"Jesus, what's your damn hurry?" asked Rocco. Her face changed and she turned like a snake, her mouth pulled down at the corners and her eyes glazed with fury, as gray as those of heart-trouble sufferers. "You going ahead with it?" she asked, glaring at Alvaro. "Sure," said Alvaro. "Well, let's go, what are you waiting for?" she asked ferociously, her red mouth looking like the pit of hell. Alvaro went on watching her, his eyes gleaming with good-humored irony. "You act as if you hadn't had any today," he said, making the gesture of kneading something with the palm of his hand. "You act like you're hard up for it," he added cheerfully.

"Drop dead," she hissed, looking as brutal as a slaughter-house laborer.

"It's all right, we'll help you with your trouble," said Rocco, following Alvaro's lead. "We got something for what ails you."

"Even Riccetto, you know?" said Alvaro. "Kid or no kid. You ought to see how he's hung!"

Riccetto gave no sign of hearing, still kneeling on the sand with his legs spread apart. He too had on a Mexican hat, pushed back behind his ears so that his curls could be seen in a tangle on his forehead, and held in place by a cord beneath his chin.

"Let's go, O.k.?" Alvaro said at last, gesturing toward the bathhouse with his chin. Nadia concealed her satisfaction under a dignified and indifferent expression, and putting her hands down and turning so as to get up bottom-first, she tried to raise, a little at a time, the hundredweight of sausage distributed in varying portions from her breasts to her calves.

"Wait!" Alvaro ordered. "I'll go first." He rose and walked off, disappearing among the beach umbrellas and sprawling bodies. After a while, Nadia, first getting onto her knees, rose to her feet and followed after him, planting her big feet in the burning sand.

Riccetto and Rocco stayed behind, waiting their turns. Rocco stretched out with his hands under his head, looking sly, as usual. Since neither Rocco nor Alvaro had said a word all morning about going in swimming, but just leaned against the bathhouse looking at the tasty dishes cooked up in Trastevere, or Prati, or Maranella, or Quarticciolo, Riccetto asked, "Hey, Rocco, can you swim?"

"What do you mean, can I swim?" Rocco said without moving. "You should see me in the water. I'm a mermaid."

"Well, what are we waiting for, let's go in, come on," said Riccetto.

"I don't feel like it, I just don't feel like it," said Rocco with a sigh. "Go in yourself if you want."

"I'm going in," said Riccetto firmly, with some emotion. He took off his sombrero and ran toward the water's edge. He stayed there half an hour, thinking it over, putting one foot in the water and taking it out, then the other one; and then he waded out till the water reached his knees, giving a jump each time a wave came by and seemed to give him a slap on the bottom. The watery mirror before him was full of people who were nearly out of their depth, and there was a horsefly dipping among their heads. Finally he made up his mind and plunged in like a duckling. The rest of his swim consisted of his standing in one place, shivering, with the water up to his nipples, watching some boys shinning up a plank and belly-flopping off the top of it.

When he came back in front of the Marechiaro dance floor, the other two had already done their business. Now it was his turn, but he sat down again, put his Mexican hat back on his head, and said nothing. But Alvaro said, shifting his jaws as he spoke, "Say, Riccetto, before you go too, don't you think you should buy us all something to drink? Just a suggestion. But you know the two of us have just enough money for the train and the bathhouse." "Why, sure," said Riccetto. He darted into the bathhouse, took the roll of bills from his pants pocket, peeled off one, came out again, and gestured to his companions to follow him. They rose, and everyone moved over to the bar to drink Coca-Cola.

The sun had already begun to go down, and the uproar was increasing. The sea glittered like a sword beyond the crowd of bodies. The buildings and bathhouses echoed with thousands of cries, and the showers were full of older and younger boys, and looked like carcasses swarming with ants. The band from Trastevere was going full blast and the Marechiaro loudspeaker was stupefying. "Hey, Riccetto," said Alvaro after a while, "it's your turn now."

Riccetto got up at once, without saying a word, ready to go into the bathhouse with Nadia. The others laughed, even Nadia, for she had grown somewhat more cheerful sitting at the table. "You want to pay first, don't you?" said Alvaro good-humoredly and rather gently, not wanting to make capital of Riccetto's mistake. "I forgot," Riccetto apologized, laughing, but his feelings were hurt. He paid, and went on ahead as Alvaro had done. The cabin was suffocatingly hot now that the air and the sand had cooled a bit; it was like an oven inside. The clothes stank a little, particularly the socks, but there was also a good smell of salt and brilliantine. After a while, when Riccetto had grown used to the relative darkness, Nadia knocked at the door and he opened it. She slipped inside, followed by those buttocks which, when slapped by some joker around the Arenula or the Farnese, felt as if a python's tail were bunching and coiling. Riccetto was in the center of the room, his Mexican hat on his head. In silence she unfastened her bra, and peeled the two-piece bathing suit from her sweating flesh; at that Riccetto took off his trunks. "O.k., let's go," he said in an undertone.

But while they were doing what they had to do, and Nadia was holding the boy tightly in her arms with his face buried between her breasts, she slowly passed one hand up along his pants, hanging on the wall, slipped it into the rear pocket, took out the wad of bills and put it into her purse, which was hanging close by.

Riccetto lived in the Giorgio Franceschi elementary-school buildings. Coming up by the street that runs from the Ponte Bianco, with a hill on the right and on top of the hill the houses of Monteverde Vecchio, first you see on the left the Ferrobedò sunk in its little valley, and then you come to Donna Olimpia, better known as the Grattacieli. And the first buildings on the right when you get there are those of the school. Rising from the crumbling asphalt is the dilapidated façade, with a row of square white columns in the center and at the corners four massive structures like towers, two or three stories high.

First the Germans had been there, then the Canadians, then the stragglers, and finally the refugees, like Riccetto's family.

Marcello, on the other hand, lived a little farther along, in the Grattacieli—huge as a mountain range, with thousands of windows, in rows, circles, diagonals, giving onto streets, court-yards, stairways, facing north, facing south, in full sunlight, in shadow, closed or wide open, empty or filled with flapping wash, silent or loud with women's chatter or the wailing of children. All around stretched more abandoned fields, full of humps and hummocks, swarming with children at play, some wearing little smocks stained with snot, some half-naked.

On Sundays, in fact, there was no one to be seen but children. None of the older boys or girls, for they all went to Rome for a good time, or if they were flush like Riccetto, to Ostia where it was lively. Marcello, who was left all alone in Donna Olimpia—broke, the poor kid—was dying of boredom. He walked along with his hands in his pockets, going through the courtyards of the Grattacieli, where he had been playing cards with little eight- and nine-year-olds—but they had soon gotten tired of that and had gone off to play Indians around the Monte di Splendore. He was all alone in Donna Olimpia in the open court in the center of the buildings, and the sun was scorching. He crossed the street, scrambled up the four broken steps of the school stairway, and started up the stairway of the building on the right. Riccetto's family didn't live in the classrooms like the squatters or the ones who had settled in first, but in a corridor, one of those that opened on the classrooms; it had been divided by partitions into so many little cells, leaving a narrow strip for a passageway along the windows that gave onto the court. Marcello ran through that passage. Those improvised rooms were full of half-made cots and beds, because the women, with all those children to take care of, had scarcely had time to do any straightening up after lunch: Rickety tables, cane chairs with broken seats, stoves, boxes, cooking implements, sewing machines, baby clothes hung up on cords to dry. At that time of day there was hardly anyone in the school buildings—certainly no children, and the grown men were all in the tavern, in the cellars of the Grattacieli, so that the only ones left at home were a few old women.

"Sora Adele!" Marcello called, as he went along the strip of corridor by the windows, "Sora Adele!"

"What do you want?" It was Sora Adele's voice, already impatient, coming from one of the cells among the partitions. Marcello appeared in the open door.

"Your son back yet, Sora Adele?" he asked.

"No," said Sora Adele, annoyed because this was the third time in the past hour that Marcello had come inquiring after her son. She was sitting in a broken-down chair, perspiring, fallen newspaper at her feet, the chair leaking straw all around her, and she was combing her hair before a mirror propped up against the sewing machine.

Her hair was parted in the middle, and on either side of her forehead were two curly scorched-looking strands, stiff as wood. She was combing them violently, frowning and tightening her mouth on the hairpins, as if it were some little girl's hair that she was combing and she could permit herself to be impatient and hurt. She was getting ready to go to the pizzeria with her friends. "Good-by, Sora Adele," said Marcello, turning away. "If your son comes back, tell him I'm downstairs." "I'll see him when he comes back tomorrow, you brat!" she muttered to herself.

Marcello went downstairs and once more found himself in the deserted street. He was feeling low as could be. He felt like crying. He started to kick pebbles around. "Damn that little shit," he thought, almost out loud, "where the hell did he go, that's what I want to know, where the hell did he go without saying nothing to nobody? Is that the way to be? Is that any way to treat your friends? Makes me so mad I'd like to knock his goddamn eyes out, the little bastard." He sat down on a stairway where there was a bit of shade. The entire area that he could sweep with his dejected eyes held nothing but four or five little boys sitting in the dust at the corner of the school buildings that was nearest the Ferrobedò, amusing themselves playing with a penknife. After a while Marcello got up, went toward them, and stood watching, his hands in his pockets. They paid no attention to him but went on playing without saying a word. After a while one of them glanced up toward the Monte di Splendore, and after staring with shining eyes, yelled, "There's Zambuia!" All the boys turned to look in that direction, and then they jumped to their feet and ran off toward the Monte di Splendore. Marcello followed slowly after them. By the time he had passed the excavations among the hillocks of the Monte, the others had already reached Zambuia, and had gathered together in the shade of a scaffolding on a slope from which one could see all of Monteverde Nuovo on the right, and straight down, half of Rome, all the way to San Paolo. The boys were all sitting around Zambuia, each one with a puppy between his knees, and Zambuia was following all their movements with an expert eye. The boys were silent and well-behaved. They laughed only when one of the puppies did something funny, and not too loudly even then. Every so often, Zambuia would pick up one of the puppies as if it were a bundle of rags, turn it every which way, open its mouth, and then drop it between a boy's knees again. The puppy would shake his skin a bit, whimper, and then jump about on his bandy legs between the boy's bare knees—or he would go bravely off on a ramble along the slope. "Look at that little bastard go!" the boys would cry gaily. One of them would stand up, and lurching along like the puppy, go and fetch it back. Then he'd play with it, trying to hide—even blushing a little with shame—the current of affection that the pup stirred in his heart. "Whose pups are they?" asked Marcello, coming forward, assuming an air of superiority but evincing a certain interest in the little dogs, a certain sympathy even. "Mine," said Zambuia noncommittally. "And who gave them to you?" "You blind?" said Zambuia, busy scratching a puppy's belly. "Don't you see the bitch there?" The boys laughed. The bitch was sitting among their legs, about as big as a mosquito and as quiet as could be. "Give 'em here," said Zambuia shortly. He picked up all the pups from among the boys' legs and slung them against the bitch's belly. All of them went for the nipples immediately and started to nurse, fat as suckling pigs, the boys watching, amused and excited, cheering them on and joking. "Hey, give me one?" asked Marcello, trying to sound casual. Zambuia, who was keeping order among the feeding pups, looked at him. "Yeah," he said. And then, after a moment, "Got five hundred lire?" "You're nuts," said Marcello, laughing, and touching two fingers to his forehead. "Don't you know that at the zoo they give you wolfhound pups free for nothing?" "Fuck you," said Zambuia, turning to his animals again. The boys were all ears. "Real wolfhounds?" Zambuia asked after a while. "No, I'm making it all up," said Marcello promptly, for he had been expecting the question. "Go ask Oberdan, the shoemaker's son, if it's true or not," he added. "What the hell do I care?" said Zambuia. "If it's true it's true, if it ain't it ain't."

Two of the pups had started to growl at each other like ferocious beasts and were now nipping at each other's noses. The boys saw them and began to laugh, rolling around on the grass as if they were puppies themselves. "Make it a hundred lire," said Marcello. Zambuia never opened his mouth, but you could see that he was interested. "O.k.?" asked Marcello. "If you want to," Zambuia conceded. "I'll take that one," said Marcello swiftly, for he had already made his choice. He pointed to a fat black one, the cockiest little bastard of them all, the one who wanted to suck up all the milk himself. The boys looked enviously at Marcello, and they tried to egg the black puppy on to bite the other dogs' noses again. Marcello fished one of the two hundred-lire notes he owned out of his billfold. "Here you go," he said. Wordlessly, Zambuia stretched out his hand and slipped the hundred-lire note into his pocket. "I'll be right back. Wait for me here, O.k.?" asked Marcello, and he went down the slope toward the school buildings. "Sora Adele!" he called again from the corridor. "Sora Adele!"

"What is it now?" she cried. She had just finished dressing. "You still here?" she asked, appearing at the door, stuffed into her good dress like sausage into its casing. "Jesus," she said, her impatience changing to good humor, "look, if I were in your shoes, you know where I would have sent that no-good son of mine by this time? What do you want him for, anyway?" "We were supposed to go to the movies together," said Marcello promptly. Sora Adele put her hand to her bosom and half-buried her chin in the folds of her throat in a gesture of distrust. "I know he won't show up around here till midnight."

"Will you tell him I'll be back?" asked Marcello, who was a little less discouraged this time, consoling himself with the idea that now he had a puppy even better than Agnolo's. " 'Bye, Sora Adele." Stuffed into her gray dress, which looked as if it was ready to split open, and with her stiff hair sticking out on each side of her forehead, she went back into the room to put on a bit of face powder and get her purse. Marcello ran down the worn and blackened stair, from whose walls sections of twisted pipe protruded, and went out into the street. But he had scarcely crossed the threshold when he heard a terrible racket behind him, like a bomb exploding, and felt a violent blow on the back, as if someone had given him a sneak punch. "That son of a bitch!" Marcello thought, and he fell on his face, an enormous crashing in his ears, and his eyes blinded by a cloud of white dust.

Riccetto had just enough money left to buy two or three cigarettes and take the trolley. He walked all the way to the Cerchi, lonely as a dog, and waited there for the number 13, which was half-empty when it came by, for it was still early, and as light and as hot as it had been in the middle of the afternoon—it couldn't have been six o'clock yet. Riccetto sat down in the rear of the trolley, where he could be alone with his gloomy thoughts, and leaned halfway out the window; during the run along the nearly deserted river banks and along the Viale del Re, the wind blew his hair into ringlets on his forehead and flattened it down around his ears, and rippled his shirt, which had come out of his trousers. He stared unseeingly at the façades of the houses as they passed, heartsick, his face sunburned, and his eyes as close to glistening with tears as they could be. At the Ponte Bianco he got off the trolley like a thief, but when his foot touched the ground he stood still, struck by the unexpected scene. Around the pillars of the Ponte Bianco, on the green lots among the construction sites on the Viale dei

Quattro Venti, all of which were usually deserted, and in the little street that ran up to the Ferrobedò and the Grattacieli, where normally the only passers-by were people who lived in the neighborhood and had no corns on their feet and weren't wearing tight shoes—in all these places there were crowds of people. "What happened?" Riccetto asked a bystander. "Who knows?" the man said, looking all around to see if he could figure it out. Riccetto broke into a run among the people down by the slope that dropped to a grade crossing and then rose again steeply and turned toward the Ferrobedò. But at that very moment sirens began to wail at the end of the Circonvallazione Gianicolense, near the Trastevere station. Riccetto turned around, made his way through the surging crowd, and reached the Ponte Bianco just in time to see the fire engines and an ambulance go by at full speed toward Monteverde Nuovo. The noise of the sirens slowly died out among the buildings and construction lots.

Riccetto ran back down toward the grade crossing, and he found Agnoletto there, walking alongside his bicycle. The two of them started to go through the crowd. "What's up?" Riccetto asked someone else, because he was dying of curiosity. "Probably a fire at the Ferrobedò," the man said, making a gesture that pleaded ignorance, and shrugging. But after they had elbowed their way to the grade crossing, they found a line of police there, blocking the street. Agnolo and Riccetto tried to argue their way past, on the ground that they lived in Donna Olimpia, but the cops had orders to let no one through, so the boys had to turn back. They tried to go down from the Viale dei Quattro Venti on the side where there was a sheer drop, taking the path that the workmen had made, down past the grade crossing. But there were policemen stationed there too. The only thing left was to go the long way around to Donna Olimpia by Monteverde Nuovo. Agnolo and Riccetto returned to the Ponte Bianco, where still more people had gathered by this time, and went up the hill by the Gianicolo, taking turns riding on the handlebars, and doing long stretches on foot when the hill was too steep. It was at least a mile and a quarter to the piazza at Monteverde Nuovo, and then another quarter-mile downhill, across fields, by the barracks-like buildings housing the refugees, and the construction lots, to get down to Donna Olimpia from the opposite side. Riccetto and Agnolo got there as the sun was setting. They rolled down the first part of the hill at a good clip, but after that they had to stop again. A little before the Grattacieli, they ran into a big crowd moving along the street at the foot of the Monte di Splendore and filling the courtyards. You could hear cries and shouts, and the voices of the people all crowded together sounded deadened and suffocated. Riccetto and Agnolo got off the bike and silently made their way into the crowd. "What happened? What happened?" Riccetto asked people whom he recognized. They looked at him and did not answer, melting away into the crowd. Then, while Riccetto pressed on, white as a sheet, one of them took Agnolo by the sleeve and said, "Didn't you know the school caved in?" At that instant the sirens sounded again from Monteverde Nuovo, and in a moment more fire engines came speeding by, cutting a swath through the crowd, and parked alongside the others by the main intersection of Donna Olimpia. When the wailing of the sirens died, the talking and shouting sounded louder. Where the corner building of the school had stood there was now a ruin, still smoking, and below in the street a mound of stones and white plaster that blocked the road and hid the line of white columns, still standing, in the center of the façade. The firemen were working a crane among the wreckage, and a score of men were digging with picks in the fading light, yelling orders and calling to one another. There was a cordon of police all around, and the crowd, pressed back, was intently watching the firemen at their work; the women in the building opposite, standing at their already lighted windows, cried out and wept.

Marcello had been taken to the hospital in an ambulance, still covered with dust, like a fish dipped in flour, and they had found two of his ribs broken. They had put him in a ward whose windows opened onto a garden where convalescents took the sun; they stowed him on a cot between an old man with liver trouble who chattered and laughed and grumbled endlessly about the nurses, as if he were continuously drunk, and a middle-aged man who, two or three days later, without his ever having said a word, was carried off to die in a room reserved for that purpose down the corridor. The next day, in the dead man's place they installed another old man who complained night and day and got on everyone's nerves; like children, they all imitated him and made faces. Marcello wasn't uncomfortable there. He spent the day waiting for mealtimes. Not out of hunger—on the contrary, he almost always let his share go to waste—but out of gluttony. His face would light up when he heard the clang of metal down the corridor, the soup cauldrons that a nursing sister pushed along on a little cart. He would turn his head in that direction immediately, and with a connoisseur's glance he would look to see what was being served that day, watching the mixture that poured out of the cauldrons to fill the metal dishes of the patients in the first row of beds. They would begin to eat carefully, making the white iron night tables, loaded with medicine bottles, ring and tinkle. You could see their jaws moving, and their narrowed eyes glittering with ill-concealed satisfaction. Nevertheless, most of them grumbled about the food, acting refined, and always finding something to criticize while swallowing down their few mouthfuls with an air of resignation. Marcello was one of these, and his main subject of conversation when his family came to visit him was the bad hospital food, as if his people didn't know what he was used to getting at home. He let most of his share go to waste and justified his lack of appetite by saying how bad it was, how badly cooked, and by claiming that the sisters gave him the worst of the stuff in order to annoy him. The truth was that he didn't eat partly because the slightest motion gave him severe pain in his broken ribs, and partly because he really wasn't hungry and no food could have appealed to him, not even the restaurant food that he so often used to dream about.

As the days went by, far from stopping, the pain in his ribs and his lack of appetite grew worse. He got paler and skinnier every day, and he could scarcely stir under the sheet. Just turning his eyes this way or that made him feel as if he were about to faint. But he didn't think about it, and bore the pain and weakness without complaining very much.

At Donna Olimpia, meanwhile, they had been piling the rubble up against the school buildings as best they could, clearing a passageway, burying the dead, and with the cooperation of the mayor shelter had been provided for those made homeless. Shelter is the word, for they had jammed ten families into a single hall of a monastery in Casaletto, and the rest were scattered, one here, one there, in the Tormarancio or Tiburtino districts, in refugee shacks, or in soldiers' barracks. A couple of Sundays later, life was going on as usual in Donna Olimpia. The young people went off to Rome to have a good time; the older ones downed their liter of wine, a quarter-liter at a time, in the wineshop: and the army of children invaded the lots and courtyards. Marcello's mother and father, and the six or seven other children in the family, went to pay him a visit in the San Camillo hospital, going on foot because it was scarcely a half-hour's walk up by Monteverde Nuovo and down again by the Circonvallazione Gianicolense. They went along slowly in the sunshine, going up the Via Ozanam—the husband and wife and the older girls all silent, walking heads-down, and the smaller children running along with them and quarreling among themselves in low tones. They passed in procession behind the Grattacieli and in front of the Monte di Splendore where, in the small cleared space among the garbage heaps, the neighborhood boys were starting to play ball. Agnolo and Oberdan were among them, all dressed up, hanging around watching the players, tired of the whole thing already, sitting on a little mound that had a bit of grass on it, taking care not to soil their trousers. When they saw Marcello's family go by, Agnolo nudged Oberdan, and suddenly filling up with emotion, he said, "Hey, why don't we go see Marcello too?" "Let's go," Oberdan said quickly, seeing that there was nothing much doing where they were, and he got up at once, putting on the appropriate expression, all fired up with his pious intentions. Then the two of them left the playing field, picking their way among the surrounding holes and trash heaps. But they were stopped by some of their friends coming over from Monteverde Nuovo. "Where're you going?" their friends asked, thinking of joining forces and taking them along someplace or other. The temptation was strong. But Agnolo said with a serious air, "We're going to the hospital to see Marcello." "What Marcello?" asked Lupetto, who didn't know him. "Marcello the laundress's boy," someone else explained. "You know he's dying?" said Agnolo. "How can he be dying?" the other boy said, not believing him. "He's got a broken rib. Do you die of a broken rib?" "Get lost," said Agnolo. "The sister told me that the rib stuck into his liver, or his diaphragm, or something." "Come on, Agnolo," said Oberdan impatiently, "we're going to get left." "See you," said Lupetto and the others, swarming down toward Donna Olimpia. Agnolo and Oberdan ran after Marcello's family and caught up with them as they were turning into the path across the field that led to the piazza in Monteverde Nuovo, and without saying a word they all walked along together in the burning sun, through streets that were deserted on this Sunday afternoon, till they came to the hospital gates.

Marcello was very glad to see them. "They didn't want to let us in," Agnolo said right away, still feeling outraged by the behavior of the guards. Marcello didn't pass up the chance to deliver an opinion in the case. "They're all nosy here. And the nuns are worse than the others, would you believe it?"

The effort of speaking made him turn paler than the sheets, but he paid no attention.

"Hey, have you seen Zambuia?" he asked suddenly, looking at Agnolo and Oberdan with eyes that were shining with curiosity.

"Who ever sees *him?*" said Agnolo contemptuously, for he didn't know about the puppy.

"If you see him," Marcello went on, a little put-out, "tell him to take good care of my puppy for me, and I'll give him another hundred lire. He know's what it's all about."

"All right," said Agnolo.

"Be quiet for a little, won't you," said Marcello's mother anxiously, seeing that the boy was tiring himself and growing paler as he talked. Marcello shrugged, almost laughing.

But he said to his friends even more enthusiastically, looking pleased and paying no attention to his mother and father, watching him from the foot of the bed, "Say, do you know they're going to give me the insurance?"

"What insurance?" Agnolo asked blankly.

"The insurance for my broken ribs. Don't you know there's insurance for that?" Marcello said contentedly.

His face flushed at the thought of what he would do with the insurance money. He had already settled it with his parents. His eyes gleaming, he said to Agnolo, "I'm getting myself a bike, better than yours."

"What do you know?" said Agnolo, raising his eyebrows.

At that moment the old man in the bed on the right began his complaint, making little groaning noises over and over, and holding his hand to his belly. The old man on the other side, who for some reason had been behaving himself all this time, roused up suddenly, turned round, grimacing with his toothless mouth, and began to groan too, "Ugh, ugh, ugh," partly for a joke and partly from pain. Then he started in with his usual tiresome complaints, sitting upright on his bed. Marcello gave his friends a cheerful look, as if to say, "Do you see that?" Then he said in an undertone, "They're always carrying on like that."

But as he spoke he seemed to fall into a kind of faint, for a little moan almost escaped his lips too. His mother came to his side and smoothed down the sheets. "Are you going to be quiet?" she asked. Marcello's sisters, who had been wool-gathering, came around him too, and his little brothers, already tired of being indoors, stopped their squabbling and came to the head of the bed.

"And Riccetto, what's he up to?" Marcello asked as soon as he had come to.

"It must be a couple of weeks since anyone's seen him."

"Where's he staying now?" Marcello asked.

"I think in Tiburtino, or Pietralata, somewhere around there," said Agnolo.

Marcello was thoughtful for a moment. "And what did he say when he found out his mother was dead?" he asked.

"What did he say? He busted out crying, naturally."

"Oh, God," Marcello said with a grimace of pain, feeling a

sharper twinge in his side. His mother was frightened, and she took his hand, and with her handkerchief wiped the sweat from his forehead and neck. Marcello was faint with weakness and pain; his family knew that the doctors gave him only two or three more days to live. Seeing his pallor, his father went to call a nurse and his mother fell on her knees by the bed, still pressing her son's hand, and started to weep quietly. His father came back with the nurse, who looked at Marcello, put her hand on his forehead, and with a dead expression on her face went away again, saying, "We must be patient." At those words, Marcello's mother raised her head a little, looked around, and began to cry more loudly. "My boy, my boy," she said between her sobs, "my poor boy."

Marcello opened his eyes once more, saw his mother crying and sobbing, and all the others standing around weeping and looking at him with a strange expression on their faces. Agnolo and Oberdan were now standing a little apart from the others, by the foot of the bed, having moved away to make room for Marcello's family.

"What's the matter?" asked Marcello in a faint voice.

His mother went on weeping even more desperately, unable to control herself, trying to stifle her sobs against the sheets.

Marcello looked around more sharply, as if he were thinking intently.

After a moment he said, "Oh, then I must be dying!"

No one spoke. "Oh," said Marcello, staring at the faces around him, "I must really be dying."

Agnolo and the other boy were silent, frowning. After a few minutes of not speaking, Agnolo plucked up his courage, went over to the head of the bed and touched Marcello's shoulder. "So long, Marcè, we have to go now, we have to meet some of the others."

"So long, Agnolo," Marcello said in a weak but steady voice.

After thinking for a moment, he added, "And say hello to everybody in Donna Olimpia, in case I don't get back there. And tell them not to feel bad about it."

Agnolo turned Oberdan around by the shoulder and they went off down the ward, nearly in darkness now, without saying a word.

3 · Night in the Villa Borghese

On the overpass by the Tiburtina station, two boys were pushing a cart loaded with armchairs. It was morning. On the bridge, the ancient buses—the one for Monte Sacro, the one for Tiburtino III, the one for Settecamini, and the 409 that turned suddenly below the bridge, going down by the Via di Casal Bertone and Acqua Bullicante toward the Porta Furba—the buses shifted gears, nosing in among the crowd, among the tricycles and the ragpickers' carts, the children's bicycles and the red handbarrows quietly returning from the markets to the farms on the outskirts of the city. The worn gangways on either side of the bridge were also full of people; files of workmen, idlers, and housewives getting off the trolley in the Via Portonaccio, carrying bags stuffed with artichokes and greens, going toward the squalid houses of the Via Tiburtina, or to some newly constructed apartment house, surrounded by junk heaps, set down among construction sites and piles of old iron and lumber, by the great Fiorentini or Romana Compensati works. Right in the middle of the bridge, in the tide of cars and pedestrians, the two boys, who were jerking the cart along behind them, paying no attention when it lurched over the broken places in the pavement and taking it as easy as they could, stopped and sat down on the sides of the cart. One of them fished a butt from his pocket and lit up. The other leaned against the arm rest of one of the chairs, striped red and white, waiting his turn to take a drag; because of the heat he pulled his black shirt out from beneath his waistband. But the first boy went on smoking and paid no attention. "Hey," the other said, "you going to let me have that butt?" "Here. Anything to keep you quiet," and he passed it over. The racket on the bridge almost drowned their voices. Even a train had joined the party, running beneath the overpass, sounding its whistle, not slowing down for the station, built low, with its bundles of track disappearing in dust and sunglare, and set against the thousands of houses that they were building in the hollow behind the Nomentana. Smoking the butt just passed to him, the boy in the black shirt hoisted himself onto one of the two armchairs in the cart and stretched out, his legs apart and his curly head resting on the chair's back. He began to draw contentedly on the inch-long Nazionale between his fingers, while around him on the high point of the bridge the stream of pedestrians and vehicles swelled in the noon heat.

The other boy climbed up on the cart too, and stretched out on the second armchair, with his hands on the seat of his pants. "Christ," he said, "I'm dying. I haven't eaten since yesterday." But just then, in all the hubbub, two long whistles sounded from the end of the bridge. Recognizing the sound, the boys lying on the armchairs turned halfway round, and where the trolley tracks curved at the end of the Portonaccio plaza, tacking swiftly among the cars and buses lining up for the bridge, they saw two other loafers coming along, pushing a cart and sweating. Besides whistling, they yelled and gestured at the two on the armchairs. They came up, their cart full of refuse, stinking like a sewer. They were all rags and dirt, with two inches of dust and sweat on their faces, but their hair was as neatly combed as if they had just left the barbershop. One of them was a slim, dark boy, handsome even in all that dirt, with coalblack eyes and fine round cheeks a color between olive and pink. The other fellow had reddish hair and a swollen, freckled face. "Since when are you herding sheep, cousin?" the boy in the black shirt asked the handsome boy, not shifting an inch from his position, sprawled on the armchair with his hands on his belly and the butt sticking to his lower lip. "Fuck you, Riccè," said the other. Riccetto—for it was the little bastard himself—wrinkled his brow meaningfully, tucking his chin into his throat with a know-it-all look. Caciotta, the boy who was stretched out on the chair beside Riccetto, got up and, as curious as a little boy, looked in their friends' cart to see what was going on there. He made a contemptuous face and then broke into a forced laugh. "Ha, ha, ha," he exploded, bending double, and falling to a seat on the edge of the sidewalk. The others watched, waiting for him to stop, half-smiling themselves. "If you get twenty-six lire for that, you can cut my throat," Caciotta said at last. The one that Riccetto had called cousin, seeing what Caciotta was up to, clicked his tongue, gave him a push, and without a word grabbed the cart-handles and started off. His partner, the redhead, whose name was Begalone, went after him, looking out of the corner of his eye at Caciotta, who was still sitting on the ground under the feet of the people passing by. "Hey, twenty-six lire," he said, "we'll see this evening who's got more money in his pocket." "He, he, he," Caciotta sputtered. Begalone stopped, his faded Arab face twisted around, and turning serious he said, weighing each word, "Hey, deadbeat, come on and I'll buy you a drink."

"Sure," said Riccetto promptly. He had been watching the scene from his armchair, not saying a word. He jumped down, and with Caciotta's help began to push his cart with its chairs through the traffic, following the two ragpickers' cart. Saying no more, the ones in the lead went like a shot along the other side of the bridge toward the Via Tiburtina and stopped at a restaurant with an arbor between two broken-down old hovels at the foot of a tall building. All four entered and drank a liter of white wine, thirsty as they were from pushing the carts all morning. Moreover, Alduccio and Begalone had dry throats from the four or five hours in the sun that they had put in fishing in a junk heap under a railroad trestle. The wine began to affect them after the very first sips. "Let's go sell the armchairs, what do you say, Riccè?" said Caciotta, propped up against the bench with his legs crossed. "Fuck this stuff."

"Where do we sell them?" Riccetto asked with a business-like air. "For Christ's sake," said Begalone, "why don't you try Porta Portese?" Riccetto yawned, and then he turned his sleepy eyes toward Caciotta. "What do you say we go?" Caciotta tossed off the glass, putting the finishing touch on his drunkenness, and hurrying out of the wineshop, he cried, raising one hand, "Hail, O Garbage!" Riccetto finished his wine too, spilling a good deal of it on his black shirt, and coughing, he followed after Caciotta.

It was a good four or five kilometers from where they were to Porta Portese. It was Saturday morning, and the August sun was like a drug. Besides, Riccetto and Caciotta had to make a big detour so as not to go through San Lorenzo, where the man who had sent them off early that morning to deliver the chairs in the Casal Bertone had his store. "All we need is not to be able to sell this stuff now," said Caciotta with false pessimism, for in actual fact he was striding along in high spirits. "We'll make out, we'll make out," said Riccetto with a scornful smile, taking a butt out of his pocket. "How much you think we'll get, Riccè?" Caciotta asked innocently. "We'll get just about thirty thousand," Riccetto said, taking the last few drags on the cigarette, and added, "and who's going to go home again after that?" Calling it home was a manner of speaking. To go there, not to go there—it all came to the same thing. As for eating, nobody ate there. As for sleeping, you could sleep just as well on a park bench. Call that a home? Besides, Riccetto couldn't stand his aunt, or her son Alduccio either. His uncle was a lush who was always breaking balls. And then, how were two whole families supposed to manage, one of them with four kids, one with six, all in two narrow little rooms, without even a toilet—that was downstairs in the center of the courtyard. Those were the arrangements under which Riccetto had been living since the school buildings had collapsed a year before, for it was at that time that he had gone to live in Tiburtino with his relatives.

They went to sell the armchairs to Antonio, the junkman in the Vicolo dei Cinque to whom Riccetto, Marcello, and Agnolo had sold the broken-up manhole cover three or four years earlier. They got fifteen thousand lire and went off to buy new clothes. A little ashamed, a little anxious not to look anyone in the eye, the boys went to the Campo dei Fiori where they sell pants for a thousand or fifteen hundred lire, and good-looking knit shirts for less than two thousand. Then they each got a pair of pointy black-and-white shoes, and Caciotta bought the sunglasses he'd been dreaming of for a long time. Limping along on their aching feet, swollen because of the long walk from Portonaccio, they went looking for a place to leave their bundle of old clothes. Finding a place around there was easier said than done. They left the clothes in an outhouse belonging to a bar near the Ponte Garibaldi, stuffing them in carelessly, and thinking to themselves as they filed by the bar under the scrutiny of the bartenders, "If we find them again, great; if we don't find them, tough."

They went off to eat pizza and French toast at Silvio's in the Via del Corso. It was getting late—time to think of how to spend the afternoon, for Christ's sake. Flush as they were, the only problem was making a choice: the Metropolitan or the Europa, the Barberini or the Capranichetta, the Adriano or the Sistina. They left in a hurry anyway, because: Go on out and get in your licks, stay at home and there you sticks. They were all excited and full of fun, not even remotely aware of the fact that the joys of this world are brief, and fortune fickle. They bought a copy of *Paese Sera* in order to look at the amusements page, and quarreled over it, pulling it out of one another's hands, each of them wanting to read it himself. Finally, in a rage, they managed to agree on the Sistina.

"But do I like to have a good time!" said Caciotta, leaving the theater in a happy frame of mind—four hours later, for they had seen the film twice. He adjusted his sunglasses on his nose, and walking loose along the sidewalk of the Via Due Macelli, he bumped into the passers-by on purpose.

"Hey, you mutt!" he would yell at some lady who, seeing him approach, had assumed an offended air. If she happened to turn around once more, that was it. Drawing himself up, standing on the edge of the sidewalk, with his hand at the side of his mouth, he would yell even louder, "Hey, mutt! Hey, bowlegged! Hey, old tore-out!"

And then there were some kinds of people he just couldn't stand, really couldn't stand. "Hey, look at them!" he yelled, eyeing a tall, good-looking woman with an enormous rear end who was coming down the street with a stocky four-eyed guy. When they came up and brushed past, Riccetto and Caciotta, grinning from ear to ear and bending down almost far enough to touch the ground with their noses, began to sputter and spit like two newborn babies. The four-eyed guy turned halfway round: And what do *you* want? Looking each other in the eye, bending double like puppets, they exploded again. "What a man!" Caciotta yelled. But a dignified lady bore right down on them, so split! And they ran off, pleased with themselves, up toward the Villa Borghese, because of all the places that had benches that you could sleep on, that was the one where you could have the most fun. Starting out by the Porta Pinciana, they went down along the avenue that paralleled the bridle path. The avenue was filled with cars and passers-by till late in the day. At the end, past the rotunda of the Ginestre, there was another avenue that ran down to the parapets of the Pincio and the Casina Valadier. Two rows of oleanders in rectangular beds, stretching in a thin line between street and sidewalk, shaded the benches backed against the retaining-wall, behind which was a slope with a bridle path at the bottom. There were people sitting on the benches, enjoying the cool air. "I'd like to rest a little," Riccetto said carelessly, and they stretched out belly-up, singing, glad to be alive, on the dry grass of the slope, waiting for it to get a bit later. When they turned into the avenue again, the benches were already rather more sparsely occupied, and fewer people were passing by, but the real life of the place was just beginning. Here and there you could see old men in their shirtsleeves, or groups of young boys, some wearing jackets on their sweating backs, some in colored sport shirts. Most of them were sitting down as if they were in a living room, holding their knees close together like women, or else cross-legged, one arm lying in their laps, leaning forward slightly and smoking in little nervous puffs, holding the cigarette with all four fingers held out straight. Farther along on another bench, also in the shade of an oleander, a gentleman was talking to a dark boy who was wearing one of those blue collarless jerseys that can be bought at Porta

Portese for five hundred lire. And still farther along, there were other figures among the trees, beneath the street lamps. "I can see all the way up my girlfriend's dress," Caciotta said suddenly, staring across the walk to where, under the cone of light cutting the darkness around the street lamp, a woman was sitting on a bench, her blood-colored skirt hiked up over her knees. "Look at that," said Riccetto, interested at once. "Hey, you bastard," someone yelled at Caciotta from a neighboring bench. "How about that?" said a young boy whose skin was as black as a skillet, and his hair blacker still, its dirty curls anointed with tonic. He was sitting spread-legged in the middle of one of the benches, a friend on either side.

"Picking up stuff?" Caciotta asked excitedly, sitting down by them.

"Where do you get that pick-up business?" the dark boy, known as Negro, said ironically, in a voice loud enough to be heard by two heavy-set men who were passing by, accompanied by two of the Villa Borghese beauties, all in high good humor. "Up yours!" Riccetto muttered after them. "This here's a friend of mine," Caciotta said, introducing Riccetto to the others. They shook hands all around. Now some distance away, the two sports and the whores were making a big production out of lighting their cigarettes. Negro and the other boys watched them out of the corners of their eyes. The smaller of Negro's two companions was talking quietly to the other, a big-headed, husky boy with lively eyes. "Get off my back, Calabrè," the hefty boy answered calmly. "Having a good time tonight, Cappellò?" Caciotta asked him, feeling him out. "Sure," said Cappellone, his mouth spreading from ear to ear, and he sprawled over the bench, stretching out his legs nearly to the bed of oleander. The boy called Calabrese was preoccupied with his own serious business at hand, and he didn't look at the new arrivals. "Let me feel it," he said in a voice that was hoarse from the cold he always had because he slept in the open every night, right there in the Villa Borghese. He was in his twenties, but his dark, warty face looked as if it belonged to a boy of fifteen. He put his hand on Cappellone's bulging pockets. "Fuck off, will you?" said Cappellone, in a sudden outburst. "Here, you satisfied now?" he asked, and pulled a revolver from his pocket. "What a nut," said Negro. Cappellone, laughing, hid the gun away again in his dusty pants. "Jesus!" said Caciotta. "It's a Beretta, huh?" said Riccetto, coming closer. But he got no answer. Calabrese went on with his interrogation, speaking in a toneless voice, his eyes at once listless and vicious. "What about the pen?" "I've got it, dumb bunny," said Cappellone. "No, Picchio's got it, hasn't he?" said Negro excitedly, reaching his arm out to Calabrese for emphasis. "He's all tanked up and giving his best to the whores," said Calabrese sulkily. "Let's go find him," said Cappellone. "Let's go," said Calabrese. Cappellone rose from the bench and stretched, laughing. Riccetto and Caciotta followed Calabrese and Cappellone, who were sauntering down the walk. But Negro, as soon as they had risen, said, "Who's gonna make me if I'm comfortable right here?" He stretched out on the bench belly-up, cocking first one leg up on the backrest and then the other.

The avenue that led to the Porta Pinciana was still crowded with women, boys in work clothes, and foreigners, who were promenading to the sound of jazz coming from the Casina delle Rose. But at the exit to the Villa Borghese, in front of the arches of the Porta Pinciana, the avenue that continued along the bridle path and then turned down along the Muro Torto was all dark and silent. Some loafers were pushing their way along, getting their bearings as if they were up to something; then came a couple of soldiers, then a young fellow on a motor scooter, and all of them vanished into the shadow of the trees. On the right ran the same wall that divided the avenue from the slope, and farther down, in darkness, before the broad stretch in the moonlight were the parallel fences that enclosed the sand-track. The playing fields were yellow and trampled. Young boys played soccer there in the daytime, and servant girls strolled there, but at this hour the action was all down around the riding enclosure—property of the army— that was studded with square-cropped bushes and reeked of horse piss. Coming out of the shadow of the plane trees into the middle of the field, or out of the maze of bushes by the riding enclosure, and climbing up across the sand-track, were sailors from Taranto, or Salerno, black and dried-up, truckers from around Bologna wearing trousers cut low in the crotch and swinging their arms, and kids from Prati or Flaminio—all of them with that caved-in feeling. At their backs, down below, it was completely still. When Riccetto, Caciotta, and the two habitués of the Villa Borghese got there, it was already late, and the periods of silence between the noises of those going down and of those coming up were beginning to lengthen. "There's Picchio," Calabrese announced, as if he had made him out in the darkness. "Where?" asked Cappellone. "You deaf?" said Calabrese. "Fuck you," said Cappellone, sitting on the railing as if prepared to stay there for an hour. And in fact, from down behind the track, nearly as far as the chestnut trees, among the wire-mesh fencing and the tangled brush in the darkest part of the riding enclosure, you could hear throat-splitting yelling. As it came closer, it grew louder. "Bitches! Bitches!" It died away for a moment, then rang out again. "Bitches!" And at every repetition the word sounded as if the man yelling it was getting more and more intoxicated with rage. As far as they could tell without being able to see him, he must have stopped every once in a while, turning halfway around toward the riding enclosure and yelling again. Or perhaps

he was walking slowly, stumbling repeatedly, looking backward all the while. In any case, he must have had his hands at
his mouth to make a megaphone; he was yelling with such fury
that you could hear the catarrh rasping in his throat.

"Bitches! Bitches!"

Then the voice stopped again, as he took a few steps, or
maybe he spit. At first, because his voice cracked on the "i,"
it seemed as if he might be yelling it for a joke. But then the
sliding tone convinced you that he was yelling for real, in a
holy rage, foaming at the mouth. They must have been able
to hear that yell from right in the middle of the bridle path
all the way to the avenue and the Casina delle Rose. The man
fell silent and rested up for a bit, and then he sounded off again,
as if he couldn't find any other word in his rage: "Bitches!"

By now he was just below the railing and you could make out
his stumbling form. He was shaking from head to foot as if
he were caught in a high wind. His hands wouldn't stay quiet
for a moment. He stuffed his shirt tail into his pants and pulled
it out again, tightened his belt, took the gum he was chewing
out of his mouth, and brushed back the hair that was falling
over his eyes.

"Filthy bitches!" he yelled even louder at an audience that
had crouched down diplomatically among the bushes, in pious
retreat and reflection. He sat down suddenly. Then he rose
again and began to climb once more, still looking behind him.
After a few steps he stopped, felt around inside the shirt, which
hung far down over his pants, and let loose a complicated outburst, chewing the words and the gum at the same time, and
spitting as he yelled.

"Hey, Picchio," Cappellone interrupted from above, "it looks
like they're letting you talk to yourself, isn't that right?" Picchio
kept climbing without answering, and then turned to look
back down toward the playing field, where his female audience

kept as mute as the Sphinx, and yelled again, "Bitches!" Then he came up by the path that crossed the track between the railings. He came up to where the others were on the avenue and sat down among them on the nail-studded railing. He chewed his gum, stretching his whole mouth in the process, grinding his jaws and leaking spit. "What you been up to, Pì?" asked Calabrese, his eyes smiling at last, like those of an animal feeding.

"Fuck those bitches!" Picchio exploded. As he yelled and chewed, the skin all over his dried-up little face wrinkled. "They won't give me any tail!"

"You let them do you that way, Picchio?" asked Cappellone. A sneer crossed Calabrese's swollen face. Picchio got up again, drew away from the others, put his hands to his mouth, and, turning to the playing field that stretched away at their feet, yelled, "Bitches!" once again.

"Where's the pen?" Calabrese asked, by way of beginning the investigation. Picchio gave Calabrese a sidelong glance as if he didn't recognize him. "What's the matter, do you think I'm so dumb I wear my ears over my nose?" he yelled at the whores. "Don't I have five hundred to pay with? Bitches!" He waved his arm at them. "I'll show you tomorrow night, I'll show you!" "What are you going to show them?" asked Cappellone. "What am I going to show them?" said Picchio, chewing away and screwing up his nose. "Bunch of cunts is what they are." Then he said to Calabrese, looking at him out of the corner of his eye and arching his brows in resignation, "Here it is."

Calabrese took the pen and looked at it in the light. "Who'd you pinch it off of?" asked Riccetto, watching him.

"Off a kid on the bus," Picchio said, chewing.

"What do you mean, a kid?" asked Cappellone. "You said you got it off an American."

Picchio paid no attention to him.

"And what can you do with that thing?" asked Riccetto, shrugging.

"Christ, won't you give five hundred lire for it?" asked Calabrese.

"Yeah, sure," said Riccetto.

"O.k., what'll you cough up for it?" asked Calabrese.

"You're making me laugh. Get off my back, will you," said Riccetto.

"Let's go have a drink," Picchio cried out suddenly, perking up, jumping up and down, so dried out that if the wind rose he'd fly away.

"He must be rich," said Calabrese.

"What do you mean, rich?" Picchio said, chewing and puffing. "I got three hundred."

Riccetto and Caciotta sat there waiting to see how things turned out.

"Let's go," said Picchio in a hoarse voice, gesturing shakily toward the Porta Pinciana. "O.k., let's go," said Cappellone, following him with Calabrese. Riccetto and Caciotta didn't move. "Come on," Cappellone said to them.

When they came to the arches at the Porta Pinciana, they found Negro and another wool-head, a little guy with a puffy criminal face and two porcelain eyes. He was from Acqua Bullicante, his name was Lenzetta, and the others all knew him. "Hey," said Cappellone, "two from Tiburtino, one from Acqua Bullicante, two from Primavalle, one homeless, and Picchio here from Hell's Acre—we could organize the Greater Rome Vice League!"

All seven of them went into a pizzeria over by the Termini station, and drank a bottle on Picchio. Then they came back by the Via Veneto, with their shirts billowing out over their pants, or with their knitted shirts draped over their shoulders, the sleeves tied around their necks, yelling, singing, insulting the rich people who were still at that hour parading around all dressed up, their Alfas waiting for them. The Villa Borghese was almost deserted by now. You could scarcely hear the violins playing in the Casina delle Rose. When they passed by the bridle path, Picchio woke up and started in yelling again at the top of his lungs, "Hey, bitches!" He vaulted the fence, went down the slope, and as soon as he hit the clearing fell face-down in the dust, and was asleep.

"Jesus, I'm feeling horny," said Riccetto. "All that good-looking stuff on the Via Veneto."

"Let's go see if the whores are still there," said Caciotta.

"For Christ's sake," said Calabrese, "they'll want money."

"Well, don't we have it?" Caciotta asked triumphantly. The others pricked up their ears.

"Let's go then," said Negro, grinning under the woolly mop that curled down to his ears. "What are we waiting for?"

They crossed the entire playing field in the moonlight, reached the riding enclosure, and looked around. But the whores were all gone.

"The paddy wagon must have come by," said Calabrese knowingly.

"Well," said Caciotta, "tonight . . ." And he made the gesture for nothing doing, shaking his hand with the thumb and forefinger extended.

Lenzetta goosed him. "Nicest ass in Rome."

"Nicest prick, you mean," Caciotta corrected.

"What, stuck on behind?" asked Lenzetta, the one from Acqua Bullicante.

"Sure, and I got a little something in front for you, too," said Caciotta.

"Fucked you that time," said Negro, as one might say "Amen." They went up the other side of the playing field and turned into the street where they had first met. But it was too busy a place for sleeping. They went on to the gardens by the Casina Valadier, stretched out on the benches, and dropped off.

The night passed quickly: The trams at the foot of the Muro Torto hadn't started running yet, the city was still fast asleep, and the sun was already beating down on the fields and trees of the Villa Borghese, shedding a white, white radiance on the walls and on the small statues among the flower beds.

Riccetto was awakened by an odd sensation of cold on his feet. He turned over onto his stomach for a moment and tried to drop off again, but then he lifted his head to see what the hell had happened to his feet. A dazzling ray of sunshine, filtering through the branches, lit up his holey socks.

"What, did I take my shoes off last night?" Riccetto asked himself, bouncing into a sitting position.

"No, I didn't take them off," he answered himself, looking under the bench, on the grass, among the bushes. "Hey, Caciotta! Hey, Caciotta," he cried, shaking the still-sleeping boy, "they stole my shoes!"

"What'd they do?" said Caciotta, numb with sleep.

"They stole my shoes. And my money, too!" he said, searching through his pockets. Still half-asleep, Caciotta went through his own pockets: not a cent, and his sunglasses were gone. "The bastards!" Riccetto yelled in despair. The others had awakened too, and were watching from where they lay.

"I didn't have a thing on me," said the kid from Acqua Bullicante, Lenzetta, sitting up on his bench. But Calabrese looked on out of his puffy face, not saying a word, just shaking his head, like someone who knows what's what but doesn't choose to tell. Riccetto and Caciotta went away without speaking, not even glancing at the others, who were playing dumb, their little crooks' faces looking so preoccupied and innocent that nobody would dare say a thing about them. There wasn't a soul to be seen in all of the Villa Borghese, bleaching under the already hot sun. They went down to the field where the bridle path was, and crossed it. Picchio was still sleeping on the far side, lying on his stomach. He was wearing blue and white canvas shoes, all frayed and with holes in the bottoms. Riccetto slipped them gently off him and put them on, though they were rather tight. Then they headed down toward the Porta Pinciana.

That day they went to the friars' to eat. They had to; though they had spent the entire morning wandering around the Piazza Vittorio, they hadn't been able to pick up a single lira.

Pale with hunger, they slouched along under the station roof and reached the Via Marsala. There was a door at number 210 with the word "Refectory" above it, of the Sacred Heart or the Blessed Virgin—one of those names. They stuck their noses in the door, and then their heads, and took one step forward and a half-step back, dressed as they were, all barefoot except for Riccetto in his canvas shoes. They found themselves in a short corridor leading to a courtyard of trodden earth, full of young penitents like themselves who were playing basketball, and you could tell that they were playing just to please the friars. Riccetto and Caciotta each looked at the other to see what expression he was wearing, and they almost burst into tears at what they saw. But instead they began to snicker, nudging each other, and entered the courtyard looking like two grinning imps.

A big-bellied friar came toward them, all sweaty and sloppy, and they hung back thinking, "What's he want?" But the friar yelled, "Want to eat, boys?" Riccetto turned away in order to conceal the fact that he was about to burst out laughing, while Caciotta, who had been to this place once before, said, "Yes, Father." At the word "Father," Riccetto couldn't hold it in any longer, and he began to chortle so hard that he had to make believe he needed to tie his broken-down shoes. The friar said, "Come on in," and led them through an entrance on the other side of the court, where there was a small table with a register and a book of tickets on it. Pulling up his cassock so that you could almost see his belly, the friar asked for their particulars. "Our what?" asked Riccetto, surprised but agreeable, and ready to cooperate in any way required. When they found out what the hell particulars were, they gave false ones, and respectfully took the ticket from the friar as a reward.

Riccetto was in a good humor, seeing how smoothly everything was going, and even a little touched and embarrassed, which was not like him at all. "Well, when do we eat?" he asked expectantly. "In a little while," Caciotta told him. Meanwhile, the other waifs were still at that game. "Hey, let's play too," Riccetto said decisively, ready to assert his rights. They went to the center of the courtyard, argued a little with the others, who looked to be no better off for clothes than they were, and started to play without knowing the first thing about basketball, a game they had never heard of. They played for half an hour, and the whole time Riccetto concentrated on not yelling out, "Fuck you!"

Then the friars called them, clapping their hands, and took them to a hall beyond the little entrance where the ticket table was; inside there were tables thirty feet long, and chairs set around them. They gave the boys two slices of dry bread and a plate of spaghetti and beans to each, made them say, "In the name of the Father, and of the Son, and of the Holy Ghost," and let them eat.

Riccetto and Caciotta went there for about ten days. Only at noon, though, for the friars closed up shop in the evening. Many times the boys ate just once a day. In the evening they managed as best they could. Maybe with money that they'd picked up at the station in the morning, or in the Piazza Vittorio market, or hooking stuff from the street stalls. At last, one evening Fortune smiled on them, and they could tell the friars to get lost. It happened on a tram. A lady had got on, carrying a bag with a coin purse inside it. That little purse, first seen through a butcher's window in the Via Merulana where the lady had been a little earlier, had appeared to bulge in a promising manner. When she came out, the lady put the coin purse into the bag, which was brimful and didn't seem to close properly. By good luck, Riccetto and Caciotta had exactly thirty lire between them. They divided it up on the run, caught the tram, which was already in motion, and climbed aboard. Each one struck out for himself, and they stationed themselves near the lady. She was standing up, hanging onto the handrail, and looking balefully at her neighbors. Riccetto drew up closer still, because he was the one who was going to work on her, and Caciotta stood behind him to conceal his movements while he opened the bag very gently, removed the coin purse with his right hand, and slipped it along his left side until he could tuck it under his armpit. Then, still protected from behind by Caciotta, he made his way through the passengers and they both got off at the first stop, cutting across the gardens in the Piazza Vittorio, and disappeared, as the saying has it, in less time than it takes to say "Amen."

They headed for San Lorenzo, going through the Santa Bibiana arch. And since they were in the neighborhood, they thought of paying a little visit to Tiburtino, to see how things had developed since the time they had run off with the armchairs belonging to the upholsterer in the Via dei Volsci. . . .

It was early evening, and a pleasant coolness helped to freshen the air at that hour when the workmen are on their way home, and the trams go by packed like sardine cans, and you may have to spend three hours waiting under the shed-roof at the tram stop for a chance to jump onto the footboard. From San Lorenzo to Verano, and all the way to Portonaccio, it's all one fun fair, a big, buzzing, blooming confusion. Riccetto sang:

> *"Rome, how beautiful,*
> *How beautiful in twilight . . ."*

at the top of his lungs, completely reconciled with life, full of big plans for the immediate future, feeling all that cash inside his pocket: cash, source of all pleasure, all satisfaction in this cockeyed world. Caciotta was walking close by his side, calm and content. They came to Portonaccio; their hands in their pockets, singing, they settled themselves in the middle of the open space beneath the overpass to wait for the bus to Tiburtino. One bus had just left, and they wanted to catch the next one. By the time it arrived, so many people had gathered that it wasn't worth struggling to try to board it. They waited for the third one; same thing. Two or three rain clouds showed up by St. Peter's, borne on a wind that blew a bit cool and a bit warm; then it thundered and a little rain fell. Riccetto and Caciotta gave up on the buses, since it was murder trying to ride them at that time of day, and decided to take a walk, along with a column of soldiers, behind the Tiburtina station, among warehouses, excavations, and building sites, through fields that were already soaked—to see if there were any whores around. When they came back to the terminal beneath the overpass, the lights of Verano were already lit, flickering with a rosy glow in lines and circles above the embankments. The bus was there, but so was the usual crowd, taking it by storm. "What time do you think it is?" asked Riccetto. "Must be eight, eight-fifteen," said Caciotta. As a matter of fact, it must have been at least ten. "It's late," said Riccetto, not losing his good spirits however. "Let's get on."

They very nearly knocked down two or three old women and two or three old men, gave the conductor a hard time, stepped on a corn here and there, and shouldered their way till they got directly behind the driver's cubicle. They leaned back against it, ironically observing the human comedy unfolding in the bus. After a while some boys they knew came aboard, and they gave them a big hello as soon as they were installed.

"Well," said Caciotta confidently and condescendingly, shaking hands with one after another, "what are we all up to?"

"Can't you see we've just knocked off work?" one of them said in a dejected voice, his clothes stinking from the factory.

"I can see all right," said Caciotta.

The other went on bitterly, "Now we go home, eat, go to sleep, and tomorrow morning get up and sweat all day again."

Caciotta said, "Yeah, I know," eyeing him with satisfaction.

"And how's things with you?" asked a blond boy, Ernestino, noticing something special in Caciotta's manner.

Caciotta looked at him for a moment, dull-eyed. Then, silently, his motions constricted by the press of bodies around him, he put his hand into his pocket and stirred it around a bit, very cool, staring ironically, detached, at Ernestino and the two or three other boys, who were watching him with amusement.

Then, very slowly, he took out his wallet, opened it carefully, and with great finesse extracted a sheaf of hundred-lire notes from one section. With surprising suddenness he slapped Ernestino a couple of times on either side of the face with the packet of bills, slap, slap, after which he put the money back into his wallet and the wallet into his pocket, all with a tired, self-satisfied air.

Ernestino's eyes were laughing. He was tickled at having

been the butt of Caciotta's sally. "And what have you been up to?" he asked gaily. "That's four hundred you got there!"

"Four hundred besides what we got stashed away," said Caciotta, twisting his mouth as he spoke, his eyes dimming even more.

Riccetto was silent, rather sleepy, though he too was giving himself airs a bit, because he hardly knew Ernestino and the others. They were old friends of Caciotta's who had been born and raised in Tiburtino.

Caciotta had known Ernestino and a certain Franco, better known as White Feather, who was there too, since they were babies, when Tiburtino and Pietralata were way out in the country, when the subdivisions were new and the fort just built. Every now and then—they were hardly eight years old at the time—they used to leave home and stay away for weeks, starving or else living on onions or peaches hooked from the vegetable stalls, or stuff that dropped from housewives' shopping bags. They ran away for no reason, just like that, to have some fun. They got smokes from the *bersaglieri* at the barracks. When it came time for sleeping, they made themselves comfortable under the watermelon-seller's awning, right in front, on top of the melons.

Good humor and gratitude toward life in general, a consequence of having all that money in his pocket, made Caciotta feel sentimental and disposed to reminisce.

"Hey, Ernestì," he said, almost tenderly, "remember that business with the melon-man?"

"No, what melon-man?" asked Ernestino, who, with no money in his pocket, was unmoved.

"Hey, Riccetto," said Caciotta, tugging at his sleeve, "listen to this. You remember, Ernestì," he said, laughing, "how scared we were at night, over in Bagni de Tivoli, and we used to sleep with clubs under our heads?" Ernestino laughed. "That melon-man," Caciotta explained to Riccetto, "was keeping a pig out in Bagni de Tivoli, in a shed out in the fields. And since we kept careful watch over the melons for him, he got the idea of sending us to guard that pig. And he kept a rabbit there too. One night the melon-man's mother comes and she says, 'Go to Bagni,' she says, 'and buy a half-kilo of bread.' You know, that meant better than a mile going and better than a mile coming back. It was dark already. Then, while we're on our way, the melon-man's mother takes that rabbit, kills it, cooks it, and eats it up. Then she takes the bones, digs a hole, and puts them in the hole. The old bitch. Then the two of us get there, and right away we go look for the rabbit and the rabbit's gone. Then the melon-man comes, the boss, and he says, 'Where's the rabbit?' So then, Ernestì and me, we say, 'Well, we went to buy the bread, and when we come back the rabbit was gone.' Then the boss says, 'Couldn't one of you have gone by himself?' And we say, 'We were afraid to go by our-selves, so we went together.' Then he's fighting mad, and he pulls five hundred lire out of his pocket. 'You're both fired, and don't ever show up in front of my foot unless you want a good swift kick.'"

"Well, a lot we cared," he went on merrily. "We went back to Pietralata, and we and the neighborhood kids got together and got taken on by the circus—you remember, Ernestì?—with lions and tigers and all. . . . And the time Rondella, the circus horse, ran away and we ran after her all night, all over the fields beyond Pietralata, and when we caught up with her, she was taking a swim in the Aniene." Riccetto was listening to him with amusement, seeing everything from the same point of view as Caciotta and his old friends. And they were all nodding, laughing, feeling larceny beginning to stir in their souls. Among the boys from Tiburtino there was one from

Pietralata, who was listening, looking discouraged. His face and hair were black as a snake. He was tall and skinny, the others came up to his armpits. He stood close by them, holding onto the handrail, looking weary and preoccupied, listening with a tender expression on his evil young face. His name was Amerigo. Caciotta knew him by sight, scarcely more than that. The bus jolted over the pavement of the Via Tiburtina, making its load of human beings dance, though they were jammed together so you could hardly slip a needle in among them, and the gang from Tiburtino was getting more and more lively. "Just look at those beautiful curls he's got there," said Ernestino during a pause in the conversation, looking at Riccetto's head. "What," Caciotta interposed brilliantly, "didn't you know that guy makes you fart in his face so's to make the curls come?" While the others were laughing, without changing his position noticeably Amerigo nudged Caciotta with his elbow. "Hey, what's-your-name," he said softly, in an almost toneless voice, "I gotta tell you something."

4 · The ragazzi

> The people are a great savage in
> the bosom of society.
> —*Leo Tolstoy*

Amerigo was drunk. "Let's get off here at the fort," he said
to Caciotta, who listened deferentially. "This here's a friend of
mine," said Caciotta, just to be saying something. Amerigo
lifted his hand toward Riccetto as if it were made of lead. His
jacket collar was turned up; beneath his curly hair, matted
down with dust, his face shone green and his big dark eyes
stared glassily. He shook hands with great force, without seeming to, as if there couldn't possibly be the least doubt that both
of them were great people. But suddenly he forgot about
Riccetto, and turning to Caciotta, he said, "Did you get me?"
He was playing the steady type, but what Caciotta got was
that you better not horse around with this boy: One day at
Farfarelli he had seen him with one hand pick up six chairs
tied together, and he knew that Amerigo had punched people's
heads in and sent more than one to the hospital at Pietralata.
"What you been up to?" asked Caciotta, talking man to man,

or bum to bum. "We'll talk about it," said Amerigo, pulling his jacket collar higher.

The bus stopped by the Pietralata fort. From the still-open bar a shaft of light grazed the asphalt surface of the Via Tiburtina. Amerigo jumped down from the footboard, taking up the shock with his knees like a tumbler, without moving his hands from his pants pockets. "Let's go," Caciotta said to Riccetto, who couldn't quite figure out the turn that things were taking, and the two boys followed Amerigo. "What say we walk it?" said Amerigo, starting off by the *bersaglieri* barracks and heading toward Tiburtino. When they had gone a little way, he took hold of Caciotta's elbow; he walked on, setting one foot in front of the other, looking so evil that you felt you'd get a shock if you touched any part of his body. He dragged his feet like a punchy fighter, and yet his tired shuffle somehow seemed as quick and agile as an animal's. For Caciotta's and Riccetto's benefit, he was still playing the steady type, as if he were quite unconscious of his strength and of his reputation as the toughest nut in Pietralata. He had the air of a man plotting a business deal with an equal, someone who didn't fool easily. "You come with me," he told Caciotta, "and you'll be glad you did." "Where to?" asked Caciotta. Amerigo nodded his head toward Tiburtino. "There," he said, "to Fileni's." Caciotta had never heard that name before. He kept silent. Amerigo went on talking, pretending to believe that Caciotta had understood him. "Today's Saturday, we'll clean up," he said in a weak, womanish voice, perhaps imitating his mother, and his face looked even yellower. "Let's go," said Caciotta, sounding like a hood; since there was no way out of it, he was going to play it for laughs.

But Riccetto was walking behind them, his eyes narrowed into a squint. When they reached the place where Tiburtino

III begins, he said, "So long, I'm taking off." "Where you going?" asked Caciotta, stopping. Amerigo stopped too, and looked sideways at him, his hands half-sunk in his pockets. "To sleep, where the fuck you think? I'm so sleepy I'll die if I have to take another step."

Amerigo came over to him, looking at him with bloodshot eyes, but it seemed as if he were laughing; he was laughing because it just wasn't conceivable that anything could be done that was contrary to what he had decided.

"Look, kid," he said in a low voice, still calm and conciliatory, "I told you already that if you go along with me you'll thank me for it. You don't know me." Caciotta, who did know him, was looking on, amused. He knew that Riccetto would go with them to that Fileni's place.

"I tell you I'm sleepy," said Riccetto.

"Sleepy? What are you talking about?" asked Amerigo, laughing under his wrinkled brows, still happily convinced that it was sheer absurdity to refuse his advice. "Let's go." He put his hand on his heart. "Caciotta here can tell you, ain't that right, Caciò? I'm a guy that nobody can't say nothing against, and if I make a promise, kid, listen, it's gonna be like I say. Why? 'Cause we're all friends here, that's why. I do you a favor, like, and another time you do me a favor, ain't that right? We gotta help each other out, right?" He had grown solemn. This was like saying that you had to be a jerk not to go along with him. But something was eating Riccetto about this business with Amerigo and Caciotta; it smelled bad to him. Caciotta was watching him with a funny expression. "Do whatever you like," he seemed to be saying, "I'm not butting in." Riccetto shrugged. "Who's saying anything?" he asked Amerigo. "You're right, you're right. Go there with Caciotta. What do you need me for anyway?" But Amerigo didn't know which of the two had the money. He looked at Riccetto very patiently, very seriously. He came so close that his breath, smelling of wine, mixed with Riccetto's. But at that moment two familiar forms loomed up against the yellowish light of the first buildings in Tiburtino, coming down toward the fountain where the boys had stopped.

"The cops," said Caciotta. "They know me. They're the ones that wanted to pinch me in the movies the other night."

Watching them out of his sick eyes, Amerigo saw them come; he put his hand to his face and gripped his forehead with his fingers. He was white as a sheet and he was grimacing as if he were about to cry. When the two figures with their carbines slung over their shoulders had passed and had gone a little farther along toward the suburbs, he passed his hand over his face again. "Oh, God, how it hurts," he said. "Like there's a nail driving right through my head." But it was already over.

He went back up to Riccetto, and put his hand on the boy's shoulder with a friendly squeeze. "Look, Riccè," he said, "if that's your name. Don't be a jerk. Better come with me." He assumed again his expansive, oratorical air. "Honest," he said, "if you was the worst son of a bitch going, afterward you'd come to me and say, hey, Amerigo, I really gotta thank you, and I gotta apologize." His hand weighed down on Riccetto's shoulder as if it were a casket.

They went down the main street of Tiburtino where the only light was the glow from two bars, and among the one-story buildings, crumbling and dirty, with some kind of cloth hanging over the windows, they heard the thrumming of a guitar. They turned down by the covered market, damp and green with fish-slime, cut through two or three identical streets that divided the low buildings, and came to a house with a balcony in nineteenth-century style, battered and falling to pieces. They went up a stair, then through an open gallery that gave onto the street, and knocked at a door that was already ajar and from behind which a bit of light was shining. A hand on the inside opened the door, and they found themselves in a kitchen full of silent men grouped around a table. Six or seven of them were playing cards; the others, leaning against the walls or against a sink that was full of dirty dishes, were watching the game.

Amerigo and the other two slipped into the group of men, who after glancing at them drew back a little to make room. Then they all watched the cards from behind the players' backs. As if he weren't thinking about Caciotta and Riccetto any more, Amerigo watched the game, each hand going quickly, with continual wins and losses, followed by some audible whispering, or even by a remark made out loud. Caciotta felt that he couldn't care less about the whole thing, but though he was dying to sleep he kept looking around in a lively way, while Riccetto, remembering when he was younger in Donna Olimpia gambling with the money he had made from selling old pipe, began to look flushed and his eyes gleamed. Whenever a hand was finished, Amerigo would turn to one side, not toward his companions but toward one or another of the older men standing by, shaking his head, or muttering hoarsely, "Jesus!" In front of him was a man named Zinzello, with hunched shoulders and sleek hair brushed straight back, a carter, who lost every time, and whose face grew harder and more wrinkled. At last he got up and someone took his place. At that moment, Amerigo, who was behind him, made up his mind. He turned to Caciotta, and as if they had already come to an understanding, confidently, with a bitter expression in his eyes, said to him, "Lend me the thousand lire you got in your pocket." "I'm not the one that's got it," said Caciotta.

Amerigo's yellow eyes fixed on Riccetto, who was standing a little farther back. "Hand it over," he said in a low voice, so as not to be heard above the rumbling in the kitchen. Riccetto played dumb. "Come on," said Amerigo hurriedly, almost exasperatedly, "I'll give it back. What do you think, I'm gonna rob it off you? You know better. Come on."

"Hand it over, what do you care?" said Caciotta.

Riccetto said, "Let's go halves on the winnings, all right?" and he pulled out the bills, holding onto them tightly. "If you lose, you give me back five hundred," he added. "I ain't gonna rob it off you," said Amerigo. "We'll do like you say. Come on." He grabbed at the bills impatiently. He put three or four hundred lire down on the table, and made his bet. The cards flowed like a stream of oil, a hand here, a hand there, and one look was enough to tell you whether things were going well or badly.

Amerigo won on the first hand, and he barely turned his eyes toward Riccetto, who was watching, looking gloomy. Caciotta laughed with his mouth wide open. "I'm dying for a smoke," he said, searching his pockets for a butt, finding one, and lighting it. Amerigo won the next hand too. Collecting the money, he turned around to say something to the man with his hair slicked back, who was standing silently beside him. He merely glanced at the other two with a satisfied look, to keep them quiet. He put all the money he'd picked up into his pocket. Then things suddenly began to go badly, and in five or six hands he was cleaned out. He looked at the other two with his corpse's stare. Riccetto's eyes were hard, pained, as if he were going to cry; he said nothing. Amerigo went back to watching the game, trying to figure it, calculating how it would turn out. Every now and then he said a word to the carter, explaining why he had lost too. After a while he turned to Riccetto. "Hand over the rest." "You crazy?" said Riccetto. "Who's going to give me some more tomorrow if we lose again?" Amerigo waited for a moment. Then he started in again. "Come on, give me the money." "But I'm telling you

I don't want to play any more," Riccetto said in a low voice. But he wasn't sure of himself. Amerigo stared at him. "Lemme tell you something," he said, grasping Riccetto's arm, which seemed no more than a twig, with two iron fingers, and leading him out among the crowd until they were outside the door to the gallery. It had started drizzling again, but moonlight was sifting through the ragged clouds and falling upon the low buildings. "To me, you're just like a brother," he began. "You gotta believe me, what I say comes right straight outta my heart. Ask anybody you like in Pietralata, in Tiburtino, ask about me, Amerigo, there ain't nobody, nobody at all, who don't know me there, and I'm the most respected guy in the place, and if I can help somebody I help him, I don't stop and think about it first, and if I need help some time, what's the difference, that guy helps me, ain't that the way it is?" Riccetto was about to open his mouth. "Now, why," Amerigo interrupted, taking hold of his lapel with two fingers, "now, why," he repeated, shaking his head, such was the force of conviction he felt in what he was about to say, "if somebody asks you a favor, why should you go ahead and do it? Another time, for the sake of argument, it might be you that needs the favor, ain't that the way it is?" "You're right," said Riccetto, "but if I lose these two hundred lire, how am I supposed to eat tomorrow?" Amerigo's fingers slackened their hold on Riccetto's lapel. He put his hand to his forehead, shaking his head as if words failed him in trying to get something so simple across. "You don't understand what I'm trying to tell you," he said, and he started to laugh. "Tomorrow you make a date with me. What time do you say?" "Oh, I don't know—three o'clock," said Riccetto. "Three," said Amerigo, "at Farfarelli, O.k.?" "Sure," said Riccetto. "Tomorrow at three at Farfarelli," said Amerigo, raising his arms. "I'll see you and I'll give you your money. How much you got in your pocket?" "Oh, I guess four hundred," said Riccetto. "Let's see," said Amerigo, getting a fresh grip on Riccetto's shoulder. Riccetto took out the few hundred-lire notes he had in his pants pocket. Amerigo took them and counted them. Then he went back into the room without looking to see if Riccetto was following him. Caciotta was talking to the carter, who was watching the game. Amerigo reached past the backs of the seated players and put some money on the table. And lost again. He bet on another hand, and lost once more. This time no one said anything. Only after some time did Amerigo defend his play to the carter and Caciotta. They stayed there for another half-hour, and then they left, and no one paid any attention to their leaving.

One part of the sky was quite clear, and big stars shone wetly, lost in its vastness, as if on a boundless wall of metal from which insignificant gusts of wind blew toward the earth. In the other direction, when you turned around toward Rome, the weather was still bad, the clouds charged with rain and lightning, but it was lifting near the horizon, which was studded with lights. In still another quarter, right overhead here in Tiburtino, the sky was stretched as if over the funnel of a courtyard, and the frightened moon leaned upon the bright edges of wandering rags of cloud. Down among the identical streets of Tiburtino there was no one stirring, and only from the main street could you hear any sounds. The three walked listlessly toward the Via Tiburtina, among the building lots with wisps of grass pushing up out of the trodden ground, and Caciotta hummed while the other two dragged along their pointed, worn-out black-and-white shoes, wordlessly. "Well, so long," said Riccetto. Amerigo turned his broad face to him, and his set jaw seemed enormous and white in the moonlight. There was no particular expression on his face, but the swollen mouth, open like a wound, more livid than red, and his discontented eyes left no doubt about the tenor of his thoughts. "We're going to the Via Tiburtina," said Riccetto, for the sake of talking, "and there it is, just a couple of steps away, so I'll be leaving you here." Amerigo's twisted face expressed, even more than genuine and natural rage at being crossed, astonishment that anyone should be so witless as to cross him. But these conversations with Riccetto were something you just had to get through, and you had to be patient about it. And Amerigo took it all, but with an expression of such dissatisfaction in his eyes that it sent a shiver up the spine. He began once more, summoning up all his good will. "Now, if we go back again, I know we'll win, now that I've caught on to the game. Understand what I'm telling you?" Riccetto didn't answer; he looked at Caciotta, whose face in the cool wind was as pink and violet as a Roman onion. "Yeah, but you'd need some money," he said hoarsely. Amerigo looked at him impatiently, and it seemed as if he were about to shake his head and smack his lips to show that not only he, but anyone in his position, would never be dumb enough to accept such a conclusion. He leaned against the glistening frame of an empty doorway. "Now, if you shell out another two hundred and fifty lire," he said, as if Riccetto had already admitted to having more money on him, "we get back everything we lost, and we make double that." His voice grew still more feeble, in contrast to his body, which looked, as he stood in the doorway, like an enormous hog carcass hanging from a hook in front of the butcher's shop. His eyes, too, had grown small and dull like those of a hanging hog; and the sneer on his handsome face indicated that his patience was growing thin. Riccetto murmured once more, his eyebrows drawn up like a little boy's, "But I don't have a single cent left!"

Amerigo sat down on the broken doorstep. "Even if I get ten years in Regina Coeli, I gotta play tonight," he said in a low voice. Riccetto thought, with a shudder, "It's our ass now," and kept quiet so as not to provoke him. But Amerigo, after a moment's silence that was supposed to emphasize his words, started in again, more hoarsely but louder too, so as to erase that impression, and began his friendly lecture all over again, from the beginning. "Boy, I've put in quite a few years in the can!" "Where at? Porta Portese?" asked Caciotta. "Yeah," said Amerigo. His face had a gloomy look, and his pouting, wrinkled lips were trembling. "They sent me up for sodomy." "Jesus, who did you play that trick on?" asked Caciotta. "A sheep," Amerigo said desperately. "And the shepherd saw me doing it, and he told the cops, the bastard." He was almost at the point of tears, his mouth half-open and his brows drawn up into a forehead that was crisscrossed with premature wrinkles and framed in sculptured curls. "Damn, what beatings I got," he said bitterly, "what beatings!" His voice had grown shrill, like that of a woman lamenting some old injustice that still makes her suffer. "What beatings!" he said again. "Here, look." He drew his shirt out from under the waistband of his pants and showed his back. "You can still see the marks." "What'd they do to you?" Caciotta asked. "The beatings they give me, beatings, the pricks," said Amerigo, grinding his teeth. "Here, look, you can still see the marks," he repeated, pulling the shirt all the way up to his neck. His back was naked, broad as a sheet of steel, with bluish reflections on it in the moonlight. There were no marks at all on the smooth tan flesh. Caciotta bent over and examined it conscientiously along the great ridge that ran from the waistband of his pants to the nape of his neck, hidden by the shirt, and having looked carefully, he went, "Hm, hm," and straightened up. "Did you see?" said Amerigo in his mother's exhausted voice. "Can't see a fucking thing," said Caciotta. "What do you mean?" said Amerigo. "Take another look." Caciotta bent over the great back again, and he had to see something this time, considering the baleful look that Amerigo flashed him from out of his anguished face. "Jesus!" he said loudly. Amerigo pulled his shirt down, and straightening up, stuffed the tails into his pants. The mist of tears had dried in his eyes and left them a hard and naked brown. That stuff about the beatings and his plaint had introduced new arguments into the discussion, in the face of which, it was self-evident, Riccetto could only yield, and without another word at that. "Let's go," said Amerigo, as if the light had just dawned and he had finally been understood. Since Riccetto still said nothing, Amerigo went up to him and carefully took the lapel of his jacket between his fingers. "Hey, fella, I said let's go. You're gonna make me lose my patience," he said, looking desperate, as if those were words that he had not wanted to say, so that it was all Riccetto's fault. So they went back to the gambling den, and when they reached the outer stair Riccetto, at a look from Amerigo, silently produced another two hundred and fifty lire. Inside, the game was still going on. No one had noticed their leaving, and no one noticed their return. But before Amerigo had lost everything again, while he was absorbed in the game, Riccetto quietly slipped through the crowd by the sink and disappeared through the door.

A good thing, too, because he had scarcely passed the door of the new building beyond the balcony when the *carabinieri* came by. He saw them just in time to cut around the corner. "Son of a bitch," he said aloud, as if he were singing—he was so pleased not to have been spotted. He started to run through the deserted streets of the housing development, down toward the Via Boccaleone, and then, still at a run, down the Tor Sapienza road. There wasn't a cloud in the sky now; lights were showing on the left, towers with signal lights, the reflectors at the power plant, and beyond them, far away by now, Tiburtino with its rows of new houses against the black sky. Before him in the warm darkness the lights of the other suburbs gleamed, all the way to Centocelle, the Borgata Gordiani, Tor de' Schiavi and Quarticciolo. Dead-tired, Riccetto finally got to the bus stop at the Via Prenestina and began to wait for the Quarticciolo bus. He fished out the five hundred-lire notes that he had managed to hang onto, and picked out the most ragged one to give the conductor.

"Now what?" he said when the empty bus let him off at Prenestino. He took a look around, hitched up his pants, and recognizing that there was nothing there for him, he philosophically broke into song. A trolley was pulling in from the Via Prenestina, and it stopped for a moment, all agleam, under a gnarled tree; then it made a circuit around three or four low houses scattered among the dirty lots, and came to a halt once more on the opposite side. Some of the passengers who had gotten off ran toward the suburban buses parked in a line before a squalid café that was still lit up; some went off quietly to their beds in the neighborhood, in the Borghetto Prenestino, with all its little dwellings like cubes or henhouses, white as Arab buildings or black as mountain cabins, full of peasants from Apulia, the Marche, Sardinia, or Calabria: They were youngsters and old men who at that hour were coming home drunk and covered with rags. Some went off to the groups of hovels piled up together in construction lots, among the slopes of the alleys that ran toward the Via Prenestina. Riccetto decided to buy three Nazionali, since he'd been dying for a smoke for some time. Completely relaxed now, he crossed the small piazza, and went into the bar, counting his money. He came out again with a cigarette stuck to his lower lip, and his crafty eyes rolling around in search of somebody with a match.

"Let me have a light, kid?" he asked a young boy who was smoking, looking decadent and leaning against a post. Wordlessly, the boy held out his lighted cigarette, and Riccetto thanked him with a toss of his head, stuck his hands into his pockets, and went off singing through the gray alley where the trolley turned around.

All about him were scaffoldings, houses under construction, big empty lots, rubbish heaps, building sites; from far away, perhaps from Maranella, behind the Pigneto, you could hear a phonograph amplified by a loudspeaker. In the field by Casilina, this side of Maranella, there was probably a merry-go-round. Riccetto headed in that direction, his hands in his pockets and his head drawn down into his shoulders by the emotion he was putting into his solitary song.

For a while around Acqua Bullicante he saw nobody, except for a few old people hurrying home. But when he came to the road that turned uphill between the walls of two factories, toward Borgata Gordiani, a group of boys appeared, walking along unhurriedly, occupying the entire width of the road, calling out and raising hell, in a group as disorganized as a swarm of flies over a dirty table. One boy was cuffing another on the head, getting him riled; one was shadowboxing, punching the air right and left, and then throwing a hook that made his eyes glaze with satisfaction; another was showing his class by acting indifferent, his hands lazily riding in his pockets, and his whole attitude announcing, "Weak as I'm feeling, who's going to make me exert myself?"—sneering at his companions. Some were arguing, twisting their mouths in disgust, thrusting out their arms and clicking their tongues, or, in the heat of discussion, cupping their chins with both hands and drawing them toward their chests, from which position they stared quizzically at their interlocutors for half an hour. All of the Via dell'Acqua Bullicante was observing them with profound concentration. As far as Riccetto was concerned, they were just a bad smell. Not that their tomfoolery had anything to do with him. If anything, it was the world in general they had it in for, the entire human race that didn't know how to have a good time the way they did. But it annoyed Riccetto that they should be showing off while he was all alone, and excluded for the time being from any such bunch of loud-mouths, forced to listen quietly to the racket they were making. He began to whistle louder, not giving them as much as a glance, and went on his way. But he had not left them more than twenty yards behind when he heard the sound of sobbing from the other side of the ditch that ran along the filthy gardens. He drew near, and saw a boy squatting on the grass, his chest bare.

"What happened to you?" he asked. But the boy went on crying and didn't answer. "Hey, what's the matter?" asked Riccetto. Coming closer still, he saw that the boy was completely naked. Skinny and wet from the dew, he had gotten down on his knees and was starting to whine through his sobs like a little child. "They took my clothes and hid them on me, the sons of bitches." "Who did it?" Riccetto asked. The boy stood up, his cock sticking out, tears all over him. "Them," he said plaintively. Riccetto started to run after the group of boys he had just passed.

"Hey, you," he yelled. They all stopped and turned around. "Hey, was it you that hid the pants on that kid over there?" Riccetto inquired firmly but politely. "They're right there by him," one of them said cheerfully. "He'll find them all right." Riccetto moved back a few steps. Neither he nor anyone else felt like having an argument; on the contrary, they felt like allies, because they were sports compared to that asshole who was crying over there. "Forget it, he's a jerk," one of them said, striking his forefinger against his nose. Riccetto shrugged. "Poor bastard," he said. Now his responsibility as defender of

the weak was over, and indeed they saw the jerk come out of
the ditch with his pants on, holding his torn shirt. But the other
boys didn't move, and one of them stared at Riccetto, laughing.
"You looking at me?" asked Riccetto. The boy had thick,
cracked lips, and a delinquent's face set on a skinny neck that
was as wrinkled as a cabbage. "What, do you know me?"
asked Riccetto, who saw the boy silhouetted against the light
of a street lamp. "Why shouldn't I know you?" said the other
cheerfully. "I'm Lenzetta," he went on. "We saw each other
last night in the Villa Borghese, didn't we?" "Oh, excuse me,"
said Riccetto magnanimously, recognizing him now, and he
came forward with his hand outstretched. "Where you going?"
he asked. "Where could I be going, hungry as I am?" said
Lenzetta. The others laughed. "How about you?" said Lenzetta.
Riccetto laughed philosophically, turned his shirt collar up,
and thrust his hands deeper into his pockets. "How should I
know?" he said. "I'm still staying away from home and I sure
as shit don't feel like going back." "Why not?" Lenzetta asked,
amused. "Think I want to get jailed?" asked Riccetto. "I was
playing cards in a house in Tiburtino, and the cops came, and
the guys they picked up, well, it's their ass now. The bastards.
You know, Caciotta was there too." "Who's Caciotta?" asked
Lenzetta. "The boy who was with me last night, the redhead.
By now he's probably in a detention cell, the son of a bitch."
"I'm still staying away from home too," said Lenzetta, "and
who wants to go back? My brother'll kill me if he sees me."
"What do you mean, he'll kill you?" asked one of the group,
"I'm telling you they picked him up Saturday night." "I know,"
said Lenzetta, "but my mother's still at home, ain't she, and
she can go get stuffed for all I care. I can't stand her." "Well,
that's your fucking trouble," said his friend, laughing and
shaking his finger at him. "Your mother's at home, your
brother's in the can—anything you do, you're in the shit. You
go home, you get busted. You run around, you get busted. You

better watch out." Everyone laughed. "What the fuck do I care?" said Lenzetta. Laughing and shoving one another, they turned up toward Maranella. "Well," someone said, "Elina isn't home tonight." "Who told you so?" said another disgustedly. "She's always there." "Shit," said the first, "she had a belly the size of a washtub. She's probably at the Polyclinic by now, having the kid." "What do you mean, belly?" the other retorted. "It can't be more than four months at the outside." "Four months your ass," said the first. "She had a belly on her like a house when I screwed her in the spring." "Shit, ten years ago, you mean," said Lenzetta. "But who gives a shit anyway? If there's a hundred lire in this whole crowd, you can cut my throat." "What, you mean it would be the first time you went there empty-handed?" someone said. "I tell her, let's do it and I'll give you the money. We do it, and I don't give her a thing." "What a bastard!" Lenzetta yelled.

They had gone along chattering in this way as far as Maranella, and they weren't thinking about Elina any more. They heard the phonograph of the merry-go-round playing near by, and a murmur of voices and trampling feet still nearer, right at the Maranella crossroads, by the tram stop. Everybody was headed in that direction, as if something had happened there, or a festival was going on, late as it was. "It's the circus people," one boy yelled, beginning to run. "What circus? What circus?" Lenzetta retorted calmly, but quickening his steps, in his lazy way, along with the others. A small crowd could be seen coming down from Casilina, black against the badly lit and broken pavement. Near the Due Allori movie house, they stopped, mottled by the torches they carried in their hands. "It's a religious procession, what the fuck," said Lenzetta in disappointment.

The boys had stopped at the crossroad, which they had reached on the run. They were undecided now whether to go to Prato, where the merry-go-round was, and maybe the shooting

gallery with the blonde in it would still be open, or to stop
and watch the goings-on here in Maranella. They sat down
with a sarcastic air on the edge of the sidewalk, among the
legs of the bystanders who were crowding in to see the procession. One boy was singing; one was punching another who had
settled himself to watch; others were rolling, locked together,
in the dust. Meanwhile the procession drew up. "Shit," said
Riccetto, "we could have stayed in Prenestino and been better
off." "What could you do there?" asked Lenzetta. "Elina's
there, ain't she?" said Riccetto with a leer. The people coming
up now were overblown old women, and some old men scattered among them, and a couple of kids. All were holding
candles inside cardboard funnels so the night wind wouldn't
blow them out. Every now and then they would burst out
singing, each for himself. When they came to the crossing, they
stopped, gathering in a group on the sidewalk near the pizza
shop. Two boys set a table against the crumbling wall, and an
old man climbed up onto it, and began to make a speech
denouncing the Communists and exalting the spirit of Christ.

There was lots of commotion around where Lenzetta,
Riccetto, and the others were camped, so much so that the old
man, who was speaking the Cispadano dialect, could scarcely
be heard. "Louder!" yelled one of the boys. "Looking to get
paid off with a drink, hey, Mozzò?" said Lenzetta. Mozzone was
silent for a moment, listening. "Listen to that guy talk," he said
after a while, his voice soft with wonder. Riccetto nudged
Lenzetta. "Hey, I've had it up to here," he said. "What do you
want?" asked Lenzetta. "Let's go back there," Riccetto said,
motioning with his head toward Prenestino. "You're crazy,"
Lenzetta said. "I got the money all right," Riccetto explained,
"but just for the two of us." Lenzetta glanced at him and then
looked around. "Wait," he said. The others were all preoccupied. "Get up," he said, "and go on down by Acqua
Bullicante, and I'll come after you."

Riccetto got up and slowly moved off through the crowd that was baiting the old man, but in less than five minutes he ended his harangue, and the procession moved off once more, singing, and turned down toward the center of the town. Lenzetta caught up with Riccetto on the run. "What about the others?" asked Riccetto.

"We shook them," said Lenzetta. "They went to the merry-go-round."

As they talked, they retraced their way all along the Via dell'Acqua Bullicante, and at their backs the sambas playing on the phonograph and the songs of the marchers faded away. Now the streets were empty except for somebody or other coming back from Prenestino or the Impero toward the Borgata Gordiani, or toward Pigneto, or some drunk on his way home, singing now "Bandiera Rossa," now "La Marcia Reale."

They found Elina in that realm of shadows where she was queen, beyond the filthy lots full of rubbish heaps where the tram turned around, among the rutted roads, in an open space darkened by the enormous shadows of two or three skyscrapers under construction on the far side, and facing one already built, but still without a road or courtyard before it, abandoned among weeds and litter. The enormous box, with all its windows alight, rose alone into the sky, where a few stars gleamed sadly. Elina was holed up behind it, next to the wire fence and the row of bushes that ran around the sub-divided lots, still no more than enormous garbage heaps, with here and there a hovel or a pile of gravel.

Lenzetta and Riccetto went up to the woman, who was small and fat as a sausage, bargained a while, and, passing through the strands of a barbed-wire fence, went forward between sodden clumps of reeds.

It didn't take long. As soon as they came out, they proceeded calmly to a fountain in the center of the little piazza where the tram terminus was, to wash up a bit. Lenzetta was going to take care of the sleeping arrangements. Beyond the Borgata Gordiani, in a field from which you could see all the suburbs, from Centocelle to Tiburtino, at the end of a dew-soaked kitchen garden, there were some great rusty oil drums, left in an enclosure with some other old iron. They were wide enough to crawl into, and as long as a person. Lenzetta had spread some straw in one of them; he took some of it out and put it in a neighboring drum. They stretched out, and slept till after ten the next morning.

Lenzetta generally hung around the Via Tuscolana, the Piazza Re di Roma, the Via Taranto, where there were neighborhood markets, barracks, and a soup kitchen run by the friars. When he was away from home, he got along by doing a little work—as little as he could—for some fish-seller or notions-vendor, or picking up a little from market stalls or on the trolley. When he was in the mood, he stayed in the suburbs, in Prenestino or Quadraro, carrying a worn-out sack and hunting for old iron or scraps of lead among the rubbish. But he didn't do that often because he got backaches from bending, and besides, it left him with his mouth so full of dust that it took just about a bottle of wine to rinse it out, and that way he lost half the profits of the enterprise. Riccetto, too, wasn't enthusiastic about the old-iron racket, for the additional reason that it was, after all, kid stuff. So they went to the suburbs just for the purpose of sleeping in the oil drums, and they spent the daytime in the city. If by chance they picked up enough money for the next day too, they said to hell with working and breaking your back. They took the bus and rode out to Acqua Santa. They slipped past four withered saplings along the Appia Nuova, went up a slope ankle-deep in dust, and pushed through a region of holes, caves, ridges, scorched fields, ravines, ruined foundations, and abandoned roads, the vast and rugged promised land of Acqua Santa. Their hope was that they might encounter some hustler on duty on top of a hillock, at the crossing of two ruined roads, waiting for beardless customers from the shantytowns or the first housing projects that loomed in the distance; or else, posted at the entrance to a cave, or among the blackberry bushes surrounding a pond, some fat German or other, with his newspaper spread beside him and his gold-rimmed glasses, from whom they could lift what they wanted. They would look at him as if casually, or else stop to take a leak; and he would come after them, up over ridges and down through gullies, to the filthiest-looking ponds, just as the great Roman poet used to sing:

"Heard the fairy call out after the punk,
'I'm exhausted, darling, slow down or I'm sunk.' "

One day the two darlings—all alone, though—on coming up to the pond with the red fence around it, found a youngster from Tiburtino there, Alduccio. Riccetto quickened his step a bit to go and shake the boy's hand enthusiastically. "What's new?" he asked cordially, while slipping out of his clothes. Alduccio was stretched out on the dirty grass in his shorts, in the shade of a clump of reeds. He answered politely, "Same as usual. The longer you stick around the more you feel like you want to give it all the fuck up and turn robber or something."

"Jesus," said Riccetto, pulling his shirt over his gleaming head.

"You don't work, you don't eat, like they say, and where the hell do you find work?" He chewed his gum with a decadent, disdainful air.

"O.k.," said Riccetto, continuing in Alduccio's humorous vein, "we get ourselves a couple of Berettas and we organize a mob." Alduccio looked at him as if he weren't joking at all. "Right," he said. Lenzetta, who couldn't bear not butting into a conversation for more than one minute, and who had pricked up his ears at the word "Beretta," exclaimed mockingly, "What do you mean, Beretta. Cappella, not Beretta!"*

Riccetto and Lenzetta stretched out on the bank of the pond too. "Well, now," Riccetto began again, "what you got to tell me about Tiburtino?"

"What's there to tell? I told you already. Same old stuff."

"Say, do you know Caciotta, the one who lives in the new development?" asked Riccetto.

"What do you mean, do I know him?" Alduccio answered. "Sure I know him."

"What's he doing?" Riccetto inquired. Alduccio's handsome face became lively. Not saying anything, with the tips of his thumb and forefinger he pinched the skin of his cheek beneath his eye. That meant Caciotta was in the can, in Porta Portese.

"Jesus!" Riccetto murmured, laughing inwardly.

"They picked him up in Fileni's joint, while he was gambling," Alduccio explained.

"I know, I know," Riccetto said wisely, "I was there too." Alduccio looked at him with interest. "Amerigo is dead," he said. Riccetto sat up on his elbows and stared. The corners of his mouth trembled as though he were smiling in amusement; it was exciting news and he was very curious. "What did you say?" "He's dead, he's dead," Alduccio repeated, pleased to be imparting this unexpected piece of intelligence. "He died yesterday at the Polyclinic," he added. That same damned night that Riccetto had cut out from Fileni's place, Caciotta and the others had all been picked up; they hadn't tried to resist. But Amerigo had let himself be led out by two *carabinieri* who

* *Beretta,* the name of an Italian arms firm, hence a pistol of that make; literally, "cap." *Cappella,* a pun on *cappello,* "hat."—*Trans.*

were holding him by the arms, and as soon as they were out on the balcony he had slammed them against the wall and made a jump of some nine feet into the courtyard. He had hurt his knee but he had managed all the same to drag himself forward along the wall of the project. The *carabinieri* had fired, and they had hit him in the shoulder, but he had managed to reach the banks of the Aniene. They were on the point of grabbing him there, but, bleeding as he was, he threw himself into the water to cross the river and hide among the gardens on the far shore, and get away toward Ponte Mammolo or Tor Sapienza. But in the middle of the stream he had lost consciousness, and the *carabinieri* had grabbed him and taken him to the station dripping blood and mud like a sponge, so they had to transfer him to the hospital and set a guard over him. After a week his fever went away, and he tried to kill himself by cutting his wrists with the glass from a tumbler, but that time too they saved his life. Then some ten days later, before Alduccio and Riccetto had met here at Acqua Santa, he had thrown himself from the second-floor window. He had lingered on for a week after that, and finally had gone on to his rest.

"His funeral's tomorrow," said Alduccio.

"Son of a bitch," Riccetto said emphatically under his breath. Lenzetta, to show that he wasn't easily impressed and that his motto was "Worry about your own fucking troubles," started in singing,

"Two-bit whores, two-bit whores . . ."

and stretched out on the grass as best he could, with his fingers intertwined beneath the weight of his big cauliflower head.

Riccetto, however, thought it over for a while and then decided that it was his duty to attend Amerigo's funeral. It was true that he had hardly known him, but Amerigo was a friend of Caciotta's, and besides, he felt like it. "I'm going to Pietralata tomorrow," he told Alduccio, "but don't tell anybody so my father won't find out."

Amerigo was stretched out on the bed in his new blue suit, white shirt, and black shoes. They had crossed his arms over his chest, or rather over that double-breasted jacket that he had been so proud of for a couple of Sundays, going around Pietralata with his tough walk. He had gotten the money from a man he had mugged in the Via dei Prati Fiscali; he had lifted something like thirty thousand lire off him, and then, just for his own satisfaction, he had stomped him bloody. That's how he had come by the blue suit, and he wore it around, looking meaner than ever. You had to watch out how you looked at him; his friends in the neighborhood, who were cowardly and hypocritical with him, knew how to butter him up without being too obvious about it, but there were some young boys who didn't know him, whom he met in the Communist Party dance hall, or in some poolroom, and who went home with their eyes swelled up and their gums bleeding. It was their good luck that Amerigo had been officially warned not to carry a knife. The trousers of the suit were as wide as a Dutchman's, and the jacket was broad and full in the shoulders. The collar of his white shirt was unbuttoned, and his hair was brushed back. He had submitted patiently to being laid out, like a sacrificial victim, his hands crossed over the double-breasted jacket, but the shirt collar was still unbuttoned like a hood's, framing the face that had looked like a corpse's even while it was alive, so much so that it seemed as if he had just fallen asleep, and he was frightening still. When his nap was over, he'd quit being so easygoing, and he'd push some faces in for having gotten him up like that. Sullen and still, he lay in the bed that was too small for him, his curly mop shiny with hair oil on the gray pillow.

Riccetto came with some friends from Tiburtino to take a look at him, and went into the little room on the ground floor of the house. In front of the entrance to the house, which had no door, and had two stairways, to the right and left, there was a small group of people wearing dark clothes: The entire Lucchetti family, come to fulfill their duty as relatives and as actors in the events of the day, were wearing their holiday clothes—bright-colored in the case of the little children and adolescents, and more suitable for a dance than for a funeral in the case of the young men. The neighbors living in the same building, ten or twelve to a room, so that they almost amounted to a neighorhood all by themselves, were standing a little farther off, and farther still were Amerigo's friends, all dressed up. There was Arduino, whose nose and one eye had been blown away by a grenade when he was a kid, the boy with T.B. who lived in number 12, and Rats, and the Neapolitan, and Capece, and Sor'Anita's boy, who played the guitar and sang, especially on nights when they had come back home from pulling some job or other, and were up late dividing the take, arguing, or taking a walk in the mud, the moon shining down on the squatters' shacks. There were a few younger boys, too, leaning lazily against the house wall, talking among themselves in low voices, or watching the little children playing ball farther down, in an open space in the center of Pietralata.

Riccetto and the others had scarcely entered the room where the dead boy lay than they were ready to leave. It was damp and dark in there, as if it were winter, and Amerigo's aunts and sisters, all of them fat, filled the room so that you couldn't even move. They glanced at the corpse, and, embarrassed because they hadn't done so since the day of their first Communion, they made the sign of the cross, and went back out into the street, where the men were standing talking. In the midst of them, but with a preoccupied air, like someone busy with his own affairs, was Alfio Lucchetti, the youngest of Amerigo's uncles, dark as Amerigo had been, and with the same cheekbones and curly hair, but taller and thinner. He was the one who had stabbed the owner of the bar by the tram stop three years before, getting him in the belly with a bayonet, and now people said he was ruining himself for the sake of a prostitute he was keeping in Testaccio. As a matter of fact, he wasn't talking to the others as much as coming out with a word or two now and again, looking remote, as if he were hinting at something, and shaking his head. And all of a sudden he would break off, as if he didn't want to discuss his affairs with all those people standing around listening. He looked beyond the circle of heads, his hands buried under his black coat in the pockets of his gray pin-striped trousers, grinding his teeth so hard that his jaw muscles swelled and subsided, just as Amerigo's used to do, and so tall that if he raised a hand he could touch the electric wires.

He was stewing quietly, brooding before them all over the secret that nearly everybody in the neighborhood had an inkling of. There were a number of things behind Amerigo's death whose implicit menace was reflected in every face there. Alfio's face, under his gray stubble, fairly glowed with it; his skin was very dark near the roots of the hair that grew low upon his forehead, and his boyish neck rose out of a turned-down white collar. It showed as well in the faces of the other uncles and cousins, filled with their sense of duty and the wordless bitterness that made them the most important people in Pietralata, determined not to talk, to keep their opinions on the state of affairs that arose from Amerigo's death in the family, or at most making some partial revelation or other in allusive and threatening language. Then, among the other young punks there was Arduino, a piece of black cloth hiding the scarred eye-socket but not the remains of his nose, and

Sor'Anita's boy, and Rats, and Capece, all with the look of beasts of prey in their shifty eyes, and beneath their serious air a hint of quiet enjoyment, like soldiers taking a shower. Alduccio picked up on the fly the half-sentences exchanged by Alfio and the other men. His face was bathed in a dignified look, and twisting his mouth and nodding with his head drawn into his shoulders, he muttered, "It's their fucking business."

"Whose?" asked Riccetto alertly, sounding a bit naïve in his curiosity. Alduccio didn't answer him.

"Whose? Hey, whose?" Riccetto repeated.

"The guy that was talking," Alduccio said, noticing him in a kindly but abstracted fashion. Riccetto thought immediately of the new building and its gambling joint, and he didn't say another word. He looked at Alfio with great respect. Meanwhile, Alfio had taken a step or two, leaving the group behind, and he was standing there, silent and self-assured, his hands buried in his trousers pockets.

The weeping of the women could be heard coming from within. The men, on the other hand, betrayed no sign of emotion; on the contrary, the features of the beardless youths, and the old bastards too, showed traces of amusement. At Pietralata, simply as a matter of good breeding, nobody showed sympathy for the living. You can imagine whether they gave a fuck for the dead.

The priest came in hurriedly, not looking at the faces around him. Behind him trotted two boys as skinny as starved cats, dredged up out of some of the ragpickers' shacks scattered here and there in the burned-over fields and among the garbage heaps on the outskirts of Pietralata. They trotted along in their surplices, swinging the censer, making their way through the people standing in the broiling sun among the houses and shacks, or walking around, or playing, or calling out. The children kicking the ball, running after it like a swarm of hornets, dressed in their beggars' rags, went on yelling in the distance, in the violet light, and in the bar by the tram stop there were the usual comings and goings of people who were idle at that hour. They jabbered away, yapping like dogs in the half-empty bar, or leaning against the dried-out young trees or the door frames, their faces leering, their thumbs buried in the waistbands of their beltless trousers, pushing them down till the crotches were at the level of their knees. Others stood around in the courtyards, under the dirty windows, near the remains of junk that had been sold to the peasants bit by bit during the war. Now they were all busy watching the funeral from afar. The priest entered the house, did what he had to do, and came out in a short time, followed by his two puppies, the crowd of women, and the coffin carried by the men. It was placed in the black car, and the cortège, on foot, went slowly down the Via di Pietralata. The marchers passed by the bar, keeping a bus that was at the stop from moving on again; then by an open stretch with two or three merry-go-rounds set upon its hillocks, by the clinic, naked as a prison, by scorched fields, pink shacks, shanties, a factory so rundown that it looked as if it had just been bombed; and then they reached the foot of the Monte del Pecoraro, near the Via Tibertina and the broken ground of the abandoned quarries.

"What do we do now?" Riccetto asked Alduccio in a low voice, from among the straggling mourners, some falling behind, some up in front escorting the automobile and the priest. "How should I know?" said Alduccio, slouching along with his hands in his pockets under his billowing shirt tails. They were walking very slowly at the end of the procession, which was itself moving more slowly now; but the boys walked more slowly still, and every now and then they had to hurry to catch up again. They walked stooped over, abstracted, looking as if their feet were hurting. Riccetto said with a pained air, "I sure didn't know funerals were such a drag. Jesus, what a drag!" "Me neither," said Alduccio, glancing at him. When their eyes met, and each saw the figure his companion was cutting in the midst of the silent cortège, they wanted to laugh, and they turned their eyes away and stretched their neck muscles trying to control themselves and not cause a scandal. The air was as soft as oil, and the pure outlines of things, the warm wind that seemed to bear an April somnolence, made it seem as if the day were a holiday—one of the first Sundays in the season of fair weather, right after Easter, when people begin to go to Ostia. Even the traffic on the Via Tiburtina seemed noiseless, deadened, as if it were enclosed in a bell jar, in the sunshine that, though colorless on the low walls and on a gray garbage dump, burned golden on the slopes of the Monte del Pecoraro. Inside the fort, the *bersaglieri* bugle gaily sounded mess call.

In front of the bar on the corner formed by the Via Tiburtina, after a brief pause, and with its accustomed disorder, the little procession broke up. The funeral car started up, and, followed by the taxi carrying the most important of the Lucchetti clan, went off at full speed toward Verano.

5 · The Warm Nights

Panza piena nun crede ar diggiuno . . .*
—*G. G. Belli*

Meanwhile, Lenzetta was waiting for Riccetto and Alduccio, sitting in the dust by a low wall, dressed to kill in his velveteen pants and his red-and-black-striped jersey, which, according to him, knocked their eyes out in Maranella. He was dripping with sweat because he had taken a kick or two at the ball with some boys who were still playing below him in a small field between the Via dell'Acqua Bullicante and Pigneto. Above the wall, squatting on the tin roof of her shanty, which looked like a sheep pen, and enjoying the view, was Elina, with two hoops of phony gold dangling from her earlobes, and in her arms her smallest baby, who was whimpering. Lenzetta paid no attention to her, for he was absorbed in contemplating life, and every once in a while cursing Riccetto for not having shown up. But he was mildly happy. He sang, his wrinkled neck pressed against the crumbling wall, now and then bringing down a bit of plaster or dust because he moved his head with great emotion from left to right, from right to left,

* The full belly doesn't believe in hunger."—*Trans.*

slowly, as he sang. His eyes were half-closed, and since he was singing in a low voice, as if he were in the confessional, or as if he wanted to give just a small sample of what he could have done as far as singing goes, anyone who was more than four steps away would only have seen his mouth opening and closing, and the cords in his neck drawn so taut that they stuck out on both sides of his windpipe.

He interrupted himself frequently, right in the middle of a trill, to yell something at those who were playing ball, dogged and panting. One of them, barely thirteen, was smoking a butt as he played; another lay stretched out on the ground exhausted, jeering at those who were running around.

"Hey, dead-on-your-feet!" Lenzetta cried, but not too loudly, so as not to expend energy. "You can't even stand up, what do you expect from us?" the goalie answered, standing idle between the posts, leaning forward, his pants torn and half-unbuttoned, making a magaphone with his hands, which were sheathed in gloves picked up from a rubbish heap. The one who was stretched out on the ground got up and walked out onto the road, abandoning the game and the boys who were knocking themselves out playing. He pulled up his pants, took off his dirty shirt and slung it over his shoulder, and went to meet another boy like himself who was coming along, gay as a lark, carrying a bottle of milk under his arm. They began to play marbles right near Lenzetta, below where Elina sat on the sheet-metal roof, outlined against the white sky like the statue of the Madonna in a procession. "Fuck you guys," Lenzetta said once more, in an angry voice, meaning Riccetto and Alduccio; but for all his annoyance he wasn't too much out of sorts, disposed as he was to say the hell with everything. The little boy who had just come up and was chattering merrily as he played, even when he got angry at the other boy who was trying to take advantage of him, appealed to Lenzetta,

who took him under his wing. The other boy suddenly started
to behave himself and play fair, without trying to cheat the
little one. They squatted down, took aim, *pock!* with the
palms of their hands on the ground; the marble skidded into
the hole. Lenzetta looked on paternally. When the little boy
won, he did a dance around the milk bottle which had been
left lying on its side on the ground; and then he got back
into position at once, with his legs spread and his seat on his
heels, shooting for the hole.

"You beat, eh, kid?" Lenzetta said in his condescending
voice. The other player was bitter about losing, and stealthily
began to win. "Hey, you letting him rob you like that?" Lenzetta said jokingly. Then an empty hearse went by at full
speed, racing by the big apartment houses and then among the
muddy hedges of Acqua Bullicante.

"So long, sweetheart!" Lenzetta yelled, by way of com-
mentary on the corpse that the hearse was going to pick up
someplace. And suddenly he remembered Riccetto, who had
also gone off to a funeral. "That shithead," he said, flushing
with anger.

Lenzetta had left home because he was scared of his big
brother. And he was right to be scared; his brother had pulled
one on him that he didn't even like to think about, and he'd
spit in his eye if he could. Not that he'd behaved badly to him,
morally speaking. Morally? What the fuck did he and his
brother have to do with morality? To tell the absolute truth,
it had been a question of honor, not just some stupid argument
over nothing at all. What the hell had come over Lenzetta that
night? Well, he must still have been punchy from the beating
he'd got, first at the police station and then in jail. When he'd
been sent to the can—Regina Coeli, not Porta Portese, because
though he looked like a kid he was already eighteen—scratching his curly head, he'd said to himself, "Jesus, it's my ass

now." And he was right, for one of the first things he heard when he got inside, from a consumptive who looked like Lazarus fresh from the tomb, was, "What a beautiful ass, kid." But it was his good luck that his brother, Lenzetta number one, was one of the most influential cons in Regina Coeli; out of respect for his brother they let him alone, cute as he was. After a couple of weeks he got out on a conditional discharge, and he went back to Torpignattara. The first thing his mother said to him was, "You don't work, you don't eat, right?" "Hey, let me rest up a little, for Christ's sake! I just got out of the can," he said, cupping his hands under his chin. And that night he went off to have a good time with his friends at the Bar del Tappeto Verde, also called the Knife-in-the-Back Bar, where the group that used to call itself the Maranella Vice League met, boys of around sixteen who had just started to haunt the bars and shoot pool. He bragged a little to them, giving himself airs because he'd been in Regina Coeli and henceforth rated a certain amount of respect. They drank a half-glass of wine apiece and went off to sleep stone drunk.

Lenzetta slept with his older brother in a little windowless room, one in an old bed like a gondola and the other on a cot. Around midnight Lenzetta, who hadn't been able to get to sleep and was high from the wine, tossed away the old patched sheets and started to sing. His brother was sleeping like a top, his mouth half-open and the sheets twisted around his legs, but after a while he began to show signs of annoyance. He turned over suddenly, catching all of the sheet under his belly. Lenzetta, stoned out of his mind, went on singing with all the steam he had. Then his brother woke up with a start and said, "Hey!" "Fuck you," said Lenzetta, getting to his feet. His brother caught on to what was happening, looked at him, gave him a shove that slammed him against the wall, and dropped off again. Next morning as Lenzetta went out into the street, he saw his brother waiting for him with his Lambretta. "Get on," he said. Lenzetta obeyed, and his brother tore through the morning traffic over to Maranella, cut through the alleys around Torpignattara, where you weren't supposed to drive at that hour because the market was open then, sprinted off at forty-five miles an hour toward Mandrione, passed it, and pulled into Acqua Santa like a maniac. He didn't dismount or even slow down to go through the alleys that were knee-deep in dust, but turned into them in high gear; once in among the fields and quarries below a tall tower, he shut the motor off, got down, and told Lenzetta, "Put up your hands." They pounded each other for a half-hour, and at last Lenzetta, just about exhausted, managed to run away.

Riccetto and Alduccio were walking along slowly because they had walked all the way from Pietralata. They were dragging their feet as if they belonged to two other people, their backs riding on legs as limp as rags, but they were making a big thing all the same out of their young hoodlum insolence. They must have covered at least three miles, from the Via Boccaleone down through the Via Prenestina to Acqua Bullicante, passing by a field full of shit, a village made up of shacks, an apartment house as big as a mountain, and a weather-beaten factory building. And that wasn't the end, the best was yet to come, for they had to go all the way through Casilina. Lenzetta, fresh as a daisy after having thoroughly cursed out the two pilgrims, and having been called jerk and shithead in return, was walking briskly in the lead, the others limping after him, in bad moods from fatigue and the pain in their feet.

The place over on the Via dell'Amba Aradam—Lenzetta had discovered it—was really first-rate. It was a little out of the way, right by the bridge where the road crossed the Viale di San Giovanni, beside green and brown walls in among gardens that were choked with leafless plants, and old, upper-class villas that had seen better days. Up on a bluff there was a whole row of low buildings roofed with rusty sheet metal, glowing in the last rays of sunlight. Far back, over in one corner, was the smallest of the shacks, but it had a large fenced-in court that was full of old iron. There was a deep silence over everything, but inside the shanties or among the junk heaps a workman was whistling quietly, or a voice was calling and another answering. The three toughs went along in Indian file, one humming and one whistling. Only when they were a little farther along, among the ruins, did they say anything at all, scarcely moving their lips. "Jesus," said Riccetto, "what a load of axle shafts!" "What did I tell you?" said Lenzetta triumphantly. "Yeah, but it's still daylight," said Riccetto, so as not to give him too much satisfaction. "And then, without a three-wheeler you can't do a fucking thing here." "Yeah, a three-wheeler. And where you going to get one, you dope?" Lenzetta grumbled, twisting his mouth. "Let's go down to Maranella and ask Remo the junkman for one," Alduccio said, suddenly piqued because of the bad reception given his idea. Lenzetta stared at him, frowning pityingly, and then clicked his tongue, not deigning to answer. "Stupid," he said suddenly a moment later, "you want all three of us to go back to Forlanini? Do it on foot again, from there to Maranella, and then back again? Is your head screwed on right?" "But who's telling you to do it all on foot again? Who's saying anything about that?" Alduccio said, flushed and angry. "Just listen to him!" "O.k., how?" asked Lenzetta, already a little more interested. Riccetto was listening attentively to the discussion, not saying a word. "Let's get a little money, why don't we?" Alduccio cried. "Oh, yeah," Lenzetta said, disappointed. "Let's go," said Alduccio. And without even turning toward his companions, he started off toward San Giovanni.

"Where's that idiot going now?" asked Lenzetta, trotting after him with Riccetto. "Has he gone crazy?" "He's not crazy, he's not crazy," Riccetto said.

It wasn't long before they figured out what Alduccio had in mind. But when they reached the piazza at Porta San Giovanni, they found the place deserted. True, there were some people on the benches along the wall that fences off the drop, but not the kind of people that the three friends were looking for. There was a fat woman who was bursting out of her cream-colored silk suit, her lips still sugary from the pastry she had just eaten, her face looking like a boiled fish, and next to her an ugly little guy, maybe her husband, with a face like a fried fish, the poor bastard, just getting over a drunk. And here and there a little kid and a nursemaid. Beyond the wall that gave upon the Tuscolano section, like a terrace, beyond tennis courts and expanses of trodden earth, the warm red evening was now descending, making the windows glow in the crowded pale blue buildings, so that the scene looked like a Martian panorama. On the near side of the wall that Alduccio and the others were leaning against, the gardens of San Giovanni, full of shrubs and flower beds stretched out in the same sad light, grazed by the last rays of sun that fell directly upon the galleries and great statues of the cathedral's façade, and gilded the red granite of the obelisk.

Discouraged, and showing it in their sneers, the three criminals were over by the wall—Lenzetta stretched out on it, belly-up, with his hands under his dust-streaked neck, singing; Riccetto sitting on the edge with his legs dangling; only Alduccio was standing, his legs crossed in a nervous pose, leaning a hip and an elbow against the wall. He was the only one who wasn't acting disgusted, for he was looking forward hopefully to the march of events. There he stood, one hand buried in his pocket, looking like the sheriff's son, his thick lips overshadowed with black down and his deep-set shining eyes resembling two mussels dripping with lemon juice.

And his faith was rewarded. When Lenzetta and Riccetto, who had suddenly decided to go get a drink at the fountain, slowly made their way back to the wall, taking it easy so as to kill a little time, they found Alduccio ready to leave, all merry and bright. "Come on, let's go," he said. He stuck his hand in his pocket and pulled out three hundred-lire notes, all worn. "A man came by," he explained. "He gave them to me for nothing, just to be friendly." Then he added gaily, "Just to feel it for a minute." The others weren't looking for such elaborate explanations; such things happened. They lost no time, and yelling and shouting so as to make themselves heard by whoever happened to be around, they went to the tram stop down by the Porta di San Giovanni, and in something like half an hour they were in Maranella again.

They drew a blank at Remo the junk-dealer's. He had already taken the three-wheeler home to Pigneto, to a courtyard swarming like an anthill with people, and had gone off to the tavern. He was sitting at a little worm-eaten table, red as a lobster under two inches of black-and-white beard, and all swollen up as if he had gas under his skin instead of blood. He was talking with a little old man who was as shriveled as a piece of salt cod, and who still talked with a country accent though he'd lived in Rome for the last hundred years. Between those two there was a third whose face was hidden because he had fallen asleep over the table and lay there like a pile of rags. Lenzetta appeared in the doorway, giving the place the once-over. He saw Remo immediately, and called to him in a sly, confidential voice: "Hey, Remo, can I talk to you a minute?" Remo broke off the intellectual discussion he was carrying on with grandpa. "Excuse me," he said, "let me go see what that young punk wants." The other put on the expression of a man who's suddenly left alone and swallowed a sip of wine, his Adam's apple jumping. The other two boys were outside the door, on the crumbling sidewalk by the trolley tracks. "These here are friends of mine," said Lenzetta, looking even more knowing, his face reddening. "Pleased to meet you," said all three, shaking hands. "Say, Re'," Lenzetta said hypocritically, coming right to the point, "you gotta do me a favor." "Why, sure," said the other, half-ironic, half-polite. "You gotta lend us your three-wheeler—I mean, if it's possible. How about it?" Remo didn't say yes or no. He had gotten the picture right away, and he had figured his own angle even quicker; in return for the three-wheeler, lent as a favor, they would have to bring him the stuff for sale, and he would know how to set a price on it. With a comradely smile, he took out a cigarette-paper, and, licking and spitting, rolled himself a smoke. You have to take it easy, you know, because in Maranella, where the Via dell'Acqua Bullicante runs into the Casilina, there're more comings and goings, both cars and people, than in the Via Veneto. . . .

It must have been around eleven, eleven-thirty, when Riccetto and the others, taking turns pedaling the three-wheeler, with one boy sprawled on his belly inside the van in the back and another trotting behind hanging onto the saddle, having gone all the way back up the Via Casilina, finally got to the place, dead tired.

A hair's breadth above the walls and the bungalows, covered with fretwork like family tombs or summer houses in watering places—built by the rich in Mussolini's time, when Riccetto couldn't have known a thing about them, any more than he did, incidentally, now that he *was* alive—a moon as big as an oil drum appeared, lighting up everything. Alduccio stayed outside with the three-wheeler, at the foot of the slope. Riccetto and Lenzetta crawled into the court on their bellies through a hole in the fence near the shed, hidden among two or three saplings and a jumble of dry refuse. Once having squeezed through the gap and raised their heads on the other side, like crushed worms, they found themselves inside the enclosure and looked around; Lenzetta decided that the occasion called for a little rhetoric: "Here we are in junk heaven," he said. Satisfaction and fear showed in the faces of the two gangsters, though they wanted to show nothing more than a natural professional interest—especially Lenzetta, who felt that he was the boss of the expedition. "Let's go," he said breathily, without losing any more time. And since the other hesitated, his ears pricked up like a dog listening for a suspicious sound, Lenzetta got annoyed. "Hey, stupid," he said, "let's go!" He went over to the pile that looked the most substantial, inspected it, picked something up, threw it down after examining it in the moonlight, and began to flit around among the other piles like a ghost. Riccetto followed him, looking around too, making no sound. Leaving behind the piles of auto tires, wheels, and other stuff that didn't interest them, they found what they were looking for in the middle of the courtyard. And they started in with the transport operation. First, one piece at a time, they piled it all up by the hole in the fence. Then Riccetto crept through, and Lenzetta passed the stuff out to him from inside. When everything was outside the fence, Lenzetta came out too, and together, at top speed, they ran up and down from the slope to the three-wheeler, from the three-wheeler to the slope, red as hot peppers, the tendons in their necks straining and their spines rigid with effort. Alduccio thought he was dreaming as he saw the stuff pile up—auto batteries, bronze gears, iron pipe, axle shafts, and a hundred pounds of lead. He helped with the loading, placing the stuff in the van of the three-wheeler while the others came and went. "There's still room for more," he said when they came back from the last trip. "Yeah, well stick this in," Lenzetta said, putting on airs, but before he had properly got the words out of his mouth his eyes turned with a hard look toward the Via dell'Amba Aradam. The others fell silent, busying themselves with the three-wheeler. A boy in a white shirt was coming toward them. When he came close they could see that he was a plump young man with a face as smooth as a piggy bank and dopey eyes. Lenzetta, seeing that he was some poor little rich student, recovered himself, and staring at the boy with eyes that had just been all watery with fright, said to him, "What you lookin' at?" "Nothing," said the other, moving by quickly, as if their words had been a simple exchange of courtesies, perfectly natural at that hour and in those circumstances.

But Lenzetta, turning after the round-shouldered form going off into the distance, returned to the attack. "Hey, Fats, if you ain't looking at nothing, beat it, or I'll make you see stars."

The student made no answer. But when he had gone far enough he turned halfway round and yelled, "Bunch of robbers!"

"That boy's spying for someone," said Alduccio, sounding scared, all his confidence evaporating on the spot. "Run Aldo, and wait for us in front of the hospital," said Lenzetta, equally shaken up, and he started to run after the fat boy while Alduccio pedaled off in the other direction, and Riccetto didn't know which one to follow. The fat boy, who sure as hell didn't think Lenzetta was running after him to apologize and make up, scampered off like a scoundrel along the walls by the Porta Metronia. Then Lenzetta turned around, caught up with Riccetto, who was waiting for him, and together they ran after Alduccio who was pedaling away, all in a lather and white-faced from the strain. They spelled one another, taking short turns, and pedaling and running they got to the Via Appia Nuova. "Oh, Jesus!" said Lenzetta, throwing himself flat in the middle of the road, right on the tram tracks.

He lay there with his legs spread and his hands on his chest like a corpse. "If I go another ten steps, it'll be the end."

The other two left the three-wheeler, laughing, and followed his example, rolling in the gravel under the trees that stretched away endlessly in two lines down the center of the road.

"Really worked your ass off, eh?" said Riccetto, his head between the three-wheeler's wheels. At that hour there was almost no one on the road, except for young fellows on their Lambrettas taking their girls to Acqua Santa.

Lying on the ground in the middle of the road, watching the couples pass by, they yelled, "Get out!" Or else, "Don't listen to him, honey!"

A soldier, coming along with a piece of tail behind him hanging onto his pants, wanted to act tough, and yelled, in a half-Neapolitan accent, "Knock it off!"

The boys exploded as if someone had stuck a pin in their backsides. They half rose, leaning on their elbows in the dust.

"Hey, you, getting civilized in Rome?" Alduccio yelled.

"You see this?" Riccetto added didactically, his hands making a megaphone around his mouth. "This here's the Basilica of San Giovanni!"

"Hey, they still use tom-toms in your country?" Lenzetta howled, increasing the dosage, and getting up on his knees to do so.

"Hey, let's go," said Alduccio when they had calmed down a little. "We going to spend the night here?"

Lenzetta sat up and lit a butt.

"Give me a drag," said Alduccio, getting ready to pedal away. After a couple of draws, Lenzetta grumbled and passed the butt to him, and Alduccio, smoking, hadn't turned his pedals four times when, slap, crack, bang, the front wheel got caught in the trolley track and was smashed to hell.

Nothing to worry about. The merest trifle. How far was it from there to Maranella? And Riccetto and Lenzetta had scarcely done any walking at all that day! While Aldo, furious and bitter, stayed behind to guard the three-wheeler and the stuff, which they had piled up on the sidewalk of a street that ran into the Appia Nuova a little farther down, Riccetto and Lenzetta put one foot in front of the other and made their way back to Maranella, to the pushcart-man's place. But the pushcart-man's place was closed. "Fuck the no-good bastard," said Lenzetta, grinding his teeth over that fathead who was God knows where.

"Oh, he closes up this time of night, huh?" said Riccetto vindictively. "We'll screw him good. That'll learn him." To tell the truth, it was after midnight, but they didn't give a damn. They went into the fathead's little courtyard and carried off the best cart.

"Tomorrow we don't bring it back, what do you say?" Lenzetta said, pleased to have his conscience clear.

There wasn't a soul about where they had left Alduccio on the Appia Nuova. But just before they came to the corner of the Via Camilla, a shadow started toward them, and as it drew near it took on the form of a skinny old man with a ragged cap on his head. He was carrying an axle shaft, and when he saw the two boys he tried to hide it.

Lenzetta turned as red as a turkey cock, and spoke to him without beating about the bush. "Hey, Pop, where'd you find that axle shaft?" Riccetto waited, his hands on the raised shafts of the cart.

The old man assumed a crafty and confidential air that made his white face look even sharper under his limp cap. "I'm hiding it," he said with a wink, "because the night watchman wants to arrest your friend. I'm giving him a hand. Could be that the watchman's gone to get help."

"Fuck you too," Lenzetta thought, but you never can tell, and he started off at a run, followed by Riccetto, toward the place where they had left Alduccio, and grandpa trailed after them, carrying the axle shaft.

But that jerk Alduccio wasn't there. They looked in doorways, behind grilles. "Aldo! Aldo!" they yelled. At last Alduccio came running out of a dark alley where he'd been hiding.

"What's the matter? The cops come by?" Riccetto asked.

"How do I know?" Alduccio said. "I just took off for the alley." The three did not investigate further but pretended to believe the old man. He was standing nearby, legs apart, looking innocent, still hanging onto the axle shaft. He smiled, and his mouth drew inward over his jaws with their toothless gums.

"O.k., let's load up," said Riccetto anxiously. While Alduccio dragged the three-wheeler into the alley for safe-keeping, Riccetto and Lenzetta, assisted by the old man, began loading the cart. When it was all loaded, Riccetto winked at Lenzetta, who said thoughtfully to Alduccio, "Say, Aldo, you go on ahead with the cart. This way, if we all go together people will spot that something's up." Aldo obeyed, but unwillingly, and protesting a bit. Sulking, but moving carefully, he started to push the cart and lead the march.

The others followed a short distance behind, ready to take off through the alleys and leave him holding the bag if there was an alert. Lenzetta was flushed, and looking at Riccetto with a satisfied grin, he said, nodding toward Alduccio, "Work, slave!" Riccetto lit up at that comment, grinning too, feeling like a big shot too. The old man walked beside them, taking long steps, dragging his canvas shoes along the pavement.

Under his left arm, tucked in tight against his armpit, he carried a rolled-up sack, which gave him a roguish, almost sporting air. "Where you going with the sack?" Lenzetta asked, just to include him in the conversation, Riccetto sneering meanwhile behind his back. "Stealing cauliflower to feed five mouths," he said. "Five boys?" Lenzetta inquired. "No, five girls," the old man replied. Lenzetta and Riccetto pricked up their ears. "And how old are they?" Riccetto asked casually, feeling out the ground. Lenzetta began to walk with more conviction, like the donkey that smells the stable. "One's twenty, one's eighteen, one's sixteen, and the other two are still little girls," said the old man, looking stupid but not missing a thing.

Riccetto and Lenzetta exchanged glances. They walked on a while, and then Lenzetta, after quietly nudging Riccetto, stopped to take a leak.

Riccetto stopped too, and moved alongside Lenzetta, while the old man's feet took him a few steps farther before he slowed down.

"Let's dump Alduccio," Lenzetta whispered swiftly.

"But how?" asked Riccetto, pained.

"Oh, make up some excuse, go on," said Lenzetta impatiently.

Riccetto was silent for a moment and then, as if he'd had an idea, he said, "Leave it to me," and after he'd hurriedly buttoned up, he started to run after Aldo, who could be seen far ahead looking like a shadow. But Lenzetta held him back. "Make him give you the money, too," he whispered.

"O.k., leave it to me," Riccetto repeated, starting off at a run.

Lenzetta, arranging his trousers with well-bred composure, caught up with the old man, and out of the corner of his eye watched to see what the other two were up to, down there under a big scaffolding by the outermost fields of Acqua Santa.

Riccetto was saying yes and Alduccio was saying no, Riccetto yes, Alduccio no. But after a while Riccetto came running back, and Alduccio started to push the cart again, bending over the shafts.

"We had him go on to Maranella by himself," Riccetto felt he had to explain to the old man. "If they saw all three of us together they might catch on to what we're up to."

"You did the right thing," said the old man.

Now they were nearly up to Acqua Santa; on the right were the empty fields and the ponds, and on the left the beginning of the Via dell'Arco di Travertino, that ran straight toward the Porta Furba, and from there to Mandrione and Maranella.

Along the Via dell'Arco di Travertino there were two great collections of shacks, and walking along the road you got a splendid view. There were pink and white shanties, sheds, huts, gypsy wagons without wheels, warehouses—all jumbled together, some spread out among the fields and some piled against the walls of the aqueduct in picturesque disorder.

Among the buildings there was one set right in the clay by the roadside, a little better looking than the others, with a branch over the door* and a signboard on which was written in red, in childish characters, "Wine." There was still a ray of light showing through a crack in the door. "It's open," said Lenzetta, glancing swiftly at Riccetto for support. Riccetto promptly winked, slapping a hand to the bottom of his pocket almost by his pecker. "Say, you in a hurry to pick up that cauliflower, Pop?" asked Lenzetta.

"Not at all, no hurry," said the old man amiably.

"Then maybe we could both go and give you a hand if you didn't mind, huh?" said Lenzetta.

"On the contrary," said grandpa. "Be a pleasure."

* The sign of a wineshop.—*Trans.*

"I believe you," Lenzetta said to himself. And then, out loud, "What do you say to a drop of wine first, Pop? That way you get oiled up a little—all that dampness in those fields!"

The old man didn't find a thing wrong with that, and his eyes gleamed cannily, for, while he played the country cousin, he didn't mind letting them understand that it was all understood. Nevertheless, before accepting he demurred a little for courtesy's sake. "You shouldn't go to all that trouble," he said, passing the sack from one armpit to the other.

"No trouble at all," said the boys, scrambling down the clay slope, and since the old man followed after them more slowly, Lenzetta remarked to the tavern wall, "Life is tough if you got tender feet."

In five minutes the two ne'er-do-wells were already loaded. They began to talk about God and religion. The old man was the audience. Riccetto, blushing with pleasure at his own originality, put the case to Lenzetta, and Lenzetta listened attentively to make it look good. "Say, tell me something. You believe in Mary, the one they call the Madonna, up there?"

"How should I know?" Lenzetta answered promptly. "I never seen her." And he looked at the old man with satisfaction.

"Well, there are certain facts," the old man said, "that go to show that the Madonna's there all right."

But one particular aspect of the question interested Riccetto. "You do know she was a virgin and she had a son, don't you?" he said to Lenzetta.

"Jesus," said Lenzetta, getting even redder, both hands stretching out toward Riccetto, "don't you think I know that?"

"What you think about it, Pop?" Riccetto asked, pressing on with the investigation. The old man's face lengthened and he drew his head into his shoulders. "Do you believe that, kid?" he asked, evading the question. Riccetto, perfectly content, started in with his speech. "You got to look at it all according to the point of view. As a human woman she could have actually existed. From the point of view of holiness and virginity, she might not have. Holiness, well, that could be too, but not virginity! Now they've invented the fact of artificial children with test tubes, but if a woman has a child with test tubes she's not a virgin any more. Then there's faith in Christ, faith in God, and all that. And if you start in reasoning from faith, then you believe in the virginity of the Madonna, but scientifically as far as I'm concerned I don't see how it can be proved." He looked at the other two with great satisfaction, as he always did when he recited that speech, which he had learned from a young fellow from Tiburtino, and he looked ready to take on anybody who might contradict him. But Lenzetta grabbed the table edge with both hands and began to make "Pff, pff, pff" noises, like jets of steam issuing from under a loose-fitting lid.

"You look like a movie director," he said, trying hard not to burst out laughing.

"You ignorant shithead," said Riccetto, feeling justly offended.

"Let's have another half-bottle!" Lenzetta cried, and offered him his hand. "O.k.?"

But Riccetto slapped away the proffered hand. "I'll spit in your eye," he said.

Lenzetta spread his arms wide. "What do you want to talk about Jesus Christ and the Madonna for, hungry as you are?" he asked, his face as red as a raw cutlet. Then, looking steadily at Riccetto, he burst out laughing. "Why do you want to drink milk when you've always drunk pure water right out of the gutter? Right out of the drains."

"You shut up," Riccetto answered. "With big feet like yours you can go around town begging."

But Lenzetta was still staring at him, and, struck with a thought that gave him an irresistible desire to laugh, he cried, shaking both his hands, fingers outspread, before Riccetto's face, "You remember when we went looking for empty tin cans, and we wanted to sell them?"

Riccetto burst out laughing too. Lenzetta was about to explode. He stood up in order to speak more comfortably. "Don't you remember when you went to the hospital, to the soup kitchen there, and you got two or three cans—" he imitated Riccetto, looking very humiliated, getting a canful of soup from the hospital porters—"and one guy ate it up on you and another guy tripped you, and you'd been hoping to sell the stuff to starving wrecks like yourself!"

Both boys began to laugh like madmen at the recollection. Lenzetta made a clumsy movement, and as he stamped and roared, something fell at his feet under the table with a dull sound. Riccetto looked, and on the tile floor he saw Cappellone's Beretta, which had fallen out of Lenzetta's trousers. "That little bastard," he thought. "Then it was him that stole my shoes on me in the Villa Borghese!" Lenzetta stooped swiftly under the table and slipped the revolver back under his waistband.

The old man looked like someone who's just been kicked in the backside and, turning round, sees that his attacker has dislocated his foot and is howling with pain.

"You got any pictures of your daughters?" Lenzetta asked him, straightening up, gay as ever. "If they're ugly," he thought, "we'll make him pay for the wine, and then we'll cut out." The old man, his face looking lengthened and puffy with drink under the lamp that was coated with fly-specks, pulled out his wallet, and exploring it with his grubby fingers compartment by compartment, showed them the picture of a little girl dressed for her first Communion.

"What's she like now?" asked Riccetto, who was still a little annoyed.

"It's true, this isn't exactly the way she looks now," said the old man, and he plunged into the wallet once more. He couldn't resist showing them his identity card. There he was, all cleaned up, in a black suit, shirt and tie, a self-satisfied look on his face. Antonio Bifoni, son of Virgilio, born in Ferentino 11|3|96. Then there were a couple of small-denomination banknotes, his Communist Party card, two welfare claims, and his unemployment card. At last he pulled out some more photos. Lenzetta and Riccetto dived at them.

"Hey, will you look at that!" Riccetto said softly, almost more in gestures than in words.

"I'll take this one," Lenzetta said under his breath, turning away from the old man, "and you take that one."

To get from the tavern to where they were going, they went by Porta Furba, turned down to Quadraro, through a group of lonely houses that looked like shacks, and arrived at a kitchen garden, bounded on one side by a white path and disappearing on the other side among some fields, with a villa and a pine wood beyond them.

There was a smell of manure and rotten straw, and the strong perfume of fennel, which could be seen spreading out like a green cloud, with the salad greens growing in the middle of the fennel beds, beyond the wire-mesh fence, and among the gaps in the hedges of soppy cane that ran along it.

"Let's go this way," said the old man with a werewolf expression on his face, and he moved off, bent double, taking noiseless steps to where the mesh fence ended in a tangle and a paling of wet, uneven poles began. Here there was a breach, a gap, covered over with spiny bushes and a few canes. The old man began scraping and scratching to widen it, down on his knees among the canes, the weeds, the mallows, and rows of spinach, all soaked with dew. They crawled through the gap and slipped into the garden.

The moonlight bathed the entire plot, which was so large that the walls on the far side were out of sight. The moon was high in the sky by this time; it had shrunk in size and appeared not to want to have anything to do with the world, absorbed instead in contemplating what lay beyond. It was as if it were now showing the world only its backside, and from that silvery rear end a great light streamed down, suffusing every object. At the end of the garden the light shone upon peach trees, willows, cherries, and elders, springing up here and there in clumps as hard as wrought iron, twisted and insubstantial in the white dust. Then it raked the garden itself, making it glisten, or else coating it with a gleaming patina, shining on the curved shapes of beets and stalks of greens, half-lit, half in shadow, and on the yellow lettuce beds and the green-gold plots of leeks and endive. And here and there lay heaps of straw, and gardening tools dropped by the field hands, in the most picturesque disorder, for the earth did so much on its own that you didn't have to break your back tending it.

But the old man had spotted the cauliflower, and he didn't care about anything else. Followed by his two partners, he stepped over the ditch without wasting time and entered the furrow, a little canal with an inch of water in it in the middle of the plot from which furrows stretched right and left, also carrying water, and dividing the plot into so many squares. Along the line traced by the furrows were the rows of cauliflower, each one as big as a peacock, stretching ten or fifteen feet. "Let's go," said the old man, his knife already open in his hand. And starting at one border, he plunged into the line of cauliflower that grew as high as his waist, and began to cut them loose. He cut them and stuffed them into the sack, using his hands and feet. The two accomplices, watching from behind, looked at each other and burst out laughing, louder and louder, until their snickers could have been heard in Quadraro. "Hey, keep it quiet!" said the old man, rising anxiously from among the bluish cauliflower heads. After a moment, as the first flush of enthusiasm subsided, they fell silent. They decided to do a little something and plucked up a couple of cauliflower each, without leaving the ditch, picking the first ones that came to hand. They slipped their booty, pulled from the rich earth, stalk and all, into the old man's sack, squashing the cauliflower, half-spilling the load, and giving it a kick now and then. "Take it easy," the old man said. Paying no attention to him, the boys amused themselves by stuffing the sack with as many cauliflower as they could, laughing and laughing. At last the old man picked up the sack, heaved it onto his back, and went off at a zigzag toward the gap in the fence. But Lenzetta called very calmly, "Hey, wait a second. I gotta do something." And without waiting for an answer, he unbuckled his belt, dropped his pants, and heedlessly commenced to let fly upon the wet grass. Seeing how matters stood, Riccetto and the old man started to follow his example, and all three were lined up in the furrow, their butts in the moonlight, squatting by a big cherry tree.

Lenzetta, finishing his business, began to sing. Then the old man gave him a cross-eyed look, squatting by his loaded sack, and said in a worried voice, "Say, what's-your-name, did you know that my nephew did six months for a cauliflower, a single one? What are you trying to do, get us all locked up?"

Lenzetta fell silent at those sensible words. "Say, Pop," Riccetto said then, taking advantage of the confidential atmosphere, while Lenzetta was already pulling up his pants, "is your daughter engaged?"

Lenzetta began to laugh, making his usual "pff, pff, pff"

sound, blaming his laughter on the stench and screwing up his nose. The old man, sedulously playing dumb as was called for by the situation, answered affably, "Nope, she's not engaged." They pulled up their pants, fastened their belts, and on their hands and knees followed Lenzetta, who was already through the gap in the paling.

Once they were on the road, the two little bastards were unwilling to let the old man do all the work, you know, and they insisted on shouldering the bulging sack themselves. They carried it by turns, very cheerful and insouciant, and making plenty of noise, as they walked along out of breath and cursing to themselves because of the effort it took, behind Sor Antonio —who, having had to play sucker and patsy, now had his own patsies to carry the load for him.

When, step by step, they had put Porta Furba behind them and had penetrated deep into a jungle of gardens, roads, wire-mesh fences, villages of hovels, vacant lots, construction sites, groups of tenements, and ponds, and were almost up by the Borgata degli Angeli, between Tor Pignattara and Quadraro, the old man said, with a polite and worldly air, "Why don't you drop in at my place?" "Thanks very much," said the two sweating derelicts, and they thought, "Wouldn't it just be the last straw if he hadn't invited us, the old creep!"

The Borgata degli Angeli was deserted at that hour, and among the regular rows of the houses of the poor, looking like big packing cases, could be seen, farther down, four dirt roads heaped with rubbish, and above, the cloudless sky and the moon beginning to set.

The street door of the tenement where the old man lived was open. They went in and began to climb a flight of stairs, two, three, with many landings, doors, windows opening on inner courtyards, everything grimy, children's dirty drawings done on the walls with a bit of coal. The old man rang the bell at number seventy-four, with his two attendants waiting behind him, and in a little while the eldest girl came to the door.

She was a pretty girl, barely twenty, wearing a nightdress that fell straight down from her shoulders. She was all rumpled, her eyes swollen with sleep, her flesh warm. When she saw the two guests, she slipped behind a dilapidated screen that stood in the middle of the hallway.

Antonio went in, stood the sack against the screen, and called in a loud voice, "Hey, Nadia!" No one came out, but from the other side of the wall you could hear the whispering noises women make when there are three or four of them together.

"Jesus," Riccetto thought, "what they got in there anyway, a tribe?"

"Hey, Nadia!" the old man called again.

You could hear louder shufflings, and then out came the eldest girl again, with her nightgown set to rights, wearing shoes, her hair combed.

"Meet some friends of mine," said Antonio. Nadia came forward smiling, bashful, keeping one hand at the neck of her gown and stretching out the other to them, with its slim little fingers soft and white as butter; the two friends grabbed at it immediately.

"Claudio Mastracca," said Riccetto, shaking that pretty little hand.

"Alfredo de Marzi," said Lenzetta, doing the same, his face reddening and softening, as it did in moments of emotion. The girl was so bashful that you could see she was on the point of tears, especially since they were all four standing motionless, staring at each other.

"Sit down," said Antonio, and he led them through a doorway covered with a curtain into the kitchen. Between the stove and the sideboard, among four or five chairs, there was a cot against the wall, and two little girls were sleeping in it, head to foot, red and sweaty, with the sheets, more gray than white, twisted around them. On the table were frying pans and dirty dishes, and a cloud of flies, awakened by the light, swarmed and droned as if it were midday.

Nadia had followed them, and she was standing to one side near the doorway.

"Don't mind the way the place looks," said Antonio. "This is a working man's house."

"You should see mine!" said Lenzetta with a giggle, to encourage him, but as a little kid who was used to talking with other dirty little kids might say it. Riccetto too laughed at his friend's feeble attempt. Lenzetta, inspired, went on without scruples, as if he were in a discussion in the Knife-in-the-Back Bar, pissing sarcasm out of both eyes: "Our kitchen at home, you'd think it was a shithouse, and the mice hold conventions in the bedroom!"

Meanwhile, Antonio had come to a sudden decision. He darted through the doorway and dragged the sack of cauliflower into the kitchen, stowing it beneath the sink with a satisfied air.

"These two fine young fellows have been giving me a hand," he told his daughter. "Otherwise, when do you think I could have brought these things here? Christmas, maybe!"

At that sally from her father, Nadia's chin began to tremble, though she was doing her best to smile. She looked as if she would burst out crying, and turned her face away.

"Oh, come on," said Lenzetta expansively, sticking out his stomach and raising his arms, "you don't want to cry about a thing like that."

But the girl, as if she had been waiting for just those words, began to cry in earnest, and ran behind the screen.

"You little idiot! You half-wit!" someone yelled from behind the wall after a moment.

"That's my wife," said the old man.

Indeed, in another minute she came into the room, also in her nightgown, but nicely combed and her chignon stuck full of hairpins, Adriana by name, preceded by two fine protuberances that put the sack of cauliflower to shame. "The mother's better-looking than the girls," Riccetto thought. She came wheeling into the kitchen, still vibrating with scorn, continuing the speech she had started inside. "That little imbecile. She starts crying because you got to manage in order to live, look at that, will you? With times being what they are nowadays! I don't know who that girl of mine takes after."

She stopped short, somewhat calmer, examining with two brief glances the somewhat shopworn guests presented for her inspection.

"I want you to meet some friends of mine," said the old man.

"Pleased to meet you," she said, frowning a bit, and complying with the formalities hurriedly. "Claudio Mastracca," Riccetto repeated. "Alfred di Marzi," Lenzetta repeated. The necessary parenthesis of greetings once out of the way, she started in again on the matters nearest her heart, although in a more confidential voice. "Where could you find a girl of twenty crying like a baby, and for what, I ask you? For four lousy cauliflowers. Will you tell me what there is to be ashamed of in that?" And she lifted her head in a gesture of defiance, her eyes aflame, her hands on her hips, confronting an invisible audience, probably composed of gentry. "Hey, Nadia," she called, thrusting her head through the doorway, "Nadiaaaa!"

Meanwhile the two little girls who were sleeping head to foot woke up, and lying there open-eyed, they began to take everything in, happily. Nadia came back after a while, still bashful, wiping her eyes with one hand, and smiling over her foolish conduct earlier, as if to say, "Please don't mind me!" "You idiot!" her mother repeated, still in that defiant voice, for the benefit of those persons she had in mind. "Would you mind telling me what there is to be ashamed of?"

"And don't we go robbing stuff ourselves?" asked Lenzetta, subtle as ever, to give her morale a boost. "We're unemployed, that's what we are."

"Nothing to wonder at," Riccetto added, almost in a drawing-room voice. "Everybody steals, some more, some less."

These consolations were just about enough to make the girl start bawling again, but luckily at that moment her sister, the eighteen-year-old, came in all dressed up. She had taken so long to put in an appearance because she had been putting on her good dress, the black silk one, and she had even put on some lipstick. She was counting on the tactical surprise of her arrival, and she came forward modestly. "I want you to meet these two fine boys, friends of mine," the old man announced ceremoniously for the third time. "This is my other daughter."

"Lucian-na," she drawled, looking kittenish like the girls in the magazines.

"Claudio Mastracca," "Alfredo di Marzi," said the two fine boys.

"Pleased to meet you," she said, smoothing her hair back with one hand.

"Pleased to make your acquaintance," mumbled Riccetto and Lenzetta, pleased and flushed as two turkey cocks. A moment later the third daughter showed up too, a redhead with freckles and a ribbon in her hair who didn't come into the kitchen but stationed herself half-in and half-out to watch the two fine boys wordlessly, like the two little girls in the cot.

And as a matter of fact, she was hardly more than a little girl herself, standing there in her flowered dress, loose as a friar's gown, and beneath it her two bony little legs. Meanwhile her mother had begun her off-stage complaining again, driven to speak by profound, deep-rooted conviction, and God knows why and whom she had it in for.

"You're absolutely right, ma'am," Lenzetta said when she had finished. "It's only natural." But his warmth arose for another reason—he was deeply stirred by that dairy she carried around with her.

"What can we offer you?" Antonio asked. "Would you have some coffee?"

"Don't bother," said Riccetto, while Lenzetta pricked up his ears at the suggestion. "You think we'd let you go to any trouble for us?" Riccetto added, with a gay and unexpected air of contempt for the starvelings they were. Antonio hadn't noticed that at the word "coffee" the four women, and even the little girls in bed, had looked at one another. So he insisted. "What do you mean, trouble? On the contrary. It's a pleasure," he said, dragged headlong by courtesy. The glances around him reflected dismay. Adriana opened her mouth halfway as if she meant to speak, but she closed it again and stood mute, her daughters watching her with apprehension and feigned indifference.

"Well, how about that cup of coffee?" Antonio asked his wife, full of his duty as the master of the house.

She didn't stir, standing among the girls who were looking now at her, now at one another, Nadia on the point of bursting into tears again and Luciana displaying an embarrassed little smile, tossing her head so as to settle the hair behind her shoulders. Adriana, shaking her head rapidly, and putting a hand to her bosom, said, "As far as the coffee's concerned, I'll be glad to fix it, only—what can I say—we forgot to buy sugar." Antonio looked stunned. "Antonio, what can you expect?" his wife said. "With all these worries, I don't have my head screwed on right any more."

"What's all the fuss?" Riccetto said swiftly, still sticking to his policy of completely undervaluing himself and his companion. "It's fine for us without sugar."

Lenzetta agreed with a laugh, red blotches all over his face. At this escape route, the entire Bifoni family felt its courage revive. Saying, "I'll fix it right away," Adriana picked up the coffeepot and lit the stove, attended by her daughters, and these activities spread such enthusiasm about that while the two fine young fellows and Antonio chatted affably, even the little girls emerged from under the sheets in their nighties and began to make a racket all over the room.

The coffee was ready quickly and was served to Riccetto and Lenzetta in two cups that didn't match, while Antonio and his wife drank theirs from large, chipped cups. Blowing on the coffee to cool it, Riccetto said, "We'll drink up, and then we won't trouble you further." "No trouble at all," said Antonio grandly. Adriana, tasting her coffee, didn't conceal her disgust, even spreading her hands before her. "What swill!" the two fine young fellows thought, suppressing a shiver of nausea under an air of cordiality and good breeding, sipping the coffee cheerfully, and at last setting the cups down on the table among the flies.

"Time for us to go," said Riccetto.

"What, so soon?" asked Antonio, astonished, as if instead of being two or three in the morning it was just after dinner.

"Be noon in a little while," said Lenzetta.

"Stick around a while, won't you?" the old man insisted, reaching out his arms.

"We'll say good-by to you," Riccetto said swiftly, extending his hand to the old man with a manly and somewhat roguish air.

"Well, I'll go a ways with you," said the old boy. Long and white as a strip of dried codfish, he went ahead of them to the door, and waited on the landing while they said their good-bys, sedulously shaking hands one by one with Adriana, Nadia, Luciana, and the last grown daughter, who came forward for the operation, still mute as a fish, but sharing in the polite buzz of farewells. She extended her hand without batting an eyelash, without saying a word, after the other two had already gone off about their business behind the screen, by this time wearing the expressions they had when they were alone.

Antonio went down the stairs as if exhausted, taking them on the slant, moving noiselessly in his canvas shoes. Riccetto nudged Lenzetta's elbow, taking advantage of Antonio's being ahead of them. Lenzetta looked at him. "Give me the money!" Riccetto said in a low, ferocious voice, for fear that Lenzetta would refuse. Indeed, Lenzetta's face darkened, and he made believe he hadn't heard. "Don't play dumb!" said Riccetto in the same hollow voice, expressing himself with his eyes more than in words, grinding his teeth, throwing a furious look at Lenzetta. "Give me the money, come on!" Lenzetta felt obliged to give it to him, and he unwillingly got it out of his pocket. They reached the bottom of the stairs in the dilapidated entryway and the old man opened the street door. It was already getting light outside; beyond the forty packing-crates in rows in the Borgata degli Angeli, beyond Quadraro, beyond the stretch of countryside, beyond the misty shapes of the Alban hills, a rosy light was suffusing the sky as if from behind a glass casement, and it seemed that, down on the other side of the skyline, there was another Rome silently catching fire.

"Well, I'll say good-by to you, boys," Antonio said. "I'm going to bed now."

"Of course," Lenzetta said. "We wouldn't want you to go to any more trouble."

The old man smiled, his head down, chomping his jaws as if he were chewing a mouthful of dry chestnuts.

"Here, take this, Pop," Riccetto said quickly, handing him one hundred and fifty lire in a crumpled heap of worn notes. Sor Antonio looked at the money, examining it carefully. "Oh, no, I couldn't," he said.

"Go on, take it," Lenzetta said encouragingly.

The old man debated with them a little longer, but nevertheless he finally took the hundred and fifty lire.

"Jesus, all that sunshine!" Lenzetta said when the old man had gone back into the house and the boys were alone among the buildings. And indeed, a thin, clear violet light had begun to shine in the open spaces of the streets, between the buildings, reflected from that remote invisible conflagration beyond the hills, while among the cornices two or three owls took flight, hooting.

Lenzetta, listening to them abstractedly, his thoughts a mixture of the fine-young-fellows-role they had played, the Bifoni family, and death, felt his knees go weak, and he stood still for a moment, preoccupied, and as if withdrawn in contemplation; then he lifted his knee to his belly and loosed a fart. But he had to force it, because it didn't come from the heart.

In the Knife-in-the-Back Bar, the Bar del Tappeto Verde, between shots or watching the game, leaning wearily against the walls of the dreary room which had two pool tables squeezed into it and a ceiling so low that if you raised your arm you hit it, the beardless delinquents of Maranella had another topic among the many on which they could deliver an opinion: Riccetto's engagement.

According to how it struck them at the moment, they might discuss it in a friendly tone, indirectly, taking it all very seriously, and at other times as if they couldn't care less. Riccetto, on his part, felt himself to be the most interesting person around; as such, he felt obliged to buy himself at least a new pair of pants. Affable, exchanging pleasantries, but keeping up an air of mystery about his private affairs, he came along with his new pants riding on hips so slim that he looked like a nail taking a walk. They were gray and pegged, with pockets cut on the slant, and he walked slouching forward with his hands on his hips and his thumbs hooked into his belt, dragging his feet a little with his weary and somewhat stupefied plowboy air. The pants looked like a couple of pipes below his butt, and they moved as he walked, one pipe here, one there, one up, one down; and when he stopped, leaning cross-legged against the wall or on the edge of the pool table, they made one solid trunk, taut, calm, menacing. For the rest, he was still sleeping, with Lenzetta, in the oil drums in the field by the Borgata Gordiani. But those living arrangements were to last but a short time longer, since they were ill-suited to his new circumstances.

Lenzetta knew of a place in the Via Taranto on the top floor of a seven- or eight-story building—a landing that opened at one end, through a lopsided door that was always ajar, into a kind of loft where the water tanks were, and at the other end into a vacant apartment whose door seemed to have been shut for months. They carried a bunch of newspapers up there, hiding them by day among the water tanks, and all their stuff, and used the landing for a bedroom.

The engagement implied a responsible attitude, and Riccetto —glad to play the role of responsible young man, which was the one that got him the most favorable comments in the Knife-in-the-Back Bar and gave him the most pleasure—had gone to work. He worked as helper to a fish-seller who had a stand in the little market in Maranella. And on Sunday, playing his part to the hilt, he mysteriously gave up roaming around with Lenzetta and the others in Centocelle or in Rome itself, and took his girl to the movies. Now his girl wasn't the twenty-year-old or even the eighteen-year-old, but the redhead with freckles, who was a bit on the ugly side too, the one who hadn't said a word that night when the two friends visited Sor Antonio but had just mooned around by the dirty curtain in the doorway. When he was with her and they weren't necking—and they didn't do much of that because they were never really alone, and at least one of them minded that a lot— Riccetto was so bored that he sometimes felt like cursing. Then he'd find any old excuse for picking a quarrel, and he always ended up giving her a slap. He couldn't wait to get to the Knife-in-the-Back Bar and see Lenzetta and the gang of hoods. He'd show up looking satisfied, naturally, like a man whose affairs are all in order, who has outlived all his worries, and has nothing more to expect from life.

At the same time, however, that he played the serious young man, he did not give up the pleasures and preoccupations of a regular tough, just like the rest of the boys. When it came to raising hell, he was always there, and he took part in the brawls they got up now and then at the expense of the owner of the Knife-in-the-Back Bar, who was a good-natured slob, and the next morning, cleaning up the mess, he groaned and moaned with the rest. Since Lenzetta and some of the others had already done time in Porta Portese, they knew all about the "modern" methods for straightening out young delinquents—which they were pleased and proud to be. So, because the owner's sister gave them a hard time, and in order to absolve themselves and keep their consciences clear—not that they gave a good goddamn but because they had a convenient way of doing it—they used to say that they got up those little ruckuses so as to punish her because she didn't know how to deal with them. Besides, the poor pay Riccetto got for being assistant fish-man didn't go very far. How are you going to keep to the straight and narrow like that? When there was something to steal, he stole it, naturally, starved as he was for cash. And now there was that ring he had to buy the girl. So he and Lenzetta decided to pull off something big, to hook enough axle shafts and scrap iron to keep them loaded for at least a month.

Four of them took off, Riccetto, Lenzetta, Alduccio, and a boy named Lello, a friend of Lenzetta's, one of the gang in the Knife-in-the-Back Bar. They took the handcart along.

As they entered the Via Casilina, the wind began to blow and columns of white dust and trash began to rise here and there among the fields and vacant lots; the wind strummed the wires over the Naples railroad line like a guitar. In two seconds flat, the sky above the clouds of white dust had turned black, and against that hellishly dark backdrop the pink and white façades of Casilina glowed like tinfoil. Then that light faded too, and all was dark, extinguished, and turning cold under the gusts of wind that filled the eyes with dust.

The four boys took shelter in a doorway just in time to get out from under the first downpour. The thunder came in crashes that sounded as if six or seven of St. Peter's domes, put into an oil drum that could hold them all, were being banged together up there in the sky, and the concert could be heard miles away, behind the rows of houses and the outer districts, toward Quadraro or toward San Lorenzo or wherever, maybe even over there in that little patch of blue sky where sparrows were flying.

In about half an hour the rain stopped, and the four of them, chilled through and soaked to the skin like drowned rats, arrived at the Porta Metronia, where they had lifted stuff the last time. Though the rain was over, the sky was still dark, as if a curtain had been placed before it to conceal something terrifying and the curtain itself was more terrifying still; red flashes gashed it now and again. Night had fallen at least two hours earlier and the Porta Metronia was deserted and dripping. The four chose lots. Riccetto had to stay outside with the handcart. The others went in, and once inside the warehouse they chose lots again to see who should go in first with the sack. Lello was it. So scared he had the shakes, he went in and filled the sack with axle shafts, drills, and other stuff till he could scarcely budge it. He came out again to call Lenzetta and Alduccio to help him carry it, since the worst part was over. He went out, but he couldn't find the other two. Then he ran out of the warehouse to Riccetto, who was waiting with the cart, and asked him where the others had gone. And Riccetto said he had seen them go in. Lello went back in again to see if he could bring the sack out by himself. Riccetto saw him disappear inside the warehouse, but when he appeared again after a while, dragging the sack, the watchman came out and jumped him. Then Lenzetta and Alduccio, who had gone into a warehouse behind the scrap-iron dump, which couldn't be seen from the street, came out with another sack loaded with things that Riccetto couldn't make out but that looked like round cheeses. But when they reached the courtyard where the dump was, they spotted Lello, and the watchman holding him, and Lello was trying to break loose and run away, but he couldn't shake the man off. So they dropped the sack of cheese to help Lello, and jumped the guard. The poor bastard began to yell for help, and the baker and his men came running out of a nearby bakery. Only Alduccio managed to make a getaway. But before he got to the street, where Riccetto was standing, looking innocent and waiting for him, other people who had come running up were blocking his path right at the gate. So he ran along the wire-mesh fence to another, smaller gate farther down. He started to clamber over it, but in his haste his foot slipped on the wet iron, and he fell on an upright stake that was pointed like a spear and drove deep into

his thigh. But he managed to jump over anyway, and Riccetto
ran up to help him. Two or three of the ones who were chas-
ing him, seeing that he was hurt, gave up so as not to get
mixed up in anything. Riccetto put his arm around Alduccio,
took him a little farther on down by the Passeggiata Archeologica, and since it was a dark spot, he bound up Alduccio's
wound tightly with a strip of his shirt. They moved on after
that, caught the tram, keeping on the platform in the back,
and got off at the Ponte Rotto. Riccetto left Alduccio at the
entrance to the Fatebenefratelli hospital. Meanwhile, it had
started to rain again gently, and to thunder in those districts
and those streets through which Riccetto, thinking that either
Alduccio in the hospital or the other two in detention cells
must have talked, prepared to wander about all night long.

It was starting to clear up. Above the rooftops of the
houses rags of cloud were shredded and pounded by the wind,
which must have been blowing up there the way it did when
the world began. But down below it merely chewed at strips
of torn posters clinging to the walls, or lifted some papers,
sweeping them along the crumbling sidewalk or onto the
trolley tracks.

As the houses spread out, among piazzas and overpasses
silent as a cemetery, among subdivided lots where there was
nothing but building sites with steel framework five stories
high or filthy little open stretches, you could see the whole sky.
It was covered with thousands of pimply little clouds, in every
shape and color, descending to the saw-toothed disappearing
summits of the skyscrapers in the distance. Black sea shells,
yellowish mussel-shapes, bluish mustache-shapes, yolk-colored
gobs of spit, and farther off, beyond a streak of blue, as clear
and glassy as a river in the polar regions, a big white cloud,

curly, fresh, and so big it looked like the Mount of Purgatory.

Pale as a sheet, Riccetto was walking along slowly toward the Via Taranto, waiting for the stalls to open up in the market and for the people to begin to do their shopping. The poor devil was so hungry he felt faint, putting one foot in front of the other, hardly aware of where he was going. The Via Taranto was somewhere in the neighborhood; how much farther was it? He came upon the Via Taranto just then, found it as deserted as a minefield, thousands of drawn blinds on the house fronts heaped up darkly along the hill, against a sky suffused with an artificial, candied light. And the cool breeze that made things look white and blue by turns before your eyes, like fennel in the wind, gave an occasional shake to the two lines of dozing tubercular trees rising together with the house fronts on either side of the street toward the sky over San Giovanni. But over where the market was, by the intersection with the Via Monza or the Via Orvieto, there was no sign of stalls. There wasn't even a scrap of paper in sight, not a cabbage stalk or a clamshell or a squashed garlic clove; nothing; it looked as if there had never been a market there and never would be. "O.k," said Riccetto, plunging his hands so deep into his pockets that he pushed the crotch of his pants down to his knees, huddling in his shirt with the collar turned up. And he took the first cross street that came along. "Fuck this shit," he said, suddenly enraged, speaking almost out loud, clenching his teeth. "Who's there to hear me anyway?" he said, with an exploratory glance around. "And if they hear me, what do I give a goddamn?" He was shaking like a leaf. The street lamps, still lit, went out suddenly. The light from the sky fell still more raw and sad, and hung upon the walls. Everyone, from the janitor to the white-collar worker, from the cleaning woman to Sir Somebody, was asleep behind the shutters of the Via Pinerolo. But all at once down the street there was a shrieking of brakes that could have been heard as far away as San Giovanni, and then, suddenly, banging noises that echoed through the quarter, now invaded by the whiteness of full day-light. Riccetto turned unhurriedly in that direction, and came to the Piazza Re di Roma. That's where the racket was coming from. Behind the trees in their black and soaking little plots, beside the row of empty benches, a garbage truck was parked, and lined up on the sidewalk there were a dozen garbage cans, and the garbage men were standing around with their sleeves rolled up, cursing. The driver had got down from the truck and was leaning against a dirty fender listening to them, his hair falling over his eyes and his hands in his pockets. A boy was standing silently a little apart, with a piece of board in his hands, and a smile twisting his mouth; he was enjoying him-self too, because he didn't give a damn about the argument in progress—on the contrary, he liked it fine, since as long as it kept up he didn't have to work. "But didn't you go call the son of a bitch?" the driver asked, turning to the boy. He flushed a little, and then said quietly, "Why, sure." "Look, you guys," said the driver to the two garbage men, "what do you want me to tell you? Settle it between yourselves." And he climbed back into the cab, stretching out on the seat and shoving his feet out through the window. But it wasn't such a terrible tragedy for the garbage men. They just had to empty the cans into the truck themselves in place of the missing boy; the other boy, with the impudent face, dirty as a gypsy, was right there. And then, after all, the bastards, if it weren't for the boys in the Borgata Gordiani or Quadraro who, for the privilege of poking around in the garbage, would get up at three in the morning and work four or five hours, wouldn't they have had to do that work themselves all the time? But by now they were spoiled rotten, and it burned them to get stuck like that. Riccetto was standing there, his hands already half out of his pockets, and his eyes doing all the talking for him.

A toothless man, coal-black stubble covering his jaws, which were white from the morning wind, and two eyes that made him look like the suffering Christ gleaming like a dog's or a drunk's even at four in the morning, said to Riccetto, "Go ahead." Riccetto didn't wait to be told twice, and while the garbage men grinned, bending over the cans full of congealed garbage, saying, "Yeah, go ahead, there's nice greasy stuff here to eat," and, "Take advantage of it, sonny, there's a feast waiting for you here," he paid no attention to them and took hold of the other board, which was sticking out of the truck, and with his colleague he set to work enthusiastically, rolling the cans of garbage into the truck and emptying them.

A stain of dirty gray vapor like diluted ink was spreading over those patches of sky visible among the roofs of the buildings and in the empty spaces of the piazzas. The remnants of the little clouds first lost their color and then merged with the dirty stain. Even the big white cloud with steely glints in it had fallen into rags and lost its radiance, and was disappearing now like snow falling into mud. Summer was ending. For three hours Riccetto and the boy from the Borgata Gordiani emptied garbage cans into the truck, the heap getting higher and higher and rasping their lungs more and more with a smell that suggested a burning orange grove. Already the servant-girls with their empty shopping bags were on the streets, and the screeching of the trolleys on the curves could be heard more often; the truck left behind the well-heeled solid middle-class section, took the Casilina road, and spread its fresh stink among the houses of the poor, doing the samba down rutted streets whose sidewalks looked like sewers, among great dilapidated underpasses, fenced-in lots, scaffoldings, construction sites, districts full of shacks, villages of hovels, passing the Centocelle trolleys, workmen hanging onto the footboards, and arriving at last by way of the Strada Bianca among the first houses of the Borgata Gordiani, as isolated as a concentration camp, swept by sun and wind on a little plateau between the Via Casilina and the Via Prenestina.

On either side of the road where the truck had come to a stop on the outskirts of the town, were stretches of ground that were supposed to be wheat fields but were full of brambles, pits, and canebrakes; father down there was an orchard whose trees were even older than the tumbledown house they surrounded, and which had not been pruned in twenty years. The ditch was full of black water, and here and there geese were wandering loose over the grass and the even blacker earth of the fields. A little beyond the old house the wheat fields came to an end, petering out as they rose above abandoned quarries that had themselves become fields once more, bare, fit only for the flocks on their way from the Sabine region and the Abruzzi, and broken up here and there by ravines and sudden drops. The path lost itself in the sand there, and there the truck stopped. "Let's go, hurry it up," said the driver when he had turned the truck's nose around toward the Strada Bianca and backed the rear over to the edge of an almost vertical drop. The two helpers opened the rear doors, and the load of garbage spilled down over the drop. When the stuff stopped rolling out by gravity, the two, sweeping exhaustedly, pushed out the rest, Prussian-blue and tomato-red, that was still stinking away inside the body of the truck.

Riccetto and the other boy were left alone at the garbage dump, the bottom of the quarry below them and the cracked fields all around. They sat down, one at the top of the heap and one at the bottom, and began to search among the refuse.

The other fellow was the practical kind; he was bending over attentively, looking serious, as if he were doing a job that called for precision. Riccetto imitated him, but since grubbing about with his hands was too disgusting, he went to pull a limb from a fig tree on the other side of a wire-mesh fence that seemed to go back to the dark ages, and crouched down with the branch and began to pick apart the filthy papers, clamshells, medicine tins, leftover food, and all the other junk that was raising a stink around him. The hours went by, and instead of turning definitely gray in the sultry wind from the southeast, the sky cleared, up there above the Borgata Gordiani, just in time for the hot nine o'clock sun to bore down into the bent backs of the two scavengers. Riccetto was soaked in sweat and every now and then things went black before his eyes; in the darkness around him he saw flashes of green and red; he was on the point of fainting from hunger. "Ah, fuck this shit!" he said suddenly, seething with rage. He got to his feet, and without saying good-by to the other fellow, who didn't make the effort to turn around either, he walked away. Limping with weariness, he went down the Strada Bianca, which was living up to its name, for it was all white with dust and sunshine under a sky that was beginning to darken once more, and with his ass dragging he reached the Via Casilina. There he waited for a trolley, hitched on behind, and after a half-hour ride he was again in the Via Taranto, circling through the market like a stray dog, moving among the stalls, sniffing the thousands of odors floating on the sultry breeze, all of them appetizing, in the little open space squeezed in among the buildings.

He watched the fruit stands, and managed to hook some pears and a couple of apples; he went off to eat them in an alleyway. Then he went back, hungrier than ever from that bit of sweetness in his stomach, drawn by the cheese smells coming from the line of white stands right in front of the alley, on the wet pavement beyond the fountain. There were mozzarella and caciotta cheeses lined up, and provolone hung up, and on the stand already cut pieces of Emmentaler, parmesan, and sheep's-milk cheese; there were also pieces of a quarter-pound or even less strewn among the whole cheeses. Riccetto stared uneasily at a slice of gruyère that had turned a little yellow—with a smell so strong it took your breath away. He moved up close to it, pretending interest in something else, waiting for the proprietor to become absorbed in talking to his customer, a woman fat as a bishop, who had been there for quite a while, examining the cheese with a venomous air—and with a lightning-quick motion, whiz! he grabbed the piece of gruyère and swept it into his pocket. The owner of the stand saw him. He stuck his knife into a cheese, said, "One moment, ma'am," came out from behind the stand, grabbed Riccetto by the collar of his shirt—the boy was wandering off innocently—and with relish, for he felt completely justified in what he was doing, he let him have two blows that made him reel. In a rage, as if awakening from a stupor, and without any warning, Riccetto plunged forward with his head down, punching desperately at the man's sides. The owner of the stand reeled back for a moment, but since he was twice Riccetto's size, he began to manhandle him in such a way that if the other market people had not come between them he would have sent the boy straight to the Polyclinic. Nevertheless, being a big, powerful fellow, he could afford to calm down fast. He said to the men who were holding him, "Let go of me, let go of me, boys—I won't touch him. You think I fight with kids?" But Riccetto, all bruised and with a trickle of blood coming from his teeth, went on struggling for a while in the arms of the men who were holding him back. "Give me my cheese and beat it," the cheese-seller said, in an almost conciliatory voice. "Go on, give him the cheese," said a fishman standing by him. Riccetto took the piece of gruyère from his pocket and handed it over dully, his face lifeless, chewing over vague thoughts of vengeance, and swallowing bile along with the blood from his gums. Then as the crowd thinned out around him—as if the incident were something that could easily be forgotten—he went off among the shoppers, amid the red, green, and yellow stalls bearing mountains of tomatoes and eggplants, and the vegetable-sellers yelling so hard they had to bend at the waist, all of them cheerful and lively. He went down the Via Taranto, and slowly mounted the four hundred steps to the landing he was using as a bedroom. He was so weak he could scarcely stand. He did see that the door of the empty apartment, ordinarily closed, was open and swinging to and fro in the intermittent draft; but he paid no attention to it. Swaying, and with the slow gestures of a man swimming under water, he pulled a length of string from his pocket, passed it through two holes and secured it, closing the leaves of the door. Then he stretched out on the tile floor, already asleep. It couldn't have been more than a half-hour later—just enough time for the janitress to make a phone call and for the cops to arrive—than Riccetto was kicked awake and found two of them on top of him. To make a long story short, the apartment on the landing had been broken into and robbed during the night; that was why the door had been ajar. Riccetto, roused from God knows what dreams, the poor bastard—maybe that he was eating in a restaurant or sleeping in a bed—got up, rubbing his eyes, and stumbled down the stairs after the cops, absolutely in the dark about what was going on. "What can they be picking me up for?" he wondered, still half-asleep. "Oh, well." They took him to Porta Portese, and gave him three years—he was supposed to stay in the can until the spring of 1950!—to teach him to behave.

6 · Swimming in the Aniene

"Tratti avanti, Alichino e Calcabrina,"
cominciò egli a dire, "e tu, Cagnazzo;
e Barbariccia guida la decina.

Libicocco vegna oltre, e Draghinazzo,
Ciriatto sannuto, e Graffiacane,
e Farfarello, e Rubicante il pazzo. . . .
Dante, *Inferno*, Canto XXI*

"I'm so hungry I could shit my pants," Begalone yelled.
He pulled off his shirt, standing in the dirty trodden grass by
the bank of the Aniene, among the burned-over bushes. He
unbuttoned his pants and took a leak right where he stood.
"What are you pissing there for?" Caciotta called from where
he himself was taking a leak some distance away. "O.k., I'll
go piss in the Via Arenula," said Begalone, "you idiot."

"Let's go for a swim," Caciotta said contentedly—in these

* "Draw forward, Alichino and Calcabrina," he/then began to say,
"and thou, Cagnazzo;/and let Barbariccia lead the ten.

Let Libicocco come besides, and Draghinazzo,/tusked Ciriatto, and
Graffiacane, and Farfarello,/and furious Rubicante. . . .

three years he had put on weight—"and then let's go to the movies." "Where you hiding the money?" Alduccio asked sarcastically. "That's my worry," said Caciotta. "He must have picked up a lot of butts last night," Alduccio yelled, already naked and his feet in the water. Caciotta, buckling his belt around his clothes, answered with a restrained, "Fuck you too."

He put down his bundle of clothes with the others', by a dusty bush, and climbed straight up the bank to the field where the grain had recently been cut, and where two or three horses were grazing. The smallest boys, who had come before noon, were playing together up there. "Hey, you're all naked!" Caciotta yelled. "Mind your own fucking business!" Sgarone yelled back. "You little bastard," Caciotta shouted at the boy, making a grab for him. But he slipped away and ran down the bank by the swimming-place. As it happened, Begalone, Tirillo, and the other boys were naked too. Caciotta had talked that way because that morning he had stolen his nephew's drawers, and had made a pair of trunks out of them, doing the sewing himself. "That's what I call dressed to kill," said Begalone, laughing. Someone was yelling at the top of his lungs from halfway across the river, which was flowing darkly beneath the sun over its narrow bed between reedy, bushy banks. The boys who meant to swim out to the dredge came along on floats made of bundles of reeds. "Let's swim across," Alduccio called from the bottom of the bank, and jumped into the water. Almost all the big boys followed after him; the little ones stopped playing and went toward the river's edge. "What's the matter, aren't you going in?" they asked Caciotta. "It ain't that I'm not brave, it's just that I'm so fucking scared," Caciotta said.

The others swam across with long strokes, crossing the path of those who were coming downstream on their floats, and reached the far shore, steep and filthy. A stream as white as

limewater sliced through the bank, flowing through the dried
mud and weathered bushes at the foot of the seaweed processing plant with its green storage tanks and tobacco-colored walls,
all windowless. Begalone went down below the factory drain to
bathe.

"That's what you need, all right," Caciotta yelled. Begalone,
making a trumpet with his hands but scarcely turning his head,
yelled across to the opposite side, "Bring your sister over here
for a bath!"

"Hey, shitass!" Caciotta called.

"Hey, clapface," Begalone answered.

The boys who had come down from the dredge on their
floats went ashore by the swimming-place, and rolled around
in the black mud under the steep bank; the younger boys came
down to join them.

There were three of the younger boys still up on the top of
the bank. They had come down from the Ponte Mammolo
district, and after stopping on the bridge to look for a moment,
they had gone to join the others on the edge of the drop to
the river, right by the bend. They hadn't yet made up their
minds to undress. They were watching the boys who were sky-
larking about in the mud and shallow water, and the others
who were paddling in the streamlet by the processing plant
on the farther shore. The two smaller boys were laughing,
having a good time just looking on. The older boy watched
quietly, then slowly began to take off his clothes. The two
others undressed too, and they piled their clothes in one heap.
The smallest boy took the clothes under his arm while the
others started down to the river. The little boy stood there
sulking. "Hey, Genè," he called, "don't I get to swim too?"
"Later," Genesio answered in a low voice. More groups of
boys came around the bend in the river, in the stubble burning
slowly here and there on the slopes by the Via Tiburtina and

at the edge of the stream, crackling into little tongues of flame. They came on two or three at a time, yelling and jumping in the empty fields, the Pecoraro hill and the white walls of the Silver Cine in the background.

They were half-naked, their trousers held up by lengths of string for belts, their ragged shirts or sweaters flopping outside their pants. They pulled off their trousers on the way, and came to the edge of the field carrying their clothes in their hands. "I can swim better than you can, I'm telling you," Armandino, holding onto his dog's collar, said angrily to a boy who was behind him. "Up yours," said the boy, intent on pulling off his grimy gray shirt as quickly as he could. When they reached the swimming-place, just above where it was all swampy and reedy, Armandino threw a stick into the water and the dog scrambled down the bank in a great cloud of dust, sniffed at the water, and plunged in. All the boys drew near to watch. The dog seized the stick, and holding it in teeth that were bared clean to the gums, came happily up onto the bank, dripping muddy water. Armandino patted him contentedly, then threw the branch into the water again, farther out, making the dog go through all that fuss again. He emerged elated, dropped the stick and jumped up on the boys. He attacked them, setting his forepaws on their chests, his tail curling about his hind legs, dripping wet, whining with joy. They backed away laughing. "Hey, you little mutt," they said affectionately. The dog fastened on Sgarone, knocking him almost to the ground, holding him with his forepaws as if he wanted to embrace him, his mouth open.

"He wants to slip it to you," said Tirillo.

"Like hell he does," said Sgarone, pushing the dog away, not at all sure of his intentions.

"Let's make the dog give it to Piattoletta," Roscietto called, laughing.

"Let's, let's!" the others shouted.

"Hey, Piattolè," they yelled down toward the shore, where Piattoletta was playing by himself in the mud and garbage of the river. "Come on up here and bend over," the boys shouted from the height of the bank. He did not answer, crouching, his shoulder blades sticking out, his arms pitifully thin, his face like a mouse's, his chin resting on his chest. He had a big, floppy cap on his head to cover the scabs; it made his pimply, hairy neck look even thinner. He had a face with a yellow cast, two huge eyes, and lips that stuck out like a monkey's. Sgarone and Roscietto came down and began pulling him by the arm. He started to cry quietly, and the tears suddenly flooded his face all the way to his neck. "Come on and give the dog a taste of it, come on!" they yelled at him. "Let's see what you got there!" He grabbed hold of bushes and clutched at the muddy soil, crying and saying nothing. But meanwhile the dog, still jumping from one boy to the next along the bare stubbled edge of the bank, whining with excitement, suddenly started to pick up in his jaws the clothes piled here and there, and race around with them. "Hey, you little bastard!" the boys shouted, laughing, afraid that he might drop the clothes in the water. Sgarone and Roscietto, laughing too, let go of Piattoletta, who slipped down among the bushes, and climbed up to make sure their bundles of clothes tied with a string were safe.

Mariuccio was holding on tightly to his own clothes and his brothers', drawing back worriedly whenever the dog came up; but the dog paid no attention to him, even when he bumped against the boy's side, almost knocking him over, and wetting him with his soaked fur. Then the dog noticed the boy and jumped up happily to pull the bundle of clothes from his hands. "Hey, Genè, hey, Genè," Mariuccio cried out in terror. The dog had got his teeth into Genesio's trousers and was tugging at them. The other boys laughed. "You little bastard!" they shouted at the dog. Genesio and his other brother came up the bank dripping water, and scared the dog off by brandishing a stick at him. Genesio took the clothes from Mariuccio and, still not saying a word, rolled them up again.

There was a moment of calm, and all that could be heard was the voice of an old drunk who had come down to drop his pants somewhere among the rubbish, and who was singing under the arches of the bridge. But the boys who had crossed to the far shore started back, stemming the current together, yelling and singing. Caciotta, who hadn't gone into the water yet, called, "Begalò, is it warm, hey, Begalò?"

"It's warm," Begalone answered, arms and legs thrashing about in the oil-coated water, "warm as piss."

"Why don't you jump?" Sgarone yelled at Caciotta.

"Probably can't swim," said some little boy.

"Yeah, shithead, teach me, won't you?" said Caciotta, his face darkening.

"Go on, cross the river," said Armandino, who had undressed meanwhile; like Caciotta, he had a pair of trunks that he had got hold of God knows how.

"*Let me stick it in just a little way . . .*" the old drunk warbled from under the bridge.

"Come on, Caciò, come on!" Alduccio and Begalone called up from the water's edge.

"Yeah, here he goes," said Armandino with a grin.

From the foot of the bank, Roscietto slung a handful of river-muck at Caciotta. Furious, Cacciotta yelled, "Who did that?" moving to the edge of the bank and looking down. The boys laughed.

"If I find the guy who did it, I'll use his head for a football."

"You can swim," said Armandino, "but I don't see you crossing the river."

"I can cross it all right, only the fucking thing scares me."

Genesio had taken a half-cigarette from his trouser pocket, and was smoking it as he watched the commotion. He and his brothers were the only ones from Ponte Mammolo, and they were on their own here. Suddenly a dozen boys surrounded them. "Give us a drag," they said, "ah, come on, lemme have a drag. What's the matter, you going to smoke it all by yourself?" They clustered about Genesio like beggars, waiting for a drag, pushing and shoving one another out of the way. "Where you from?" Sgarone asked, to get things onto a friendly footing. "Ponte Mammolo," Genesio answered. "That's where we live," Mariuccio announced. After taking a couple of drags, Genesio passed the butt to Sgarone, and the others crowded around him, waiting for their turn.

"First we go swimming," Caciotta repeated with satisfaction, "and then we go to the movies."

"What're they showing in Tiburtino?" Armandino asked.

" 'The Lion of Amalfi,' " said Caciotta, stretching out contentedly in the dust and rubbish.

The hundred and fifty lire in his pocket accounted for his good spirits. From time to time the buses from Casale di San Basilio and Settecamini passed along the Via Tiburtina, beneath the silent sun that wrapped the Tivoli hills in haze beyond the shimmering fields. An odor of rotten apples, coming from the processing plant, hung over everything, clinging like an oil stain spreading out from the factory building—that looked like a spider with its walls and storage tanks—over the banks of the Aniene, the asphalt of the roadway, and the stubble, burning with a flame that was invisible in the glaring sun.

"Hey, Borgo Antico," Riccetto called patronizingly to Genesio's middle brother. Riccetto had come down from the bridge along the path, erect, his chest swelling out under his polo shirt, wearing his out-for-a-stroll air—so much so that a boy from Tiburtino, catching sight of him, yelled, "Well, will you look who's here!" "Hey, Borgo Antì," said Riccetto gaily and mockingly from the edge of the steep bank, for Borgo Antico was paying absolutely no attention to him, and as if he had not heard at all had squatted down on the dirty shore and turned his frowning face toward the river. Riccetto, looking scornful, began to undress. He piled his clothes at his feet, not hurrying at all. Then he pulled on a pair of loud trunks, took a cigarette from his pocket, and lit up. He squatted down in the hot dust and looked again at the boys milling around below the bank. Mariuccio was standing near him, holding his brothers' clothes against his ribs. "Hey, Borgo Antì," Riccetto began again. "Here's where I came in," sneered the little kid, who had it in for him. The other boy paid no attention whatsoever. "Hey, sing us a song, Borgo Antì," Riccetto called. But Borgo Antico didn't even turn his head, crouching immobile, his chocolate face dark and shining. "What, he sings too?" asked Sgarone sarcastically. "Why, sure," said Riccetto in the same voice. Borgo Antico was still silent, and Genesio too was quiet, as if they had no idea what was going on. Mariuccio, the smallest of the brothers, said, "He don't feel like singing." "Hey, shithead," said Riccetto to Borgo Antico, "what's the matter, your throat dry?" "What'll you give him?" Genesio asked suddenly. "I'll give him a cigarette, how about it?" "Sing," Genesio ordered his brother. "He's going to sing now," Mariuccio announced. Borgo Antico lifted his skinny dark shoulders and pressed his bird's face even tighter into his chest. "Sing, why don't you?" Genesio said, already angry. "What am I supposed to sing?" Borgo Antico said hoarsely. "Sing 'Luna Rossa,' go ahead," said Riccetto. Borgo Antico sat down, pulling his knees up against his chest, and began to sing in Neapolitan, producing a voice ten times his own size, and so full of passion that he sounded like a thirty-year-old. The other boys, who had been out of sight under a hump in the bank, right in the mud, came around him to listen. "Jesus, how he can sing!" said Roscietto, and all over the river you couldn't hear anything but that voice. At the song's high point, when everyone was standing stock-still, another handful of mud struck Caciotta's head—he still hadn't made up his mind to jump into the water. "Who did that?" he began again, getting mad. "Let's see what you got in that hand," he said, catching sight of Armandino, who, with his dog at his side, had one hand hidden behind his back. Armandino stared right into his eyes, his own mocking and just a little scared, defiant, pretending he couldn't care less. He was silent a moment, refusing to show his hand. Then suddenly he pulled it from behind his back and showed it, palm up. But Caciotta jumped behind him, and grabbing hold of him under the arms, forced him to get up.

Taken by surprise, Armandino pushed the hair away from his eyes, still looking at Caciotta with a mixture of insolence and nervousness. "What's the matter with you anyway?" "What's that you were sitting on?" asked Caciotta, getting even angrier, picking up a handful of mud that had been kneaded and shaped for throwing. "Stop breaking balls, why don't you?" Armandino stammered. "It was you, right?" said Caciotta. Pointing his hand stiff-fingered at Caciotta, Armandino burst out, "Look at him, will you? Who the hell's fucking with you anyway, you jerk?" But he moved back about ten steps, just in case. Caciotta watched him, speechless, choking with rage, and moved threateningly toward the boy—who had behind him the whole field and the riverbank as far as the dredge to retreat in, all the way to the Fisherman's Rest in Tiburtino, but who stayed where he was, hunched a little, red-faced, ready for anything for pride's sake. When Caciotta came close, he bent down suddenly, almost crying, picked up a dried turd, and slung it at him. But he couldn't get away immediately because Caciotta, beside himself, was on him in two jumps and had grabbed him by the seat of his underpants as he turned. Armandino ran away, his underpants hanging down in tatters from his bare backside. He went a long way off, amid a storm of laughter, as far as the bend of the river, and sat himself down while Caciotta turned back to the others with scarcely concealed triumph. Armandino began to slip his underpants around back-to-front. He didn't give a damn if he was bare in front; the main thing was to have his butt under cover. The other boys went on jeering at him, standing together at the top of the bank. "Hey, look, even Piattoletta's laughing!" said Begalone, who had come up from the water to join the others, and who now saw Piattoletta with his mouth open. As soon as he heard this, Piattoletta stopped laughing and turned to go back down the bank. But Begalone's hand stopped him. The contrast between the two boys was immense. Squint-eyes, freckles, reddish skin and all, Begalone could still be considered the toughest of the group, and you can bet that's just the way he was considered, patiently holding on to Piattoletta by the back of the neck without even looking at him. He had spent part of the night sleeping in Salario and part in the Villa Borghese, among the whores and bums, or picking pockets on the trolley. The other boy had come down to the river after spending the morning with his grandmother, picking through garbage heaps in the stinking fields or among the shanties down where the drains from the Polyclinic spill into the Aniene. Now, with Begalone's hand forcing him down to the ground, he squatted silently like one of those animals that plays dead, ready to start bawling under the filthy white cap that was so enormous it reached down his back. Only his flapping ears kept the cap from sliding down over his nose.

"Even Piattoletta's laughing, the little jerk," Begalone repeated in a gaily patronizing voice, slapping his hand hard against the bony knobs of the boy's spine. Piattoletta watched him, jolted by the slaps. "You're going to break him in two," said Riccetto. "What? Are you kidding? How'm I going to break a tree trunk like that?" And he gave him another shot in the shoulder. Piattoletta laughed a little, his mouth twisting.

"You want to know what he's laughing at? You want to know?" said Sgarone. "He's laughing because he saw Armandino's nuts."

"Is that right?" said Begalone. "The little bastard! I didn't know you had to put blinders on when he was around. You like nuts, huh? I hope they kill you—you and that Arab you got for a father."

Piattoletta hung his head down, looking around out of the corners of his eyes, while everyone laughed.

"What do you mean, nuts?" asked Tirillo, shaking himself, legs spread, his belly against Piattoletta's nose. "This is what he wants, the little fag."

"Give it to your sister, why don't you?" muttered Piattoletta, who had already started crying. Tirillo struck him two or three times in the face with his naked belly, knocking him over in the dirt. "Let him go," said Begalone. "He's going to give us a speech in German, ain't you, Piattolè?"

"What, is he German?" Riccetto asked.

"That little shit is German, English, and Moroccan—go ask his mother!" said Begalone.

Piattoletta's face was bathed in tears, and he let them run down his face and throat without wiping them away.

"You ought to see how he talks German," said Sgarone. "Say something, Piattolè."

"Go on, say something," yelled Begalone, "up yours and your grandmother's."

"If you don't say something," said Tirillo, jumping to his feet, "we'll ream out your asshole for you."

"Yeah, because right now it's just a little one," said Roscietto.

"Are you or ain't you?" said Begalone, grabbing hold of Piattoletta. "Because if you don't start talking German, I'm going to throw your clothes in the river, and you can go home bare-assed to Pietralata."

Piattoletta went on crying. "Where's this shit-ass hidden his clothes?" asked Begalone. "Down there, in the mud," Sgarone yelled, and ran to get them. "And this cap too," said Begalone, pulling it from Piattoletta's head, exposing his shaven skull, crisscrossed with white scars.

He made a heap of the clothes, and holding them up with one hand, jumped into the river and swam across. When he reached the other bank, beneath the drain of the processing plant, he yelled to Piattoletta, "If you don't talk German now, you can get these crummy clothes tomorrow morning!"

"Go on, say something, why the hell not?" Riccetto said cheerfully.

"Damn you!" Sgarone yelled, giving him a kick in the back. Piattoletta began to cry louder, his monkey-face growing even more distorted and disgusting; but he decided to talk. "Ack rick grau ricke fram ghelenen fil ack ack," he said, as softly as he had been crying.

"I can't hear you! Talk louder!" Begalone yelled from the far shore. "Ir zum ack gramen bur ack minen fil ack zum cramen firen," Piattoletta said a little louder, suddenly beginning to cry again. "Now talk like the Indians!" Begalone yelled. Piattoletta obeyed immediately, and, tears still streaming from his tightly shut eyes, he began to hop and flutter his arms, crying, "Eeyoo, eeyoo-oo-oo-ooh, ee-oo." Begalone set the clothes down under a bush and jumped into the water, yelling, "Now do it with your asshole and I'll bring the stuff back."

The sun had sunk a little over toward Rome; coal dust seemed to hang in the air. "Let's go," said Genesio to his brothers. He made Mariuccio hand him his clothes, and he slipped on the trousers that had a rip in the cuff where the dog's teeth had torn them. "Son of a bitch," he said between his teeth, looking at the rip. "What's Mamma going to say to you?" asked Mariuccio. Genesio didn't answer. He took half a cigarette from his pocket, and when they had gone a little way farther along the path that climbed the slope to the Via Tiburtina, he lit up. "Hey, wait!" Riccetto called at that moment, seeing them going off. The three boys turned part way round and stopped for a moment; they were undecided whether to wait or not. "Let's wait for him," Genesio said in a low tone, still frowning, and without even looking to see what his brothers were doing he sat down cross-legged in the dust, smoking, his eyes lowered.

Riccetto dressed calmly, pulling on one sock after the other and taking time out to sing a little and shout at the boys who were taking racing dives and headers. Finally, after putting his clothes on backward two or three times, he was ready. He rose to his feet, and step by step, moving his shoulders lazily, he came up to the three boys from Ponte Mammolo who were waiting for him, and making a sarcastic gesture with his head, he said, "Let's go." They walked in single file along the path by the Aniene, went up the high bank where it very nearly overhung the Via Tiburtina, and went onto the bridge.

Riccetto, in his polo shirt, took the lead, plump, shining from his bath, still walking like a tough. He was feeling gay, and he sang, his eyes full of sarcasm, his dripping trunks swinging from his hand. The three boys followed him—Genesio by himself, his skin the color of licorice and his coal-black eyes looking crafty, and the others trotting along behind like puppies, as if they were forming a procession with Riccetto in the lead. They turned out of the Via Tiburtina to go up by the Via Casal dei Pazzi, which ran among the flat expanses of cultivated fields with their zigzag furrows, small factories painted with whitewash, construction sites, and the stumps of houses. There was no one about, and all that could be heard beneath the sun that was cooking the fields and the asphalt of the road was Riccetto's voice as he sang.

The workmen who were excavating to lay sewer-pipe along the Via Casal dei Pazzi—since election time was at hand —were sleeping on their backs, stretched out in the shadow of a low wall. "Hey, look!" cried Mariuccio in his little bird's voice, leaning over to look down into the pit where the line from the winch hung motionless. Borgo Antico hurried over to look, equally impressed by the depth of the hole. Genesio glanced down at it sourly. "Hey, let's go," said Riccetto, seeing the three lingering behind, busy observing the separate pits, each with saw-horses around it, along the length of the road.

"Your ass has had it when your old man sees you," Riccetto called brightly, moving one hand energetically up and down.

"Who pays any attention to him?" asked Genesio hoarsely.

"Yeah, yeah, just gossip is all," said Riccetto mockingly, still shaking his arm. He was alluding to the beatings that the three boys caught every day from their father, who was an ill-tempered, drunken peasant. Riccetto knew him well, because he had been working with him as a laborer at Ponte Mammolo since spring. They turned into the Via Selmi, leaving behind the line of fenced-in pits stretching out of sight in the sunlight.

"He's going to give you a fat lip!" Riccetto went on, enjoying himself.

"Oh, yeah?" Genesio said, wounded to the quick, and not at all anxious to accept Riccetto's predictions. But he had no good arguments handy, and Riccetto took advantage of the fact to have a good time.

" 'Specially if he's had a drink," he went on in a pathetic voice, "he'll pick up a great big stick and you'll be seeing technicolor all right."

"Oh, dry up," said Mariuccio, who was still too little to say fuck you to Riccetto, and he looked up uncertainly at him. "Oh, yeah, you're joking now, but you'll be crying pretty soon," Riccetto said.

"Oh, dry up," Mariuccio said again, undecided whether to take it as a joke or get angry. Riccetto began to hum a tune, as if he had forgotten about the three brothers. Then, "I wouldn't like to be in your shoes!" he said merrily, twisting his mouth and drawing his head down between his shoulders as if to avoid a rain of blows.

"Oh, dry up," Mariuccio repeated angrily. Genesio kept silent, taking a last drag from a cigarette that was reduced to a smoldering butt, kicking at the pebbles of the Via Selmi, which was sunken among tiny shriveled kitchen gardens, half-abandoned houses, and rutted fields.

"Here we are," Riccetto said mockingly as they came down the road and approached the Pugliese's house, one-storied and without whitewash. But they were building onto it and it was surrounded by scaffolding, while there were piles of dark-colored sand on the trodden earth of the garden, and a quick-lime pit. None of the two or three workmen was still on the job. Riccetto, walking in the lead, came forward calmly. Pugliese had just been dealing with his wife, and he was seated on the steps, the blood showing in blotches beneath the skin of his face, his eyes glaring and shining like a dog's. The three boys, having caught sight of their father from a long way off,

were keeping their distance among the stone-piles by the roadside and the tumbledown walls, expecting an outburst. But
Riccetto went into the garden, calm and good-humored, took
a comb out of his hip-pocket, dipped it in the fountain, and
began to comb his hair, beautiful as Cleopatra.

"The dogs! The dogs!" Roscietto cried, coming out from
under the bank of the Aniene, a whole flock of boys behind
him. Zinzello, the carter who combed his hair straight back, and
Miccia, with two grown dogs, male and female, were coming
along the path from Tiburtino. When they reached the bend
in the river, while the dogs went dashing about in the stubble,
they undressed, took soap out of their pockets, and walked into
the stream to wash, chatting together.

They paid no attention to the little boys or to the older
boys. Both Zinzello, with his stony face, and Miccia, who was
already running to fat, a beard rimming his well-nourished
cheeks, had started to sing, the cold water running down their
backs the whole time, and they took no notice of the boys
playing with their dogs.

Armandino's dog had begun to snarl but kept some way
off, his tail laid along his ribs, turning so as never to present
his wet flanks directly to his two colleagues as he curled up
into a ball or stretched out.

All the boys, including Piattoletta, had gathered around
them.

"He's scared shitless," said Roscietto jeeringly.

"Ah, he's only a pup," said Sgarone, taking the dog's side.

"Pup, what do you mean, pup, you dope," said Roscietto
resoundingly. "He was born before I was."

Armandino clucked his tongue and raised his brows in a
gesture of sympathy. "He's not even a year old yet."

"So what?" said Roscietto. "Does he have to be scared of another dog?"

"Where do you get that scared stuff? You give me a pain," said Armandino.

He went over to the dog, grabbed him by the collar, and dragged him toward the other two dogs, who were snarling and had begun to circle around in the stubble.

He bent over his dog, and began to urge him on furiously, so softly he could hardly be heard, his mouth dripping spit.

"Get 'em, Lupo! Get 'em, Lupo! Get 'em!"

Lupo was trembling from the sound of the low voice that scarcely reached his pricked-up ears. His chest was thrust forward, and his whole body was vibrating like a running motor. Suddenly Armandino let him go.

All the boys were watching, hardly saying anything. Of Zinzello's two dogs, the male was the smaller and skinnier, and seeing Lupo being encouraged and egged on by his master, he beat a lazy retreat toward the middle of the field, turning now and again to snarl and bark.

But the bitch was a terror. Skinny, black, sharp-nosed, scabby-tailed, slant-eyed, she stood motionless as a statue, waiting for Lupo. Coming up at full speed, Lupo stopped dead in his tracks, barking madly at her.

She waited a moment, listening to him balefully, among the shouts of the boys. Then she turned away and took a couple of steps to go off about her business, with an air that plainly said, "Let me get out of here, because if I don't there's going to be a massacre!"

Moving off, she turned now and again, her head stretched along her skinny shoulder, her eyes dull, dark, and mottled with red.

"Get 'er, Lupo! Get 'er!" Armandino whispered, still bending to the dog's ear, while the boys egged him on too, yelling like apes, raising a clamor that could have been heard all the way to Tiburtino. Lupo, in his innocence, darted after the bitch, who was still keeping quiet, barking his head off and whining.

"It seems to me like you're pushing it just a little," she appeared to be thinking, and she stopped. "It really does." And a moment later, "Why, you little jerk!" she howled, losing her patience suddenly. The howl was so ferocious that Lupo stopped, and it even intimidated the boys. The bitch turned halfway round, and looked darkly at that clown Lupo, who started to back away.

"What did I tell you, Sgarò?" said Roscietto.

Armandino bent down lower still. "Get 'er, Lupo! Get 'er! Get 'er!" he said, very nearly trembling himself. Lupo plucked up his courage, suddenly forgetting his fear, and began to bark again, even more threateningly and incautiously than before. "Here's where I came in," the bitch seemed to be thinking. "You slut, you two-bit whore, what do you think you're staring at?" Lupo yelled in fury. "Trying to impress me or something?" The bitch was still silent. "If you don't say something quick," Lupo threatened, "I'll knock your goddamn head off!"

"Ain't you a little sweetheart, though!" said the male dog, butting into the conversation.

"Yeah?" asked Lupo, taking a swipe at the other, who slipped away. "What does that little creep want with me?" The bitch let out a growl. "Shove it up your ass!" Lupo yelled.

"That does it," said the bitch, "I've had it up to here, you know what I mean?" She turned to face him squarely. "You may do your damnedest," she howled ferociously, "but I'm going to straighten you out if it means thirty years in Regina Coeli!"

"They're going to tear each other apart!" said Sgarone, but he hadn't gotten the words out before the two dogs were at each other, their hind legs planted on the ground and their forelegs drawn back to their chests, their muzzles gaping open and their teeth bared to the gums. Growling the whole time, they tried to bite each other behind the ears, and between bites they howled so loud that the noise drowned out the boys' shouting. Lupo rolled over in the stubble, raising a cloud of dust, and the bitch was on top of him, snapping at his throat. But Lupo got up again and after jumping backward, leaped on her from almost his full height, waving his forepaws as if he were drowning. They howled and writhed, mad with rage. But at the height of the battle, Zinzello came up from the bank and whistled. Immediately, as if her rage had magically evaporated, the bitch ran up to him, followed by the other male dog, running swiftly, jumping, wagging her tail, submissive and almost joyful. Zinzello cursed at the boys, and when he had finished speaking his mind, he went back to soaping himself, taking the dogs with him. Lupo was hurt. "Look at those slashes!" said Tirillo loudly, astonished. "Just look at those slashes!" They all bent over Lupo, whose neck was nearly hairless; there were swollen red bites with black edges here and there among the black hair plastered against the skin. "Jesus!" said Sgarone, in the same astonished voice. "Let's throw him in the water," said Roscietto, and they all went down the bank, pulling the dog along with them.

Meanwhile Caciotta was coming up along the shore where the older boys were playing cards and every now and then looking over to see if they could spot the janitor's daughter at a window in the factory walls, so they could give her a hard time, bare-assed as they were. Caciotta looked around and said, "Now, where have my clothes gone to?"

"O clothes, where are you?" he sang out, as high-spirited as usual.

"You going already?" asked Alduccio.

"What's there to hang around for?" asked Caciotta, looking for his clothes among the bushes and clumps of reeds.

"Let's go for a swim again, come on," Alduccio cried.

"Uhuh," said Caciotta.

"Forget him," Begalone told Alduccio, giving him a nudge. Caciotta had found his clothes and was turning them over in his hands, looking at them.

"Who's been at these things?" he said to himself. "Beats me."

"What, is somebody around here going through people's pockets?" he asked out loud.

"Oh, no!" Sgarone called sarcastically.

"If I catch anybody going through my pockets I'll kick his head in," Caciotta said cheerfully.

"What a man!" said Begalone from down by the shore, in response to that. Caciotta began to put on his socks and his shoes, singing meanwhile:

"Two-bit whores, two-bit whores . . ."

"Hey, Caciò," said Begalone, "Claudio Villa's got nothing on you."

"Don't I know it," said Caciotta, breaking off his song, and then starting right in again.

"Console yourself by singing," said Alduccio.

"I'll console myself all right," said Caciotta.

"Two-bit whores, two-bit whores . . .

Why shouldn't I console myself? What, I gotta ask permission from somebody before I can sing a song?

"Two-bit whores, two-bit whores . . .

Now we get dressed, and then we take a stroll, and then we go catch a flick." While he sang and chattered to himself, he drew on his socks and shoes, and then he unfastened the belt that he had buckled around the bundle of clothes.

"You're going off to the flicks, but you don't say nothing about inviting your friends, right?" said Begalone.

"You clown, all I got's a hundred and fifty lire."

"Sure, sure, have it your way," said Begalone.

Caciotta started to sing again, "*Two-bit whores, two—*" He broke off suddenly. He was silent for a moment, and then he came forward holding his clothes, white as a corpse.

"Who stole the money I had in my pocket?"

"Hey, jerk! You looking at me?" asked Begalone.

"Who was it?" Caciotta insisted, his face pale.

"I'm sure the guy that did it will tell you," said Zinzello, going off with his dogs, shaking his head.

"Let's see what's in your pockets," said Caciotta. Begalone jumped to his feet in a rage. "Here, you stupid bastard, take a look!" He picked up his pants and threw them at Caciotta, who caught them and went through each pocket carefully, not saying a word. Then he looked through Begalone's shoes and socks.

"O.k., what'd you find?" Begalone yelled.

"Found your fucking ass," said Caciotta.

"I'll give you a kick in the head in a minute," said Begalone. Caciotta went to look through Alduccio's clothes, and then one by one through those of all the little boys, but he didn't find a thing. He dropped them in the dust, not looking at anybody. God knows how many weeks it had been since he'd seen a hundred lire and felt as good as he had this afternoon. He dressed in silence, deep in thought, and then took off. There were more cars going by on the Via Tiburtina now, though the sun, already low, was still burning hot above the sooty clouds piling up over Rome. The shutters were being raised at the Silver Cine, and here and there among the buildings of the district, far-off voices and noises began to be heard.

Alduccio and Begalone went for another swim, and then they took off too. The little boys were the last to leave the river.

Some of them went straight home by the Via Boccaleone, while others wandered around for a while. Slowly they went along the river up to the outskirts of Tiburtino, and stopped for a half-hour or so by the Silver Cine to look at the ads outside and horse around. Then they went down again among the big bushy oleanders of the Via Tiburtina, all the way to the bus stop, which was the meeting place for the gangs of little boys and the groups of older boys, in the piazza by the Pecoraro hill.

There were a bunch of little girls down in the yellow field stretching out between the four or five ridges of the hill and the Via Tiburtina, which was filled with workmen cycling home, some of them going on toward Ponte Mammolo or Settecamini, some turning off right by the field, over toward Tiburtino III and Madonna del Soccorso. By this time, too, there were some who had already been home and had gone out again to take a walk with their friends toward Pietralata or one of the two movie theaters in the neighborhood, their polo shirts or dress-shirts flopping outside their trousers.

The younger boys, leaving the river still half-undressed, went up by the dark road that split the craggy crest of the hill in two, starting at the edge of a limestone pit and then winding among the brambles of the Pecoraro hill.

The little girls followed them, and the two groups met halfway up the hill, where the road was no longer in sight, at a flat place full of abandoned excavations that deepened in the middle into miniature ravines. Since a squall was coming up from around St. Peter's, it was almost as dark as evening; the sinking sun was already obscured by clouds split here and there by lightning, although the sky above was clear, ruddy with reflected light and heat. And instead of sun, the hillside was now being bathed by the south-west wind, freighted with the sounds of all the suburbs. Even Piattoletta was walking along behind the gang of boys, laughing under his floppy cap, staying by himself so that he could be with them without their noticing him. But by now they had calmed down a bit, since the girls were there. They gathered around the lamppost, and Sgarone and Tirillo began to play the finger game; at first they played good-humoredly, but then they grew excited and began to call the numbers loudly, one of them kneeling and the other squatting on his heels on the bit of grass at the foot of the lamppost.

Armandino stretched out in the thread of shadow cast by the lamppost, hardly noticeable now that the sun had disappeared behind the storm clouds—though its glow still lingered in the air. The other boys, scabby as a band of apes, had begun teasing the girls. They kept their distance, however, because no matter how tough they acted they were still a little shy, and they bunched up together, their arms about one another's shoulders, making wisecracks and slouching about. But the girls always had an answer to shut them up.

Armandino said in a self-satisfied voice, "Ah, send them on their way," and began to sing. But the other boys acted as if they hadn't heard, and went on horsing around with the girls. Roscietto, running out of things to say, grabbed one of them and gave her a slap on the head that nearly knocked her down. Then the girls, angry and offended, went off to the other side of the lamppost, to where Pietralata could be seen, the boys following behind them, growing more outrageous as the girls became more reserved. Below, on the other slope of the Pecoraro hill, among the old limestone quarries, was the Fiorentini factory, making the air tremble with its running engines. From time to time the white flashes of the automatic welding-machines shone through the patched panes of the factory windows. Pietralata lay farther away, its lines of pink shacks, housing squatters, encrusted with dirt and filth, and farther still were the tall rows of huge yellow project-buildings in fields so parched by the sun that they were as bare as in winter.

But the girls moved off by themselves to a little clearing between the edges of two large pits, and they didn't answer any more, hardly talking among themselves until the boys would make up their minds to go away. The boys were gathered together farther up on the slope, cutting up; but the girls' calm restraint enraged them, though they tried not to show it. For that reason they became even more quarrelsome and provoking: Since they couldn't assert their superiority in words, they began to throw sticks and branches at the girls, who were dressed in torn pull-overs, their hair full of dust but nonetheless combed just like that of young ladies.

The girls did not respond, but merely moved off once more, farther downhill, but not before giving the boys a piece of their mind. "Why don't you go screw around with your sisters, you stupid idiots?" Their voices shook with rage, sounding more strident now, and at the same time their drawls were more marked than ever. Hearing them, the boys began to snicker and answer back in the tone of voice they had caught from their older brothers when they talked about Via Veneto hustlers, and the most sophisticated one yelled, "Hey, you cunts!" And moving off up the hill, they walked with long, slow steps, their left hands on their hips, and the right now extended before them, now brought back to caress the hair at the napes of their necks.

Under the lamppost, Armandino was still singing at the top of his lungs, full of passion, and the other two were still playing the finger-game, standing up now, the fingers of their left hands out stiff to count their points. "Well, for Christ's sake, what's going on here?" cried the group coming up the hill. Some of them fell upon the three by the lamppost, excited, wrestling and rolling around. One lit a butt, and the match, tossed away burning, set fire to a clump of grass that shriveled and flamed in the gusts of air blowing on those heights.

The clouds were swelling with rain, and glowing with flashes of lightning. The bursts of light from the welding in the factory below were swifter and more frequent now—since in the darkening air they showed more boldly—and the engines covered the sounds of the poverty-stricken life of Pietralata and Tiburtino with their constant hum.

Piattoletta was sitting on the ground, his legs crossed, his floppy cap pulled as far down as possible over his ears, and a laugh came from his long, pendulous lips.

"Hey, Piattolè," yelled the others, rolling around on the cracked mud, "look at this, will you?" But then they went on wrestling with one another, not bothering with him any further. Sgarone was stretched out on his back, Roscietto on top of him, belly to belly, holding him down, his hands pinning Sgarone's wrists to the ground on either side.

Sgarone tried to get loose. "Don't move," Roscietto said, red in the face from the effort of holding him. But Sgarone, who was beginning to get bored with the whole thing, started squirming like an eel. "Fuck you!" he yelled. "Hold still, Sgarò," said Roscietto. "Well, get off my cock," said Sgarone, getting really mad now, his voice beginning to break. Roscietto began to jiggle around on top of him as if he had St. Vitus dance. "Watch it, for Christ's sake, Rosciè, it's getting ready to stand at attention," said Sgarone, laughing. Roscietto let him go, jumping up excitedly. "Let's play Indians!" he yelled. "Ah, cut it out!" said the others disgustedly. "Come on, we'll have fun," Roscietto insisted. "What a bunch of shit," said Armandino with a sneer. "Eeyee, eeyoo-oo-oo-oo, eeyoo," Roscietto yelled, jumping up and down. "Come on, Piattolè."

Piattoletta stood up and began to yell too, hopping now on one foot, now on the other, "Eeyoo, eeyeeyoo." Roscietto stood next to him so that they could jump up and down together. "Eeyoo, eeyeeyoo-oo-oo, eeyoo," they yelled, laughing.

The others began to jump around too, leaning over far forward and far back, yelling, "Eeyoo, eeyoo." The girls had come up to see what was going on, and watching the commotion, they made a circle around the boys and said, "What a bunch of idiots!" But the boys jumped and yelled all the more in order to annoy them.

"Let's do the dance of death, the dance of death!" Roscietto cried. The others began to shriek even louder, "Eeyoo, eeyoo," and as they came near the girls they aimed a kick or a slap in the head at them. But the girls were alert and ducked away smartly. "Gee, what a bunch of jerks," they said. "Why don't you stuff it, you idiots?" But they didn't go away, and stood watching the dance; and the boys, though exhausted from yelling and jumping, nonetheless redoubled their efforts, showing off.

"Burn 'em at the stake!" Roscietto yelled.

"Yeah, burn 'em at the stake," the girls said, sneering. "It's ridiculous." And they looked on, contemptuous and annoyed.

Roscietto pounced on Piattoletta, who was in the middle of the mob, hardly moving his feet because he was dead tired, but still yelling "Eeyoo, eeyoo." "To the stake!" Roscietto yelled, as soon as he had caught him.

Yelling, the others helped him, and they dragged Piattoletta up to the lamppost.

"Tie him up!" someone cried. Piattoletta was struggling,

and then he went limp. Roscietto was holding him under the armpits, and he yelled, "Stand up, you little shit!"

But Piattoletta didn't want to play, and fell to the ground kicking; the others went on screaming around him. "I've had enough out of you," said Roscietto, kicking him in the belly.

Piattoletta began to cry so loudly that he could be heard over the boys' yelling. "Now he's crying, the little prick," said Armandino. "If you don't get up . . ." yelled Roscietto. But Piattoletta paid no attention and went on struggling furiously, crying at the top of his lungs.

"Ten of them, and they can't handle that little runt there," said the girls. But Roscietto pulled him upright by his shirt-collar, and when Piattoletta yelled, "Lemme go, you fuck!" he said, "Here!" and spat in his eye, and then grabbed him, and with Sgarone and Tirillo helping, pushed him against the lamppost, and with a cord tied his wrists to an iron spike protruding from the concrete.

But even though he was tied up, Piattoletta went on kicking out, squirming and screaming. The others started dancing around him again, but far enough away from him to avoid the kicks. "Jesus, doesn't anyone have another piece of rope?" cried Roscietto.

"Who the hell would have one?" asked Tirillo.

"Piattoletta, Piattoletta," said Sgarone. "He's got one holding up his pants."

They jumped on Piattoletta, who was groaning and pleading, and while the laughing girls cried, "Just look at them, will you?" they took the cord that held up his pants and tied his ankles together.

"O.k., I'll set fire to the stake," Armandino yelled, lighting a match.

But the wind blew it out. "Eeyoo, eeyoo, eeyoo," the others yelled with all the breath in their bodies.

"Let's see your lighter!" Sgarone cried to Tirillo.

"Here," said Tirillo, pulling it out of his pocket. He lit it, and while the others kicked together a heap of branches at the foot of the lamppost, still yelling and dancing, he set fire to the dry grass here and there.

A strong wind was blowing from every direction on the nearly dark Pecoraro hill. As the flashes came from the welding plant and lightning flickered from the squall, a peal or two of thunder sounded, and the air smelled damp.

The dry grass caught fire at once, the blood-colored flames took hold of the branches, and a bit of smoke began to rise around the screaming Piattoletta.

His pants, no longer held in place by the cord, slipped down, exposing his belly, and fell to his bound feet. From the burning grass and the branches that the boys were still kicking at, the fire seized on the dry cloth, crackling merrily.

7 · In the City

Opposite the Pecoraro hill there was a broad piazza, and right by the sign reading "Zone Ends—Zone Begins," just before the broad expanse of fields stretching toward the Aniene, was the old tram-line shelter of the route 309 that turned off at that point, leaving the Via Tiburtina, and cut through the district housing project toward Madonna del Soccorso. Alduccio lived in Block IV, as did Begalone, toward the end of the project's main street, a little beyond the market place, with a line of street lamps that, lighting up at dusk along the building fronts just two stories high, gave the place the air of a poor quarter in some summer resort, the road climbing for a short way and then seeming to lose itself in the darkened sky, and the sounds of the householders echoing among the walls or in the court-yards as they had their dinner or made ready for the night. At that hour there were many boys and young men walking around, but the real toughs were off in groups here and there, in the cafés or on the street corners, waiting for night—not to go to the movies or to the Villa Borghese, but to get together in some gambling house or other and play cards till morning. And while some young men strummed guitars here and there in a courtyard, there were women still washing dishes or sweeping up, their children whining; and the buses were still pulling in loaded with men coming home from work.

"So long, Begalò," said Alduccio when they reached his friend's house. "So long," said Begalone, "see you later." "I'll look for you at nine," Alduccio said. "Whistle for me." "O.k., but you be ready," said Begalone, going on up the dilapidated stairway that was crowded with little boys. Alduccio lived three or four doors farther down, on the ground floor. In front of the entry there was a sort of open gallery, as in all the buildings, its walls and columns battered and falling to pieces. Alduccio's sister was sitting on the stair. "What are you up to?" Alduccio asked. She didn't answer, but went on watching the street. "Well, up yours," he said, and passed into the kitchen, where his mother was busy at the stove. "What do you want?" she asked without turning around. "What do you mean, what do I want?" said Alduccio. She turned around in a rage, all disheveled. "You don't work, you don't eat, you hear?" She was a tall, fat woman, almost naked under her sloppy bathrobe; the perspiration had plastered her hair to her forehead, and the bun tumbled down behind over her neck and the collar of her bathrobe. "O.k.," said Alduccio, playing it cool, "you don't want to give me anything to eat, is that it? So who gives a damn?"

He left the kitchen and went into the only bedroom, the one in which his entire family slept—Riccetto's slept in the other room—and began to undress, whistling in order to show his mother that it didn't bother him a bit. "Whistle some more, you bum," she yelled from the kitchen, "and I hope you choke, you and that lousy drunken father of yours." "Yeah, and that sewer-mouthed mother of mine," Alduccio muttered, as he sat naked on the bed, pulling on his moccasins. "If you're upset because of that whore you've got for a daughter, just button it up, will you, instead of taking it out on me. You don't want to give me any dinner? Then don't give me any dinner! What the hell do I care? Just so long as you shut up." "Shut up? Shut up? Just show me another son who's nearly twenty years old and ready to be a soldier and doesn't bring home a single cent, not one, the loafer!" "Man, what a pain!" Alduccio yelled as he dressed. Screams could be heard from out in the street, the voices of quarreling women. Alduccio's mother was silent for a moment, listening; in the bedroom, where Alduccio was, the voices sounded indistinct. "Ah, you stupid idiot!" she said, talking to herself at the stove. She dropped something in her hurry to go outside, and went to the door. She stood there a moment in silence, listening, and then she went out and you could hear her voice too, yelling with the others. "Listen to them! Why don't they all go piss up a rope?" said Alduccio to himself. After nearly ten minutes of yelling and shouting, in the street or perhaps on the stairway landing, the door banged open again—but it didn't close, for Alduccio's mother had stopped in the doorway, perhaps because she still had something she wanted to get off her chest. Instead she turned back toward the landing. "You slut!" she yelled in the direction of the street. "You've been a whore all your life, and now you come and call my daughter a tramp!" A voice answered her from above; the words were hard to make out. "Boy, do they burn my ass!" said Alduccio bitterly. "And a good thing, too!" yelled his mother, putting her hand on her hip, in answer to the jumbled words that Alduccio couldn't distinguish. "Just look who's talking! You who get your boyfriend to give the kids money to go to the movies so you can stay home alone with him!" The voice from the courtyard or the landing went up two or three tones in fury, and at that high pitch began to vomit out a splendid collection of insults. When the voice stopped, it was the turn of Alduccio's mother again. "Do you remember," she shouted, in a shrill voice that the suffering

Christ himself couldn't have persuaded her to moderate, "you slut, when your husband came home and found you in bed with your boyfriend right in front of your two little kids?" She came into the kitchen, slamming the door behind her, and there she went on, talking to herself, her voice vibrating in her throat with a cutting-edge like a knife's. "So just shut up, you miserable whore, and when I see you in the street tomorrow, I'll pull every hair out of your head, and I hope you croak!" After a moment the door opened again, and Alduccio's father came in. He was drunk, as he was every evening. He went up to his wife and tried to catch hold of her, but she put her hand against his chest and pushed him away; he spun completely around and collapsed into a chair. But he got up again, and tried stubbornly to grab her. Riccetto's little sister came out from the farther room, where Riccetto's family lived, to see if anything serious was afoot. She was just in time to see her uncle fall into the chair once more. "What do you want here?" Alduccio's mother asked, turning on her in fury. "What do *you* want?" The child, carrying another little Riccetto in her arms, turned on her heels and went straight back to her room. "You and your whole miserable family of spongers and deadbeats," Alduccio's mother yelled after her, "it's four years you been here and not once did you ever say, here, take these thousand lire, pay the electric-light bill!" The father, after some moments of reflection, managed to get his voice working again, and after a couple of tries managed to say something like, "Always yapping, that tramp!" He stood up, and delivered an address all in gestures, weaving back and forth, lifting his hand two or three times from breast-level to his nose, then making his fingers do a pirouette as if to indicate that some highly original idea was going through his mind. At last, running so as not to fall down, he went into the bedroom where Alduccio was dressing, and fell flat on the bed, fully clothed. The wine he had been drinking all afternoon had made his face as white as a sheet and seemed to have singed the two inches of bristly whiskers, dark, damp, and rough as a dog's, beneath his nose and at the corners of his mouth. He was completely limp— arms stretched out on the bed, half-open mouth, slack jaw, and drooping eyelids, and lank hair, still black, and shining with sweat as if with brilliantine. The lighted lamp which hung over the bed showed up each separate chocolate-colored stain of ancient grime on his face, together with newer incrustations of dust and sweat upon his forehead; the web of wrinkles shifted about upon his face, stretched and swollen with wine, yellow from God knows what kind of liver disease hiding somewhere in that frame draped with old rags. Here and there were the shadowy traces of wounds, dark-colored, encircled by little spots, that went back to his childhood, perhaps, or his young manhood, when he had served as a soldier or worked as a day laborer, ages ago. And over all that was a grayness that came from going hungry and drinking wine, plus the stubble of a four-day beard.

By now Alduccio was dressed, sporting his pegged pants and his striped shirt with the open collar, the tails hanging outside his pants. Now he had to comb his hair. He went to the mirror in the kitchen, and after wetting the comb under the faucet, he began to primp, standing spread-legged because the mirror was set too low for him. Finding him in her way again, his mother started in on him once more, choking with fury. "Good-for-nothing hog!" "That's enough, Ma," Alduccio burst out, "I've had just about enough of that now!" "I've had enough of you!" his mother retorted, louder still. Alduccio began to sing, bending over the mirror. "He doesn't work, he doesn't help out in the house . . ." "Ma," Alduccio interrupted her, "I'm telling you I've had enough. How about dropping it now?" "I won't drop it. If I want to complain, I'll complain as much as

I like, understand, you no-good loafer!" "Let me out of here!"
Alduccio said in a fury, and he went out, all neatly combed,
slamming the battered door. He didn't even glance at his
sister, who was sitting huddled up on the stair with her skirt
pulled down to her ankles. Her face was sickly green, and her
painted mouth looked like a wound. Her hair fell to her neck,
smooth and dry, and a few locks hung over her eyes. "That
pig!" Alduccio said to himself as he went by. From the time
she had got into trouble with Sor Anita's son, the fruit-seller
who lived on the corner, there hadn't been a minute's peace
in Alduccio's house. Now she had to get married, but the
fruit-seller's son couldn't stand her any more. The night she
had been kicked out of her parents' house, he had kept her
company, sleeping by her side conspicuously on the stairway
in front of his house in Block III—but that was just to impress
people. After she found out that she was pregnant, they got
engaged, even though neither her parents nor his had been
willing before. Out of shame, she had cut the veins in her
wrists with a piece of glass, and she had nearly died. She still
had two nice fresh scars on her wrists.

Waiting for Begalone, Alduccio strolled around the neighborhood. The storm had blown over and the air was warm,
almost springlike. Begalone had changed his clothes too. He
had knotted a kerchief around his neck like a tough, and had
combed down his tow-colored mop just as smooth as smooth, so
that it looked as if it had been baked that way, parted on one side
and long on the neck. "Hey, Begalò," Alduccio called. "How
much you got on you?" Begalone asked him immediately.
"Thirty lire," said Alduccio, "just enough for the bus." Begalone
said, "Me too." "What about the rest of it?" Alduccio asked
suspiciously. "Right here! Right here!" said Begalone, slapping
his back pocket where he carried the hundred and fifty lire he
had lifted from Caciotta. "We can get two cigarettes," Alduccio

said as they went by a bar. "Wait, Aldo!" Begalone said, and then, "Farewell forever!" to the bus that was going past them. "There'll be another one coming," said Alduccio, stretching contentedly.

Begalone had not eaten either. Beneath his yellow hair his face was a greenish yellow that made his reddish brows stand out all the more. He was so weak that not even his fever could give him a bit of color—he had at least a degree or two of temperature every night, since the time he had been discharged from the Forlanini hospital. He had had TB for two or three years now, and nothing could be done about it. They gave him a year or so to live.

Walking along with Aldo, he put his hands over his empty stomach, leaning forward, cursing his brothers, his father, and most of all his poor mother, who one night—the first of a succession of terrible nights—had jumped out of bed screaming like a madwoman that she had seen the devil. She said a snake had come into the bedroom and coiled about the foot of the bed and gazed at her fixedly, forcing her to strip naked. And she had started to scream. And then, all the next day, she had burst out yelling repeatedly, whining like a dog about the headache that was killing her, seizing on her daughters or whomever was around and begging them to protect her from God knows what. The following night she woke up screaming again, but this time it wasn't the devil. She had moved to one side in the rumpled bed, to make room for somebody, though her body was as dried up as an anchovy and didn't take up much room. Beside her on the gray sheets, as she told it later, a dead girl had sat down—at least she must have been dead, seeing that she was wearing her best dress, white wool stockings, and a crown of orange blossoms, because she was supposed to have been married in a few days. She had begun to weep and told Begalone's mother that the slip they had made her wear was too short, and the wreath of flowers they had put on her head was too tight and hurt her temples. Then she complained that they were saying too few masses for her, that little Pisspants, her baby cousin, never came to visit her in the cemetery, and so forth and so on. Begalone's mother had never met the girl before, but the next day the neighbors, talking about the yells that streamed through the broken windows of Begalone's apartment and echoed among the courtyards in the middle of the night, learned that the dead girl was a relative of some people who lived just a few doors farther down in the same block. All the details matched exactly, including her little cousin Pisspants, who was living, healthy and happy, in Prenestino. Then the devil began to appear again, in various forms: one time a snake, another a bear, still another a neighbor whose teeth had turned to tusks—and these apparitions came and went in Begalone's apartment as if they were quite at home there, tormenting his mother. Then the family had decided to take steps, and they sent to Naples for an old relative of theirs who was skilled in such matters. First, the old man had them boil every single thing that belonged to Begalone's mother. In a few days they used up twenty kilowatts of gas for all that boiling business, and nobody bothered about fixing a meal. The three brothers and four sisters and all the neighbors were concentrating on getting rid of the spell. In Begalone's mother's pillow they had found feathers twisted into dove-shapes, crosses, and crowns, and they had boiled them all right away. They had put bits of iron in boiling oil, and then poured cold water into the pot to see what shapes would emerge, and for several days all that could be heard in that house were knockings on the tile floor to make charmed circles around the possessed woman, who did nothing but moan and beg for help.

"If only they'd given me a slice of bread, just a slice of bread, the bastards," Begalone said, pressing his hands over his stomach. "Here we are, each a more miserable pauper than the other," said Alduccio with a laugh, his handsome face distorted with a sneer of ironic resignation. They buried their hands in their pockets, and went on foot as far as the Pecoraro hill.

The heat wasn't sultry and it wasn't dry; it was just hot. It was like a warm hand laid on the light breeze, on the yellowish walls of the district, on the fields, the carts, the buses with clusters of people hanging on outside. A warm hand that was all the joy and misery of summer nights past and present. The air was as taut and reverberant as a drumhead. The sprinkling that traced wet lines on the sidewalk dried immediately; the garbage heaps were baked and odorless. The only smell came from stone and ironwork still hot from the sun, perhaps where wet rags had been spread out and then had dried in the heat. In the few remaining gardens here and there, full of vegetables growing fine and plump, untended as if in an earthly paradise, there wasn't a drop of moisture. And in the center of each district, by the trolley tracks, as here in Tiburtino, there were crowds of people running about and shouting so that you thought you were in the slums of Shanghai. Even in the most deserted places there was a bustle, with gangs of boys out looking for whores, stopping to talk at the doors of workshops that were still open. And after Tiburtino, there was Tor dei Schiavi, Prenestino, Acqua Bullicante, Maranella, Mandrione, Porta Furba, Quarticciolo, Quadraro. . . . Hundreds of neighborhood centers like the one in Tiburtino, each with a crowd by the traffic light, flowing off into the streets round about that buzzed with their comings and goings like an entrance-hall, on the broken sidewalks and along colossal ruined walls with lines of hovels at their bases. There were young men racing on their motor scooters, Lambrettas, Ducatis, or Mondials, half-crocked, their greasy jumpers open on their hairy chests, or else dressed to kill as if they'd just stepped out of a show-window on the Piazza Vittorio. There was a great encirclement of Rome and of the countryside around about on the part of hundreds of thousands of human beings, swarming among their blocks of dwellings, their squatters' shacks, or their skyscrapers. And that teeming life wasn't confined to the suburbs but invaded the city itself, the city's very heart, even under the dome of St. Peter's. Yes, right under the dome, all you had to do was to peer out through the colonnade of the Piazza San Pietro toward Porta Cavalleggeri, and there they all were, shouting, horsing around, acting up in crowds and gangs around the movie houses and the pizza joints, fanning out farther down in the Via del Gelsomino and the Via della Cava, in the empty lots of trodden ground bordered by garbage heaps where the little kids play ball, lying in couples among the bushes, covered with sheets of newspaper, between the Via delle Fornaci and the Gianicolo. And farther down, once through the damp tunnel, here there is the same scene again, in the Piazza della Rovere, where lines of tourists are going by, walking erect and arm in arm, wearing knickers and heavy shoes, singing mountaineers' songs in chorus, while the young punks in their pegged pants and pointy shoes, leaning against the Tiber embankment near a flooded public toilet, watch the tourists pass, looking angry and sarcastic, calling words out after them that would kill them on the spot if they understood. And down below by the river where an occasional empty tram goes by under the arcades of plane trees along broken pavements, and Lambrettas bank on the curves, carrying a young fellow or two looking for trouble; over by the Castel Sant'Angelo, with Ciriola's all lit up at its feet, reflected in the river; over by the Piazza del Popolo, the Pincio, elegant as a great theater, and the Villa Borghese, its violins murmuring softly to the whores and hustlers walking by in groups, singing "Sentimental," eyelids lowered and mouths drooping, and looking around out of the corners of their eyes to see if by chance the paddy wagon is cruising around. And again, in the opposite direction by the Ponte Sisto where, beneath the dirty, glittering Funtanone, two teams of young boys from Trastevere are playing soccer, yelling furiously, surging like a flock of sheep among the swell cars driven by pimps who've brought their girls from Cinecittà to have dinner in Antica Pesa—while from all the alleys of Trastevere beyond can be heard the sound of male and female jaws chomping on pizza or French toast in the open air, in the Piazza Sant' Egidio or by Mattonato, and babies whining or children quarreling and running along the pavements, as light as the bits of dirty paper that the wind drives here and there.

"Hey, Aldo, let's get off here," said Begalone, jumping down from the cowcatcher, bone-weary but as fast on his feet as a witch.

Aldo stood up on the footboard so that the conductor could get a good look at him, and tapping on the glass, he called, "So long, pie-face!"

He jumped down from the trolley to the pavement, and the conductor treated himself to the pleasure of sticking his head out and yelling—clutching his sheaf of tickets while the passengers waited to get theirs—"Young punks!"

"I got something here for you," Begalone yelled, kneeling down, and thrusting out his stomach, and with his fingers at the level of his chest he made the sign for two black eyes.

On their right was the Colosseum, as hot as a furnace, and out of the hollows of the arches rose ruddy smoke in puffs and columns, pomegranate-colored and bright as candy wrappers, rising up and up and covering the sky over toward the Celio and the Oppio, above the Via Labicana, gleaming with cars, above the Via dell'Impero, in the crossfire of searchlights.

"What do we do now?" asked Alduccio.

"Let's take us a little walk," said Begalone.

"Let's take us a little walk," repeated Alduccio. They went over by the Colosseum, circled around it, and went off under the Arco di Constantino along the Viale dei Trionfi, dark and hot, sunk among the ruins and pine trees of the greenish Palatine hill that ran along smoothly, making a great curve toward the Cerchi.

They walked along some distance apart from each other, their hands in their pockets, swaggering and slouching, and, as was their custom, each of them singing a different song.

"Two-bit whores, two-bit whores . . ."

Begalone sang. Interrupting himself, he said, "Did you get a load of Caciotta's face?

"Two-bit whores, two-bit whores . . ."

he began again, more loudly, making a whole stretch of the deserted street resound under the umbrella pines, green as pool tables, among the broken stones of the ruins. But Alduccio paid no attention because he was too busy singing himself, leaning forward, his hands thrust into his pockets, his head high and swaying, his eyes half-closed, and his neck sunk into his shoulders.

A tiny, dusty moon shone down upon the Cerchi, endlessly lighting up the whole empty field, the black bushes, the pebbles, the piles of stone and rubbish. Everybody was looking at the moon out of the corners of their eyes, disgusted because the only places in shadow were the ones at the foot of the walls that surrounded the enormous oval of the Circo Massimo. On the wall just above Alduccio and Begalone, beyond which the Circo stretched away in the powdery moonlight with here and there a ruined tower, some men were already seated, some young boys, and even a few kids; farther along, by the trolley stop, but out in the field, shadows were moving about, coming together and dispersing.

"Hey, the cops!" Begalone shouted for a joke, making a megaphone of one hand, and guffawing. They both went on laughing even when the whores could no longer hear them, bending over, leaning against the wall, or shoving at each other; besides laughing, they made raspberries with their mouths, and spat. But they got over that quickly because they would have been glad to go with those fat whores, or at least tear off a piece on the run. By now they were both so worked up that they would have gone for an old woman of seventy. That's why the laughing jag broke off suddenly, and they walked on very seriously, almost angry, glancing over the wall with tough expressions on their faces, exploring the great oval space full of ruins and brush that looked black in the powdery white glow of the moonlight. There were rows of soldiers there, some young boys, and the usual prostitutes screaming at one another bitchily as if they were fighting over their purses.

"We come all this way for nothing!" said Begalone as he walked along gloomily. "We ought to get ourselves committed to the poorhouse, that's what. Jesus, how I'd like a piece tonight. Fat chance of that. Fuck this being without any money! Hey, look at that," he said, pointing to a man driving by in a custom job, "he's got it made. How do you like that, him riding around with that swell cunt, all dressed up, lousy with cash, and we got nothing! Those pricks! But that stuff ain't gonna go on forever. There's gonna to be some changes made." And he walked on for a while in silence, his mouth twisted in an expression of disgust.

But as they turned into the Via del Mare by the little gardens on the slope in front of the Tempio di Vesta, Begalone said, "Look at that!" And he stopped to stare into the gardens with his eyes half-closed.

"What's up?" Alduccio asked, undecided whether to ignore him or to show some interest.

Begalone started to whistle, bending over double. "What are you doing, calling the cows home?" asked Alduccio.

"What dishes!" Begalone exclaimed. The "dishes" were two girls sitting on the steps of the little temple, two well-endowed blondes wearing come-hither skirts that were about to split, and blouses cut so low in the bosom that you could see the best part of what they had.

They were roosting there in grave silence, turned toward each other, but as if they couldn't even see each other, staring at the gardens and the flower beds that ran down to the Tiber, way off yonder, by the Piazza di Bocca della Verità, by the Arco di Giano, by the old church—all bathed in moonlight; you could see everything as clear as day.

Going down from the Cerchi toward the Ponte Rotto, Begalone and Alduccio swaggered by, humming as they went. But after they had walked a little farther, they thought better of it and turned back again.

The two beauties had not stirred; it seemed as if they hadn't even breathed. Walking side by side, like two mongrels who have just been driven off with a stick and stop by some filthy sidewalk, their tails plastered to their rumps, the boys came back along the Via del Mare, and then separated again. They stationed themselves in the gardens, and stared at the two flaming roses. But the girls seemed not to be aware of their existence. The boys moved down toward the temple once more, but approached it from the opposite side, the one facing the slope; they entered the shadow of the small colonnade and slipped quietly toward the side that faced the Piazza Bocca della Verità, glowing in the moonlight.

The two damsels ignored them this time around too, sitting motionless as before. Crestfallen, the two mongrels sat down with their backs against the crumbling yellow wall of the temple, partly in shadow and partly in moonlight.

"Which one would you like to plow," Begalone asked, "the blonde or the redhead?"

"Both."

"Not asking for much, are you?" said Begalone.

"Double or nothing," Alduccio explained gaily, "because if I take just one, the other girl will get jealous."

"They're waiting for a cash customer," Begalone muttered.

"Well, what of it? Can't we be waiting to ball around too?" Alduccio said optimistically.

"Want to give it a try?" Begalone asked after a moment.

"Let's give it a try," said Alduccio. But neither of them moved; they stayed there, talking quietly and snickering, their knees pulled up to their chests, their bottoms planted in the dirt, their cowlicks and the tips of their shoes touched by moonlight. But when the two girls at last exchanged a few words with each other, the two boys took heart and began to kick up a little verbal dust.

"Hey, give me a smoke," said Begalone loudly.

"When we've smoked this one, that's all she wrote," said Alduccio, lighting the cigarette.

"There's more where that came from."

"Yeah, but unless you pay for them, you better hook them off a blind man."

"Boy, it's hot," Begalone said, gasping. "It's enough to split a turtle's ass! You know," he added after a moment, "I'm dying in this heat."

"Yeah?" said Alduccio.

"Let's take a dunk in the fountain," said Begalone.

"You out of your mind?" Alduccio was amused.

"I'm not kidding," Begalone said disgustedly.

"Ah, fuck off," said Alduccio with a laugh.

The two girls had a fit of the giggles.

"Come on, Aldo!" Begalone shouted.

They rose to their feet in the shadow, and jokingly began hastily unbuttoning their shirts. They slipped them off, and threw them to the ground, back into even deeper shadow. In their undershirts and with their long hair, they looked like Samson and Absalom. So as not to lose their balance while pulling off their pegged pants, they sat down once more.

"Let me take my shoes off first," said Alduccio softly, feeling sentimental about his new shoes, and talking like a man who's getting ready to horse around a little all by himself. He took off his shoes and gave them a toss. At last, they both slipped their undershirts off their black, sweaty chests, and were dressed in nothing but their shorts.

"Get a load of this build, buddy," said Begalone, sticking out his chest.

"Solid as a truck," said Alduccio.

"*Two-bit whores, two-bit whores,*" Begalone sang, gathering up the clothes that they had tossed around for the hell of it. He tied them into a bundle with the belts, and slipped them under his arm. Ready for their act, they moved out of the shadow, paused a moment in the full splendor of the moonlight, and then began to run through the flower beds, yelling and screaming. They threw the clothes down by the chain that encircled the fountain, scrambled up onto the basin, which was at least three feet off the ground, and stood upright on the fountain's edge.

"Jesus, I'm shivering already," said Begalone, twisting up his mouth and hunching his shoulders.

"Go on, it's warm," said Alduccio.

"Yeah, warm as soup all right," said Begalone, balancing himself with his toes curled on the fountain's rim like a monkey's. Alduccio gave him a shove, and he fell into the water like a sack of potatoes.

"Christ, what a belly-whopper!" Begalone said, coming up, his head streaming with water.

"Let me show you how it's done," said Alduccio, and he took a plunge that sent the water sloshing from the basin to pour down the marble pedestal beneath the fountain. Begalone was singing at the top of his lungs, his head and shoulders raised above the water.

"Hey, shut up, you nut!" Alduccio said. "If a guard hears you, it's our ass."

"Watch this, the drowned chicken," said Begalone. He sank beneath the surface, and came up again half-drowned, wiping his face madly, his hair all over it, stiff as bristles and longer than Mary Magdalene's.

"You want to do things in a big way, but you don't have what it takes," said Alduccio, laughing. In three minutes, they had soaked the pavement, flower beds and all, for ten yards around.

"Hey, I'm getting out," said Begalone.

"Me too," cried Alduccio. "I ain't getting pneumonia if I can help it."

They clambered up onto the basin's edge again, their shorts sticking to them, transparent, took one more header, and then crawled out of the fountain.

"Jesus," said Begalone, his teeth chattering.

Dripping as they were, they picked up their clothes and started to run across the mowed lawn, hurdling the low bushes. They raced along laughing, trying to warm up. Then they took the steps of the temple in two jumps, went under the colonnade, and passing behind the two girls, went into the shadow to slip their clothes on again. They started to slap each other around a little. The girls hardly bothered to notice, uninterested, or smiling scornful little smiles.

"Come on," said Begalone, "let's wring out these shorts." Laughing, their teeth still chattering, they drew back a little farther, around the curve of the temple, slipped off their shorts and started to wring them out. As always when dressing after a bath, Begalone was overcome by a wave of sentiment. "*Never, never before—have I loved you as I love you now*," he sang, his wet shorts over his shoulder, pulling on his socks. But while the boys were quietly getting dressed, the two turtle doves took off. They walked up toward the river, each with a book in her hand, wide pleated skirts floating in the bright moonlight. Still half-undressed, and holding his pants up with his hand, Begalone went over to the steps where the girls had been sitting.

"Hey, you beauties!" he yelled.

Alduccio too, also half-naked, came up, put his hands to his mouth like a megaphone, and yelled loudly: "Look at those lovely tomatoes!"

"Come on," he said, "let's get dressed and go pick them up."

The girls were already at Monte Savello when Alduccio and Begalone, their clothes sticking to their wet bodies, caught up with them.

"O.k., let's see how you make a woman," said Begalone, as they hurried after the two chicks, who were walking along calmly and briskly.

"Damn them, look how they're running," said Alduccio, who was moving as if his feet were hurting him. "Why don't you talk to them?" he said, panting.

"Yeah, sure, weak as I'm feeling," said Begalone, sounding even more exhausted.

"You're such a great pick-up artist, say something to them, for Christ's sake."

"Balls," said Begalone disgustedly.

Meanwhile, however, the two girls turned onto the quay, walked up to a car that was about thirty feet long, got in, started up the motor, and took off.

The two young toughs were left leaning against the guard-rail, all tired out, looking like a couple of plucked turkeys.

"You look like a beggar," Alduccio said after a moment, glancing at Begalone and bursting out laughing. "And you look like you've been in solitary," said Begalone. "Shit, we'll never make out tonight, not at this rate," he went on.

"Yeah, well, with a hundred and fifty lire in your pocket, what do you want?" Alduccio sadly smoothed out in his pocket the hundred and fifty lire stolen from Caciotta. "Let's go get a drink in the Cerchi," said Begalone. "We'll draw lots for it." "Idiot!" said Alduccio, striking two fingers against his forehead. "And then I suppose we walk back to Tiburtino." "For Christ's sake," Begalone burst out, "you mean we can't pick up another hundred and fifty lire somewheres? You can't find a clown with a little money on him around here?" "When are we going to find him, next Christmas?" asked Alduccio. "Fuck, what do you want to bet we find him?" said Begalone. They turned down toward the Ponte Garibaldi, looking like a pair of hungry wolves. By the urinal on the hill above the bridge, on the Via Arenula side, an old man was hunched up against the low wall. Begalone went inside to take a leak, and then went over to lean against the wall too—Alduccio was already there. They stood there without talking for a little while. Then Begalone fished a cigarette butt from one of his pockets, and leaning courteously toward the old man, he said, "I beg your pardon, would you have a match?" In five minutes' time, they'd gotten fifty lire off him.

They got another hundred by the Ponte Sisto, off an old man who was carrying a sack under his arm. He started in whining piteously, enough to bring milk to an old woman's tits. Begalone decided it was time to cut the comedy. He said, "We're dying of hunger, son-of-a-bitch, we haven't had nothing to eat since morning." The gentleman gave them a hundred lire to buy four buns with, and they immediately took off by the Via dei Giubbonari. They walked along swiftly in the direction of the Campo dei Fiori. They were in deep discussion. "Well, are you a man too?" Alduccio said angrily. "Will you listen to him!" Begalone cried, stopping in the middle of the street and thrusting out his hand toward him. "Who got the money, you or me?" "O.k., so what?" said Alduccio. "Nothing at all," said Begalone. "I find the money and he gets huffy about it. You idiot," he added, striking two fingers against his nose. But at that moment they came to a barbecue place. Begalone said, "Fuck it!" and went inside. They bolted down three meatballs each, and when they came out again, they were exactly where they had started. But since they were in the swing of it, they kept at it, walking apart down the Via dei Giubbonari. When they reached the end of the street and turned into the Campo dei Fiori, Alduccio gave Begalone a nudge, and with a gesture of his head and a sleepy, knowing look in his eye, he pointed out a queer who was walking ahead of them giving them long looks every now and then. "We've made it now," said Begalone. The man, walking slowly for a while and then speeding up for a while, turned into the Campo dei Fiori, then turned to the left among a crowd of kids who were playing in the wet piazza with a ball made of rags; he stopped for a moment by the opening in a public urinal, and looked around. Begalone and Alduccio examined him thoroughly. He was pretty well dressed, wearing a fine shirt and handsome sandals. Undecided, the queer went on toward the Piazza Farnese, and then up again to the Campo dei Fiori by a dark little street—and so on, two or three times running. He went around and around through those streets like a mouse drowning in a bucket.

"Hey," said Begalone, coming forward, "what the hell are you doing here?"

"What the hell are *you* doing?" asked Riccetto, lowering his eyes to take in Begalone, Alduccio, and the joker they had in tow.

"Give me a light and cut the crap," said Begalone, coming close to Riccetto with a cigarette in his mouth. Riccetto held out his own lighted cigarette to him, without shifting his position an inch, but simply dropping his eyelids a bit, since he was a little higher up than Begalone and the other two. He was sitting on the guardrail of the quay-side street, one leg swinging back and forth and the other pulled up against his chest.

"What, you got a date with somebody?" Begalone asked.

"Date? What date?" said Riccetto.

"Just an idea," said Begalone.

Alduccio and the other man were keeping very quiet.

"He likes Alduccio," said Begalone, snickering, but a little envious. In any case, the other man was giving Riccetto the once-over as he purposely sat in that provocative posture, his legs apart.

"You looking at me?" Riccetto said to him.

He smiled. "Yeah," he said, half shy and half putting it on.

"Oh," said Begalone, suddenly affable and gracious, as if he had only just noticed something he'd forgotten, "meet my friend."

Riccetto let the leg that was pulled up to his chest slip down, and stuck out the hand that had been holding it toward his new acquaintance. The man shook hands with him, flashing a finishing-school smile. "Pleased to meet you," he said, alluding to the pleasure he expected to have in the future if all went well, and looking up and down at the dispenser of that pleasure, who sat there calm and unruffled, as if he were ready to burst into song.

"You're looking at me," Riccetto said, taking in the glances.

The queer pretended he'd been caught out, feigned an embarrassed smile, with the suggestion of a dare about his pale mouth, and the tongue inside it darting around like a snake's. He put a hand to his throat, nervously fingering his open shirt-collar, as if he wanted to protect himself from the damp of the night air, or as if to modestly conceal God knows what from the sight of the boys.

"You'd like him, huh?" said Begalone.

"O.k., so I'd like him," said the fairy, shrugging and pretending to be annoyed.

Alduccio began to get restless, feeling somewhat slighted. "What do you say we go?"

"Where you going?" the queer asked, drawling the words.

"Down by the river. Let's go," said Alduccio. They were at the railing on the quay-side between the Ponte Sisto and the Ponte Garibaldi.

"You out of your mind, baby?" said the queer in a hurt voice.

"Come on," Alduccio insisted. "Let's go on down by the stairway and under the bridge and do our business."

"No, no, no, no, no," the fairy said, waving his hand and shaking his head, with an expression on his face that showed he was dead-set against it.

"Why the hell not?" Alduccio went on heatedly. "Where you going to find a better place? We don't have to take a half-hour over it. Two minutes and good-by. We just make out we got to take a leak, and who's going to bother anybody down there?" As Alduccio spoke, the queer paid no attention to him. All smiles and showing his teeth, he went on contemplating Riccetto—sometimes looking deep into his eyes and sometimes you know where. When Alduccio fell silent, the queer remembered him again, and he said drily and abruptly, as if the whole business were now beyond discussion, "No, I'm not going down there."

And he smiled again at Riccetto, casting sheep's eyes at him.

"Jesus, what an ugly bastard you are," said Riccetto.

Alduccio took the offensive again. "Well, what do you want to do then?" Begalone backed him up too: "Say, let's not waste any more time, buddy-boy!" The queer was fiftyish, but he was trying to make himself look at least twenty years younger. He went on clutching his shirt collar close to his chicken-breasted little chest, like a man who's worried about his health. "O.k., let's go," he said condescendingly to the two boys.

"Yeah, you say let's go, let's go, but you don't move!" said Alduccio.

Almost nobody ever came down between the Ponte Sisto and the Ponte Garibaldi any more, but Riccetto remembered what used to go on around there back when he was a kid just after the war. There used to be at least twenty young boys sitting on the rail the way he was now, ready to sell themselves to the first comer; the fairies used to come by in bunches, singing and dancing around, all plucked and peroxided, some of them still very young and some of them old men, but all acting crazy, not giving a damn about the people walking by or riding by in the trams, loudly calling out one another's names— "Wanda!" "Bolero!" "Railroad Rosie!" "Mistinguette!"—as if they were hailing one another from a great distance, running up and kissing one another delicately on the cheek, the way women do so as not to spoil their make-up. And when they were all assembled in front of the boys who were sitting on the rail and watching everything with mean looks on their faces, the fairies would begin to dance, some sketching out a ballet step, some doing the cancan, and as they went on horsing around, every now and then they'd scream, "We're free, girls! We're *free!*"

In those days you could go down the stairway and on the muddy flats covered with scraps of dirty paper under the Ponte Sisto or the Ponte Garibaldi you could do whatever you had a mind to, and no problems. Sometimes the paddy-wagon would come around, and everybody scattered, but afterward everything would start up again just as before. Tonight, Riccetto wasn't there looking for business; he was just passing the time, feeling nostalgic.

"Tell you what, I'll show you a good place," he said, moved by an excess of generosity.

The fairy set the mask of his fixed smile even tighter, throwing little sidelong glances in every direction, but feeling that he was a brilliant success, like a model being photographed with her shoulders bare. In fact, he made the same gesture that women make, tossing his hair back, and he started off, a little bit bowlegged, ready to follow Riccetto wherever he might lead.

Riccetto made them take the number 44 bus and ride up to the section where he used to live when he was a kid. They got off at the Piazza Ottavilla, which used to be practically out in the country when Riccetto had lived around there, and then they turned down to the left along a road that hadn't been there before, or had just been a path going along through broad fields with clumps of reeds ten feet high and willows here and there, as if growing on the slopes of a valley; but now there were buildings here, already completed and tenanted, and more buildings going up. "Let's go on a ways," said Riccetto. They went on, and beyond the last building sites they came to a path that led to Donna Olimpia, passing first through the yard of an old tavern that had an arbor, full of drunks. They walked past it, but the little path ran only a short way beyond, for just after the fields that were now all built over with houses, there was a new street, and a number of buildings here and there along it, either completed or still under construction. Immediately on the left the slope of the Monte di Casadio plunged down, the slope where Riccetto used to spend the whole day when he was a kid. Now they walked in that direction, and when they came to the very edge of the hill that fell away beneath them almost in a sheer drop, they found themselves facing the Ferrobedò. It lay at their feet at the bottom of a valley bathed in white moonlight. Beyond it, against a background of whitish clouds, you could see the great semicircle of Monteverde Nuovo, a black mass of jagged buildings, and to the right, beyond the Monte di Casadio, the roofs of the tall buildings of Donna Olimpia.

"Here you go," said Riccetto. "You go down there to the right," and he pointed to a kind of path among the bushes, winding down along the spine of the hill, looking as if it had been designed for goats. "It takes you right to a cave. You can't miss it. Nobody'll bother you there. So long now, take it easy."

"Where you going, you leaving us now?" cried the fairy, looking downcast and hunching up his shoulders. "He's going to attend to his own fucking business, what's it to you, fellow?"

asked Alduccio, who didn't mind Riccetto's departure one little bit.

"What?" said the queer. "Is that any way to be?"

"O.k.," said Riccetto magnanimously, "I'll go as far as the cave with you." They went down by the path, holding onto the bushes, and soon they were in a small clearing, green and muddy—for a little stream ran out of the cave close by, carrying black drain-water. "There you are, right in there," said Riccetto. The fairy couldn't bear to see him leave, and he took hold of Riccetto's arm, smiling invitingly at him, and coyly keeping his face tucked behind his shoulder so he could pitch Riccetto a covert little smile.

Good-humoredly, Riccetto laughed too. Since he had been in Porta Portese he had put on weight, and he wasn't as touchy any more. By this time he was a man with a broad experience of life. "Jesus," he said, almost in a tone of complicity, "what's the matter, two not enough for you?"

"No-o," drawled the fairy, bending one of his knees like the girl who says no because she wants to be coaxed.

"Jesus," said Riccetto again, "you really like a good time, don't you?" Full of understanding, and full of the sense of his own superiority, he went on down the path, waving jauntily without turning around.

Halfway down the hill, the path ran another twenty yards and then turned right into the center of Donna Olimpia. Just one hop over a crumbling wall and then a little way down the road brought him right smack in front of the Franceschi Elementary School. There was still a great pile of rubble, as if the building had caved in only a couple of days ago, except that garbage had accumulated upon the rain-washed, sun-scorched stones. His hands in his pockets, Riccetto stopped by the heap of ruins to look things over. It was true that the masses of stone that had rolled out into the middle of the street, and the tide of rubble, had been more or less piled up to one side. There was only an occasional stone still in the roadway; it could be seen that when election-time had come around, they had given a lick and a promise to rebuilding everything, and those few stones had been left behind, and then the elections were over and nobody bothered to come and shift them out of the way.

Riccetto looked all around him with great interest. He went around in back to inspect the courtyards with their washbasins and outhouses, and then he came out again to the foot of the hill of rubble and the corner buildings that were still standing, deserted, with rotten boards nailed over the windows. He stayed there a while, for he'd come to Donna Olimpia expressly to look around again. Then he pulled his shirt collar up and hunched his shoulders slightly, since it was beginning to be a little chilly, and started walking slowly through Donna Olimpia, seeing the crumbling sidewalks and the closed newsstand, and just a few people coming home, silent and sleepy, and right by the entrance to the Case Nòve, something new: two policemen on guard, shivering and bored to death, sometimes standing still and sometimes walking a few steps either way, like two shadows in the shadow of the buildings, with pistol-holsters on their belts.

Riccetto had nothing on his conscience. He was in the neighborhood for sentimental reasons only. He walked by the two cops very slowly, looking as if he didn't give a damn; and he went off toward the Grattacieli—four buildings so designed that the levels and diagonals formed by the rows of windows were uninterrupted and made lines hundreds of feet long, and so did the stairwells that could be detected from the outside by the long verticals of rectangular windows. Below them, among arcades, passageways, and porticoes done in twentieth-century fascist style, a half-dozen interior courts stretched away, all of trodden earth, showing the remains of what must once have been flower borders, strewn with rags and paper, forming the bottom of the vast funnel of the building-walls that stretched up as high as the moon. At this hour, in these courts with their darkened passageways, almost nobody was coming in any more through the gateway that opened onto the Via Donna Olimpia, or if anyone did come in he walked swiftly along past the basement gratings, slipped into some archway, and made for his own apartment up the long flights of stairs smelling of dust.

Riccetto wandered around among the courtyards, hoping to meet someone he could talk to for a bit. And in fact after a while he saw the outline of a young fellow coming down the iron stairway from the Via Ozanam. "Maybe I know that boy," Riccetto thought, and he walked toward him. He was a redhead, covered with freckles, two bushy red eyebrows hiding his eyes, and his hair carefully parted on the side. Riccetto watched him as he came up to him, and the boy, feeling eyes on him, looked attentively at Riccetto, ready for all eventualities. "Say, we know each other," said Riccetto, going up to him with his hand outstretched.

"If you say so," said the boy, taking a closer look.

"Isn't your name Agnolo?"

"Yes."

"I'm Riccetto," he said, as if he were revealing a great secret.

"Oh," said Agnolo.

"Well, how's things with you?" Riccetto asked courteously.

"So, so," said Agnolo. You could see he was dead on his feet.

"Well, what's new?" asked Riccetto, who, for his part, was feeling full of beans.

"What could be new? Same old stuff. I just knocked off work, and I'm so tired I can't see straight."

"You're a bartender, aren't you?"

"Yup."

"And the others? Oberdan, Zambuia, Bruno, Lupetto?"

"Well, they're all more or less working, and that's about it."

"Rocco, Alvaro?"

"What Alvaro?"

"Alvaro Furciniti—you know, old Straw Boss."

"Oh, him," said Agnolo. Rocco was living in Risano, and he was only seen once in a blue moon. But Alvaro was in a big mess, and the whole thing had ended just a few weeks before. It was during the early part of March. It was raining. Alvaro was in a bar down in Testaccio, where a group of weary-looking boys were shooting pool. He was playing too, passing the time. Everybody in that bar was a hood, including the owner, who was a fence, a fat guy with curly hair running all the way down his neck like the Emperor Nero. All the boys playing pool were in their work clothes because it was a weekday—Monday, as a matter of fact—but every one of them had just pulled off at least two or three big jobs, and now they were living on their capital, that day anyway. So they'd been playing in that damp room behind the bar all afternoon, and they were bored with the whole thing, so they decided to take a little trip into town. When they went by the Piazza del Popolo, they saw a chance to steal an old heap, an Aprilia, so easily they'd have had to be real jerks to let it go. There was nothing in the car, not even a pair of gloves, but they were thinking of joy-riding around that evening and then dumping it someplace. They'd had a few drinks in the bar in Testaccio, they had some more while strolling around the Piazza di Spagna and the Via del Babuino, and then they had some more, running around Rome in the Aprilia they'd just liberated. They got stinking drunk and started to drive like madmen. They headed for the Piazza Navona to play race-track, but since the circle around the piazza was too small, they buzzed off toward the Cerchi by the Archeologica promenade, keeping the engine in top gear and doing seventy-five, eighty through the wet streets. Two cops on motorcycles took off after them, but they shook them by turning in by the Anagrafe and then through the alleys around the Piazza Giudia. They went back to the Piazza Navona, and racing around it they smacked into a baby carriage and sent it sailing off fifteen or twenty feet; it was empty, as luck would have it, because the baby was holding onto its mother's hand and walking. A man yelled something after them, they stopped short, got out, jumped him, stomped on him, left him with blood running out of his mouth, got back into the car, and took off at top speed for Governo Vecchio and Borgo Panigo. They turned into the Lungotevere and sped up toward the Ponte Milvio. Around the Naval Ministry, one of them spotted a good-looking woman, all dressed up, walking by herself beside the railing. They slowed down; one of them jumped out, went over to the lady, grabbed her purse, and they were off again. They turned around, crossed the bridge, and turned down again toward Borgo Pio. They careened around a while in the Piazza San Pietro, and landed back in Testaccio to have two or three shots of cognac. It was night by this time, and they decided to take a spin out to Anzio, or Ardea, or Latina—somewhere out in the country. They climbed back into the Aprilia, gunned off toward San Giovanni, and turned into the Via Appia. In half an hour they were in a little town that they didn't even know the name of, and they went into a tavern to drink some wine, and after that they spun up and down those country roads, always doing better than sixty, until, almost by chance, they found themselves in a place near Latina that one of them knew about. It was well on into the night by now. They left the car parked on the shoulder of the road, and broke into a farmyard where they grabbed about twenty chickens and shot the dog dead. They piled the chickens into the car, took off at eighty miles an hour, got back onto the Via Appia, and about twenty miles from Rome, just before Marino, they smacked into a trailer-truck, God knows how. The Aprilia was a heap of twisted metal, and the inside was a mess of bloody bodies and chicken feathers. Alvaro was the only one who got out alive; he lost an arm and he was blind.

While telling this story, the redhead began to feel a bit chilly, maybe because he was so sleepy, and looking rather pale-faced, he glanced impatiently out of the corner of his eye at the people coming in from time to time, going silently into their doorways, all hunched up.

"Let me go on home and get some sleep, or my old man will raise hell," he said at last, stretching.

"O.k., see you," said Riccetto, who was sorry to see him go but didn't want to show it.

"So long, uh, Riccè," said Agnolo. He shook hands and disappeared into the broad black maw of stairway M or N, with its dusty steps, splashed at intervals by the light of a feeble electric bulb.

Riccetto went off across the courtyards in a quiet, thoughtful mood. In the Via Donna Olimpia he passed by the policemen again, and whistling, hands in his pockets, he took the road at the foot of the Casadio hill that led down to the Ponte Bianco, beyond the Ferrobedò. He had no further business in that neighborhood, and he quickened his step a bit, still whistling. He was in a hurry to get to the Ponte Bianco and take the tram home and go to sleep.

The Ferrobedò—or, to speak properly, the Ferro-Beton*— stretched out on his right in the sugary moonlight, that fragrant

* Literally, reinforced concrete.—*Trans.*

white powder; everything was as it should be, and so still that you could hear a night watchman singing to himself behind some warehouse. Beyond him, raised on a sort of plateau against the light and looming above some huge black mounds, the enormous semicircular outline of Monteverde Nuovo could be seen, dotted with lights, under wisps of cloud that looked like shards of porcelain in the smooth, smooth sky. Riccetto hadn't been in that district since the old school buildings had collapsed; it was a little hard to recognize the place. Everything was too clean, too orderly. Riccetto could scarcely make out where he was. Beneath him, the Ferrobedò was like a mirror—with its tall chimneys that rose nearly as high as the road from the floor of the little valley, its yards full of railroad ties piled in neat rows, perfectly aligned, its lengths of track gleaming near some dark motionless freight car, its rows of warehouses that, at least when seen from above, looked like ballrooms, all clean, with neat rows of reddish roofs.

Even the wire-mesh fence that ran along the road, following the bushy slope above the factory, was brand new, not a single gap in it. Only the old watchman's shelter by the fence remained as foul and smelly as ever; people passing by still used it as a toilet—the shit was inches deep inside and even outside, all around the hut. That was the only place that looked familiar to Riccetto, just the way it used to be when he was a kid right after the war.

Begalone and Alduccio were again walking swiftly toward the Campo dei Fiori, their hands in their pockets, their open shirts flopping outside their pants, but not horsing around any more, and not singing.

"What kind of a guy are you, anyway?" Alduccio said again, walking with his shoulders hunched.

"Will you listen to him!" cried Begalone, stopping short in the street, and thrusting out his hand with the fingers spread stiff. "Were you all by yourself, for Christ's sake?"

"What's that got to do with it? He was talking just to me, like a decent guy!" Alduccio hollered, putting his hand to his mouth like a megaphone.

"Oh, what a little sweetheart you are!" said Begalone, starting to walk again. "Goddam idiot!" he added, striking his fingers against his forehead.

"And besides, I never said it had to be only me," said Alduccio. "You dope, I said let's toss for it!"

Arguing like that, they got to the Campo dei Fiori, where the pavement had been wetted down but there were still cabbage stalks and empty shells lying around, and the boys were still playing soccer with a rag ball. At the far end of the piazza, in deep shadow, there was an alley, the Via dei Cappellari, lined with crumbling entryways, crooked windows, and sagging arches, its cobbled pavement splattered with stale urine. The two friends moved into the last patch of light before the intersection, near two old ladies sitting in a doorway under a rickety lamppost, and Begalone produced a coin, turned it over in his hand a couple of times, and tossed it into the air.

"Heads!" Alduccio cried.

The coin struck the cobblestones that stank of fish, and rolled over by a manhole cover. Begalone and Alduccio, giving each other the elbow and grabbing at each other's flapping shirts, both threw themselves on the coin.

"I win," Alduccio said calmly, and feeling pretty full of himself he led the way into the alley. Begalone was right behind him. The only light on the pavement, which looked like the floor of a stable, came from some tiny windows let into the sooty wall, and it could have been a real trick finding the door to the cathouse. But as it happened the door was painted pea-green, so it could have been picked out among a thousand, and besides it was ajar, opening onto a white-tiled corridor that looked like the ones in the public baths.

They went up the stairs and got to the first-floor landing. On one side the stair, covered with a threadbare carpet, continued upward under a white vault; on the other was the door to the parlor. In the center of that room, the madam had her presiding-officer's chair.

Since there was no one in the hall at that moment, and the parlor door was closed, the two friends went calmly up the second flight of stairs. But a roar stopped them in their tracks. "Hey, you lousy bums!" The madam was doing the roaring, hard enough to bust her bladder. "Will you look at that! Making yourselves right at home, aren't you?"

Laughter and jeering voices issued from the smoke-filled parlor. A couple of customers got up and leaned against the doorway, grinning.

Begalone and Alduccio ran back down the flight of stairs they had climbed, and, laughing themselves, went to pay their respects to the madam, who had already turned back toward her throne, her fat thighs waddling. She wasn't amused one little bit, and neither was her servant-girl, who glumly stuck to her like a leech.

"Imbeciles!" said the madam in choice Tuscan, for she considered herself high-class because she was a property owner. "You want to close the deal without laying out one lira, don't you? What are you, crazy?"

"Ahh, lady, we just made a mistake is all," said Begalone conciliatingly.

"Mistake my ass," she replied. When it came to money, she

could talk the Trastevere dialect loud and clear, even though she was from Frosinone. She shoved her hand out toward them. They pulled out their identity cards and showed them to her. Then, looking cheerful in spite of the asshole trick they had pulled, they mingled with the customers, who were sitting on couches along the walls, smoking, red as lobsters, most of them looking like born losers, silent and horny.

And on an upholstered stool in the center of the room, a couple of greenish veils draping her belly, an old Sicilian whore was sitting smoking a cigarette daubed with lipstick.

The company stared at her in silence, and she stared back in a rage, puffing smoke all around her, her tits reaching down to her navel.

When he came in, Alduccio marched right up to her, turned his back on the audience, and motioning with his head, he muttered, "Let's go."

"What a jerk!" Begalone thought, moving over toward one of the couches and sitting down. "All these guys have been here an hour and none of them goes upstairs. He comes in and right away he's got to go up to her room." Meanwhile, Alduccio and the whore had left the room and gone up the stair with the threadbare carpet. Begalone had a smoke, sitting with one ham on the couch and one off it, next to two soldiers from the country south of the Po who didn't say a word and acted as respectful as if they were in church instead of in a cathouse. "When the hell is he coming back down, a fucking year from now?" Begalone mused darkly. "The next time, if he don't lay out the money, I'll break his balls." He took the last drags on the cigarette that was scorching his fingers, and dropped the butt at the foot of the couch, crushing it with his heel.

Everything was as usual: The madam was cursing out the servant-girl in the corridor. She yelled as if she were being disemboweled, and the words couldn't be made out too well.

"Hey, big-mouth, shut up!" a couple of young men yelled at her from a corner of the parlor—also as usual, after some of that racket. Their voices were so deep and powerful that they sounded as if they came from down in the guts somewhere, stretching the cords in their necks and making their eyes go bloodshot. They immediately assumed their ordinary expressions again, and nobody could have known who had shouted. The madam paid absolutely no attention—just went on screaming at her handmaid. Everything as usual, in short. After a while, two more of the girls came downstairs; one of them took the unoccupied stool, and the other sat down on the lap of one of the young men who had called out and then shut it off quickly, making a sacrificial face so that he looked as if he had just swallowed the Host. The two soldiers left, followed by insults from the two whores. The younger men all laughed, getting as red in the face as peppers. The stench of tobacco smoke, sweaty clothing, and sneakers got worse and worse—but that was as usual too. Suddenly . . .

Right at the height of the racket going on in the parlor, above the voice of the madam, who was working on the last paragraphs of her speech, and those of the girls, who were bitching, suddenly laughter was heard upstairs, and it went on and on. At first, nobody paid any attention. Not the madam, or the girls, or the customers, or Begalone. But since the laughing kept up, they all began to prick up their ears. The madam started throwing suspicious glances up the stairs from the vantage-point of her throne. Then she put all the money away in a drawer—she had been counting it all the time that she had been giving the servant what-for—and she walked as far as the staircase, looking up. The girls fell silent, too, and gathered in the doorway, dragging their trains behind them, and their plump flesh shaking beneath their skins, which smelled of powder and fried food. The young men from Panigo also got up and crowded together in the doorway, leaning on the door frame or piling up behind each other. The other clients crowded behind them, and after them Begalone, stretching his neck to see what was going on.

The one who was doing the laughing was still up on the third flight of stairs, out of sight under its little plaster vault beyond the landing where the threadbare carpet gave out. But she was coming slowly downstairs. She must have been stopping every once in a while to throw her head back or to double up, in order to laugh better. She was laughing hard enough to be heard out in the street, but you could tell she didn't mean it all that much. She'd go ha-ha-ha-ha-ha for a good while, then she'd stop, and she'd start in again, ha-ha-ha-ha-ha, a tone higher, till you thought the wench would split her gullet. At last she got to the landing, and there she stopped again, to laugh for the benefit of the audience, who were watching from the foot of the stair. Open-mouthed, they watched her going through her spasms up there, her heart not in it any more but carrying on more than ever just for the hell of it.

"Hey, loud-mouth, you mind telling us what you're laughing at?" yelled one of the young men. She looked down at him and the others, and laughed at them too.

"Shut up and give your ass a chance!" one of the others said.

She turned toward the stair above her, which was out of their view, and still laughing she screamed, "Hey, come on, shake it, what do you need, a wet nurse?" Then Alduccio showed up on the landing next to the Sicilian woman, his head bent over as he tightened his belt another notch.

"Go get yourself an eggnog," she said between explosions of laughter.

"Fuck you," said Alduccio in an undertone, having found

the right hole at last. The Sicilian woman came slowly down the carpeted stair, leaning against the wall in order to laugh at her ease, and he followed her down as if he were hiding behind her. The ones below, who had all caught on by now, were laughing too, but not very loud, rather discreetly, and muttering among their laughter, "Well, damn her anyway, what's all the fuss for?" But she kept it up, laughing fit to die, in order to spite them all. "He's in such a tearing hurry, and then he just shoots blanks. Ha-ha-ha-ha-ha." "I'm just run down is all," Alduccio stammered by way of excuse, but in such a low voice that he was the only one who heard it. Now they were down on the lower landing among the others. The Sicilian woman went into the parlor laughing hysterically, pushing her way through the crowd around the door, while Alduccio—in a towering rage, but not daring to look anyone in the face—tore down the last flight of stairs to the street door, and Begalone, having hastily paid the madam, who was already beginning to yell, ran after him.

"Now we got to walk all the way to the terminal," he said worriedly to Alduccio when he had caught up with him and the door of the cathouse had closed behind them.

"So what?" said Alduccio. He walked on without turning around, like a mangy wolf with its tail tucked in between its hind quarters. They were all alone in the Via dei Cappellari, walking one ahead of the other, along the housefronts decorated with two courses of encrusted soot, sopping wet, black, and pierced with windows out of which rags were hanging; the alley was so narrow that hands stretched out could touch two facing windows. It was so dark that they had to walk along like blind men. "Hail, hail, the gang's all here," said Begalone. "We're going to end up with our faces in a puddle of piss at this rate." Almost feeling his way along, being careful where he set his feet down, he suddenly burst out laughing.

"What's so funny?" said Alduccio, turning halfway around in a hurry. Begalone went on snickering, moving along the pavement that seemed to be smeared with grease. "Keep it up, why don't you," said Alduccio weakly.

Still walking one behind the other, they crossed the Campo dei Fiori, quiet now, and went by the Largo Argentina and the Via Nazionale toward the terminal, and got there after half an hour of forced march. "Should we grab a hitch here?" Alduccio asked dully. "Be better farther down," said Begalone, his face sagging and yellow with fatigue. They grabbed a ride on the number 9 farther down, by the Macao barracks. Begalone was in high spirits. Hanging onto the cowcatcher, he started in singing, over and over, "*Two-bit whores, two-bit whores . . .*" If by chance someone passing by turned to look at him, he tried to start something right away. "What you looking at?" he said. Or else, according to what the man looked like, or how fast the trolley was going, "Yeah, chief, I'm stealing a hitch, what's it to you?"—and he thrust out his hand in a questioning gesture, the fingers spread stiff. Or if it was a young boy, "Hey, you going to lend me the fare, buddy?" Or if it was a woman, "Hey, good-looking!" And carried away with enthusiasm, he'd start in singing louder than ever. "Why don't you cut it out?" Alduccio said to him seriously during a stop, while they wandered around the trolley, looking innocent. "Or why don't you just phone the cops and tell them to pick you up—there's a stupid son of a bitch hitching a ride on the trolley, on the number 9?" "What do I care if they stick me in the can? You think I'm any better off at home?" asked Begalone, catching hold of the cowcatcher on the run.

The lights of Verano glowed around them, twinkling, calm, thickly clustered, hundreds of them, through the cypresses and the tombs that jutted out above the retaining-walls. But Portonaccio, at the head of the line, just the other side of the overpass by the Tiburtino station, was deserted—just a couple of empty trolleys and empty buses parked there, showing like dark stains in the dim light, made more gloomy rather than illuminated by some street lamps and the calm sky. A 309 car was stopped in front of the shut-down newsstand, and beyond it was the station shelter. There wasn't a soul around.

"Let's see what I've got in my pockets," said Begalone, turning them inside out and pulling out the money. "Fifty-five lire," he said, "forty for the bus, and with ten more we get ourselves a bun, what do you say, Aldo?" "O.k., let's get a bun," Alduccio said hoarsely. He was dying of hunger, but he didn't care one way or another about that bun; he stood behind Begalone, all bent over. Begalone bought the bun from an almost empty stall. "Here you go," he said, lifting the cold bun to Alduccio's mouth. Alduccio took a bite with his mouth twisted up. "Take another one," said Begalone. "No, that's enough," said Alduccio, turning his head away. "O.k.," said Begalone, "so much the better. I'll eat the whole damn thing." And he began to eat it, laughing with his mouth full. "Laugh, laugh, and fuck you too," Alduccio muttered, looking even grimmer. "What do you say we hop on?" said Begalone after a while, when he had finished chewing. And he jumped up onto the bus platform, lively as you please. Alduccio followed him into the half-empty bus, not saying a word, dragging his feet, not even taking his hands out of his pockets. But Begalone was whistling a Charleston. "Two tickets, conductor!" he yelled. "I can hear you, I can hear you," said the conductor, slowly pulling two tickets from his pad. "You don't have to shout."

There were a dozen passengers on the bus, all half-asleep. There was a blind woman who had been begging, accompanied by a man who looked like Cavour; two musicians with their instruments encased in black cloth bags, nodding as they sat;

a *carabinieri* officer; two or three workingmen; and some young boys on their way home from the movies. Begalone and Alduccio sprawled out on the front seats, and while Alduccio kept quiet, Begalone began to sing half out loud. The driver was chatting with the dispatcher, and beyond them, beyond the retaining-walls, the lights of Verano glowed and twinkled. Suddenly, in the midst of the silence and the depressing stink of poor people's clothes, a young fellow wearing a jacket entered the bus, a little blond with a face that looked like the seventh generation of a race of starvelings, and set himself in the center of the platform, facing everybody. While everyone ignored him, he cleared his throat conscientiously a couple of times, and then started to sing. So everybody turned to look at him, and, undaunted, he went on singing in a loud, nasal voice, pronouncing all the words of the song very distinctly. "*Fly away! Fly away! Fly away!*" he sang. Out of the corners of their eyes, Begalone and Alduccio observed their colleague at work. Here and there, someone started to laugh, and some sat with their mouths open, staring; some, on the other hand, felt embarrassed, and kept their faces turned toward the window.

"You don't hurry up and fly away, the bus'll start up, and that'll be all she wrote," said Begalone, by way of breaking the ice. Alduccio took advantage of the distraction afforded by that idiot who had come here to sing, and concentrated on his own thoughts. But the boy sang his song right through, in the silent bus in the silent square, and then he went around among the passengers to collect what he could. Begalone shook his gravedigger's head, swelling up his neck like a turkey, and pulled the last five lire out of his pocket. His duty done, the blond kid jumped down from the bus platform as quietly as he had climbed in. "Yeah, now you've got the money, scram," said Begalone, broken-hearted about the five lire. "Fly away, fly away," he called after him, though the kid couldn't hear him any more, "fly away, damn you!" Then he thrust his yellow face under Alduccio's nose. "Fly away, fly away," he repeated. Alduccio gave him one with his elbow under the chin, so that Begalone's head struck the back of the seat, and he looked at him in a rage, ready to come to blows if the other said one more word. But Begalone dropped the whole thing. Then the driver climbed slowly into the bus, but instead of starting up he stretched out in his seat with a vacant expression on his dark Judas face. He put his hands between his legs, and seemed to be dropping off to sleep. A dismal voice sounded from the rear of the bus, "Hey, buddy, what are we doing here, digging in for the winter?" But the driver didn't respond. "Hey, fly away, fly away, fly away," Begalone said loudly. With those two sallies, the atmosphere in the bus perked up, and everybody more or less put in his two cents' worth. When they had joked around a while, one after another contributing an observation on the Korean War or on Rebecchini, the driver began to show signs of life. He straightened up, and lazily released the brake; the bus began to shake and spit, and jouncing over the pavement, it took off down the dark and empty Via Tiburtina.

"So long, Aldo," said Begalone when they were well into Tiburtino, near their own neighborhood, and he went up the crumbling stair. "So long," Alduccio muttered. He walked on toward his own house a little farther on down the empty street. But even if it had been crowded with people, he wouldn't have seen one of them. The street lamps poured out their spattering of light on the pavements and the yellowish walls of the buildings, stretching out in rows of ten, all alike, and with little courtyards of beaten earth, all alike. A half-dozen kids came by playing music, one with a harmonica, one with a drum, one with a pair of maracas, and they went off among the buildings until their samba sounded like an echo in a ghost town. A drunk whose face looked like a burst of flame under his dirty cap let out a whistle now and then, signaling to his girl-friend to let him in while her husband slept. Two young fellows were quietly talking over some private business—their voices distinctly audible, nevertheless—in one of the courtyards, with its row of stone supports for clotheslines, looking like so many gibbets in the shadows.

The door to Alduccio's place was ajar, and the light was on. His sister was sitting on a chair; inside the messy kitchen his mother was still shouting. The dishes on the drainboard were still unwashed, there was garbage all over the floor, and on the table, in the light of the lamp shining on the wet surfaces, there were still some chunks of bread, a dirty bowl, and a knife. The door to one of the inner rooms was ajar too, and in the gloom Alduccio's father, still dressed, could be seen lying spread-legged on the double bed, where the youngest girl was also sleeping; the other young children were sleeping on mattresses on the floor. But the door to the other room, where Riccetto's family all slept, was closed, and nobody seemed to be in there.

"I'm going to kill myself, I'm going to kill myself," his sister cried out, winding her skinny bare arms about her head as if she were suffering from cramps. "You bet," Alduccio muttered, not looking at anyone and moving toward his cot over against the wall in the room where his father was lying. Suddenly the girl jumped up from the chair and hurled herself toward the doorway. "You stay where you are," said Alduccio, catching her round the waist and flinging her back into the center of the room with such force that she fell to the floor.

She lay where she had fallen, between the table and the overturned chair, sobbing tearlessly with rage, twisting about on the wet tiles.

"Close the door," Alduccio's mother said to him.

"Close it yourself!" he said, taking a piece of bread from the table and stuffing it into his mouth.

"You bum," his mother cried, not too loud so as not to be heard by the neighbors, and for that reason even more infuriated. She was disheveled and half-naked as he had left her, sweaty breasts nearly out of her open gown. She went to close the door, trailing her bare feet over the tiles.

"That shameless hog," she went on, while Alduccio's sister, still stretched out on the floor, gasped as if the death-rattle were upon her, saying over and over in a half-whisper, "God, God." Alduccio swallowed a mouthful of bread and went to the faucet to get a sip of water. Wearing his undershorts and the black jacket of his work clothes, Alduccio's father reeled across the kitchen, blind with drink, his uncombed hair plastered down on his forehead with sweat. He stood still a moment, perhaps because he had forgotten what it was he had meant to do. Then he raised his hand to his mouth and waved it about in the air, from somewhere around his heart to an indeterminate point in the neighborhood of his nose, as if he were giving emphasis to a long and complicated speech that never got past his lips. At last, realizing that he wasn't managing to express himself, he took off at a run toward his bed. Alduccio went out for a moment to relieve himself, for there were no toilets in the project apartments, and when he came back his mother lit into him again. "He's out of the house all day long," she said. "He drinks, he eats, and not once does he bring home a single lira, not once!"

Alduccio turned suddenly. "I've had it up to here. Can it, Ma!" he yelled.

"And if I can it," she cried, tossing the hair out of her eyes, and freeing the locks that stuck to her sweaty bosom, bare almost to the nipples, "you'll make sure I have something else to yell about, you lousy good-for-nothing!"

Blind with rage, Alduccio spat out at her feet the mouthful of food he had been chewing. "There!" he said. "Take it back! You can have it!" Turning to go into his room, he bumped against the table, and knocked the bowl and the knife that had been lying on it to the floor. "You give it back to me, do you?" said his mother, moving toward him. "You think you can get even that way, do you?" "Fuck you," said Alduccio. "Fuck you too, and that filthy sewer-mouth you've always had!" screamed his mother. Alduccio saw red. He bent down to grab the knife that had fallen by his foot on the dirty tile floor.

8 · The Old Hag

...The withered hag
*of the Via Giulia lifts her claws.**

It was a Sunday afternoon. The fine view that could be enjoyed
from the San Basilio bus on the long express run from Tiburtino
to Ponte Mammolo seemed to be composed of wonderful shapes
bathed in the light of the blue sky, from here at the foot of the
slope to the Tivoli hills, vaguely outlined against a patch of
haze, encircling the countryside with its trees, small bridges,
gardens, factories, and houses.

Here and there along the Via Tiburtina, and almost grazed
by the bus that at that point speeded up to forty miles an hour
with a great clatter of glass and metal, young fellows could be
seen going by in lazy, noisy groups, all dressed up, on foot
or riding bicycles, and groups of girls, too. After the rain of
the night before, everything looked as fresh as a new coat of
paint—even the Aniene, curving among the fields, the reedy
stretches, and the clumps of shacks, and uncoiling in the Prati
Fiscali to flow down toward Monte Sacro.

Two *carabinieri* were taking in the splendid panorama from

* The hag represents death; the Chiesa della Morte, or Church of
Death, is in the Via Giulia.

inside the empty, stifling bus. Men from the Campagna or from Salerno, running sweat like fountains, with their summer uniforms unbuttoned wherever they could be unbuttoned, their caps in their hands, their reformed hoodlum faces frozen in bored expressions, thinking disgustedly about all this fuss made over a kid with a couple of scorches on him. After the bus crossed the bridge over the Aniene at top speed, brushing by the seaweed processing plant, and came to a stop in front of an old tavern, they got off, moving at a leisurely pace; wiping the sweat away with their handkerchiefs, they prepared to walk all the way up the Via Casal dei Pazzi, which started below the tavern and stretched out endlessly to the horizon shimmering in the hot air. Way off in that direction, Ponte Mammolo, like an Arab town, had its white houses spread along the gentle curves of its fields.

Eventually the two *carabinieri* got under way, walking on asphalt that was softened by the heat, and when they reached the crossroads they took the Via Selmi and entered the district proper. But the boys they were after weren't around. They weren't in one of the last houses in the Via Selmi, half-built and half-unbuilt, with curtains where the window-sashes should have been, and women quarreling around the outside water faucet. And they weren't playing with the other boys in the street or in the fields. If the two cops had known that, they could have spared themselves the hike. But how could they have known? And to think that if they had just taken a look around as the bus was turning onto the bridge, they would have seen the vegetable gardens just beyond the bend in the river where the gang of boys all went swimming, and might have spotted the ones they were looking for.

The ones they were looking for were in fact right there among the vegetable gardens, or rather in a kind of jungle of bushes, willows, and reeds between the gardens and the bank that fell in a sheer drop to the Aniene. Mariuccio, who was still so small that he hadn't started school yet, was playing there quietly, squatting on his heels, stirring up a couple of ants with a stick. Borgo Antico was watching him, and Genesio was squatting down off by himself, smoking gravely. Seated by them was their little dog, Fido by name, and he too was caught in a moment of repose. He sat with his hind legs under him, his front paws planted vertically on the ground; every now and then he scratched under his front legs with one or the other of his hind ones. With his easy, almost elegant, manner he looked about him, far off to right and left, watching the whole scene, from the houses of Tiburtino to the bend in the river, and casting a calm eye occasionally on his three young masters, who were after all just boys compared to him, and had to be indulged a little when they acted dumb.

Suddenly, in the midst of his contemplations, he rose and went over to sniff at Mariuccio's heels. "Here, Fido," Genesio said, but without a trace of a smile. He took hold of Fido, who had run over to him at once, and set the dog between his knees, petting him. The dog contentedly let himself be fondled, half-closed his eyes, and seemed to sink into a half-sleep in which he could enjoy to the full the special treatment being accorded him by his favorite among the boys. And it was unusual, because Genesio, who was good-hearted and an easy prey to his own emotions and affections, poor boy, habitually kept everything inside, and spoke as little as possible so as not to give himself away. His younger brothers had caught on to him, and they always did what he said, though not at all out of fear, and occasionally, while following instructions most respectfully, they still took the liberty of kidding him a little. The dog was just about to drop off on his lap. All four of them were dead for lack of sleep that morning. It was their first day of freedom; close by in the dry grass, among clumps of crushed reeds, you could still see the lairs where they had slept like sparrows in their nests, or little rabbits. They weren't the least bit sorry that they had left home. On the contrary, the two younger boys were perfectly happy; Genesio would look after everything. And Genesio was frowning, looking after everything, while they played with the ants.

"Let's go," said Genesio, getting up suddenly. As usual, without asking where or why, Borgo Antico and Mariuccio got up too, full of curiosity, waiting to see what would happen next. The dog ran about wagging his tail, pleased that things were stirring again. He ran back and forth, barking continually, the sound coming out of his open mouth with its lolling tongue. But the place that Genesio had in mind wasn't very far off. For a while they followed the rugged curving bank of the Aniene, jumping from one hummock to the next among the stands of reed, as far as the Fisherman's Rest and the dredge. Then, crossing the river on the little old cobblestone bridge, they walked back along the other bank, which was much more open and where there was a narrow path running among the leafless bushes, until they were directly opposite where they had been on the other bank, over by the swimming-place. Like the day before, the old drunk was singing all by himself, "*Let me stick it in just a little waaaay . . .*" under the arch of the bridge—a place he must have taken a liking to. There wasn't a soul to be seen anywhere in the large expanse blackened by fire, leaving charred wheat stubble all around; not even the four black horses were in sight. But then they heard voices, and in fact, at the foot of the bank by the water's edge, where the ground was still dirty and ploughed up as it had been the day before, there were three or four swimmers who must have come up while the three brothers and Fido were going around the dredge. They chattered and moved about quietly in the still pure light, in which, however, a stench was just beginning to spread in the sultry air. They were stretched out in the dust, their legs apart, turning lazily every now and then, and their voices resounded in the quiet air, for there was little traffic along the Via Tiburtina, and the factory opposite them was closed.

One of the group was Caciotta. When Genesio and the other boys came up, he was saying nostalgically, "If only that song had been popular last year!"

The song in question was being sung by Zinzello, who, perhaps dissatisfied with his Saturday bath, had come down to give himself a good lathering again, this time without his two dogs. Behind a bush, naked and skinny as an anchovy, he was bawling out desperately with all the breath in his body, "*Here I am in jail, and mother's dying . . .*"

"Why do you wish that song had been popular last year?" inquired Alduccio, who was there too, his eyes as red as two wounds for lack of sleep.

"Why?" said Caciotta. "Because when I was in Porta Portese last year, I could have been singing it."

"You bet," said Alduccio, grinning.

"Boy, how I would have liked to sing that song," Caciotta went on in a tone of enthusiasm blended with pathos, "when I was in jail myself, you know what I mean? Christ! I would have sung it at night, before going to sleep." And he began to sing it after Zinzello, with fervor, but they sang it independently, each more passionately than the other, Zinzello on one side of a patch of bare and garbage-littered bushes and Caciotta on the other.

"They really broke you when you were in jail, didn't they?" asked Begalone.

"You looking for trouble?" asked Caciotta menacingly, breaking off his song for a moment.

"Well, fuck those guys, anyway," Genesio muttered, frowning, and speaking as if to himself as he squatted a little above them on the crumbling edge of the slope. Mariuccio and Borgo Antico stared at him. It was the first time he had ever said the whole phrase like that. Looking thoughtfully at his brother and sighing, Mariuccio said softly, "What would Mama do if she heard you say that?" Genesio turned one of his expressionless glances on him, and then went back to contemplating the Tiburtino hoods. The boys' mother was a woman from the Marches who had married a mason from Andria during the war, God knows why. She drudged away all the time, poor woman, and led a life that was worse than an animal's. But, as she told the neighbors sometimes at moments when she was catching her breath, she wanted the boys to act as if they had had a decent upbringing. At that moment, she was weeping, first because she had realized that her boys and their dog were no longer living at home, and then because she had had a visit from the *carabinieri,* who were looking for them. But the three boys, each of them her spit and image, inside and out, were too excited just then to spare any thoughts for her. "Hey, Borgo Antì," Begalone called from the foot of the bank, "let's hear you sing that song."

"I don't know that song," Borgo Antico said quickly, his dark face hardening.

"That's not true," said Mariuccio. "He knows it!"

Begalone got mad. He came up and chucked Borgo Antico under the chin. "You're annoying me," he said. Then he added, a menacing look settling on his Arab features, "Sing it if you know what's good for you." Pulling a long face, his head sunk down to his knees, Borgo Antico began singing "The Prisoner" with all his might.

Aldo took advantage of the diversion to go off a little way, as if he wanted to take a nap. He stretched out on the grass, washed clean by the rain the night before and burned by the sun again today, belly down, his face on his crossed arms.

While Borgo Antico was singing, Genesio went down the bank without a word, and Mariuccio and Fido followed him, both sliding down the crumbling slope on all fours. At the water's edge, Genesio stopped a moment, looking abstractedly at the river flowing before him at the foot of the walls of the processing plant, and at the white furrow cut by the flow from the sewer on the opposite bank. Then he began to undress slowly; Mariuccio and Fido, squatting on the ground, watched him respectfully. Carefully, he slipped off his trousers, which were stiff with sweat and dust, his shirt, pink undershirt, shoes, and socks. Slim, a bit skinny even, his shoulder blades sticking out a little, he stood there for a moment, almost naked. Not quite, because he wasn't a shameless little bastard like the Tiburtino kids his own age. He was still wearing his shorts, keeping thoroughly covered, front and rear. "Here," he said to Mariuccio, handing him his clothes, carefully folded and tied in a bundle with his belt. "No, wait a minute," he said shortly. He unloosed the belt, undid the bundle, and took a butt from his pants pocket, and a comb. He lit the butt and as he smoked he combed his hair carefully, asking Mariuccio if the part was straight or crooked, and then gave himself a kind of wave effect over his forehead—black, shining, not a hair out of place. At last, handing back the tied bundle to his brother, he announced drily, as if he were not speaking of himself, "Going to swim across today." Mariuccio looked at him for a moment, aware that something exciting was afoot. Then he began to yell in his puppy-voice, "Hey, Borgo Antì, hey, Borgo Antì!" Borgo Antico hastily sang the remaining words of the song, really stepping on it, and leaned over the edge of the bank without saying anything.

"Hey, Borgo Antì," Mariuccio said hurriedly and gaily, "Genesio says he's going to cross the river today."

Borgo Antico waited in silence for a moment, and then came sliding down the bank on his bottom, right by the swimming-place of sun-baked mud.

"You crossing the river, Genè?" he asked gravely.

"Yep," said Genesio, smiling a little, rather excited.

"Right now?"

"Not right now, later. I'm going to take a rest now."

All three sat down on the black sand, and the dog, seeing them occupied with higher matters that he couldn't grasp, couldn't keep still a single moment, but ran from one to the other, nosing each of them in turn. Genesio, smoking gravely, kept silent for a bit, and then he said to his brothers, "Now, when we're grown up, we're going to kill the old man."

"Me too," said Mariuccio promptly.

"All three of us, together," Genesio assented, "all three of us have to kill him. And then we'll go live somewhere else with Mama."

He spat his butt out into the water, his serious and candid eyes shining wetly.

"He must have beaten her up again this morning," he said. He fell silent again until he could control himself, and then he said in his ordinary toneless, inexpressive voice, "When we're grown up, we'll show him all right.

"Now I'll give it a try," he said then, in the same tone of voice.

"You're going to cross it?" the smallest boy asked excitedly.

"What do you mean, cross it? I'm going to practice."

"You're going all the way out to the middle?" Mariuccio insisted.

"Sure," said Genesio. He rose and scrambled up the bank.

"Where you going?" Mariuccio asked, wondering.

"Farther down," said Genesio, without turning around.

His brothers followed him up the bank and then back down to the water's edge beyond the swimming-place, where Zinzello was finishing the soaping-up process, while, as if to spell him, another poor devil arrived, a balding man with a long beard that half-covered a face that seemed to have been burnt by a fever. It was Alfio Lucchetti, the uncle of that boy Amerigo from Pietralata, the one who had killed himself.

"Where'd all these jokers come from?" Zinzello asked good-humoredly. Alfio, who was still dressed, wearing pin-striped black pants, looked at him, shaking his head ironically, holding his rolled-up towel and soap against his side, a smile swelling out a jaw that was stubbled over with stiff hairs, his sideburns running down below his protruding ears from a head of hair that was combed in a youthful style, although a gray streak showed here and there. Genesio walked into the water, as though he had not been included in Zinzello's remark. He paused for a moment, looking at the river. Then he waded in, his arms raised, till the water was up to his waist, and then he started to swim a quick dog-paddle.

"He's practicing to swim across the river," Mariuccio announced to the grown-ups, full of naïve enthusiasm, looking up at them as if he were staring up at a couple of mountain peaks. But they were discussing their own affairs by now, and they didn't even hear him. Genesio swam to the middle of the stream, where the current made little wavelets, flowing more swiftly and gathering up all the filth of the river—black streaks of oil and a kind of yellow foam that looked as if it were composed of thousands of gobs of spit. Then he turned around, let the current carry him down a bit while he rested, till he had floated past the swimming-place, and then he began to swim back to the bank. A little farther downstream, toward the bridge, he reached some thorny bushes that hung down over the water from the almost sheer bank.

Borgo Antico and Mariuccio ran toward him, not caring where they set their feet, slipping, falling, jumping up again out of the mud, up and down the slippery hump of the swimming-place. The dog followed after, barking, without knowing whether he was supposed to feel worried or pleased.

"Hey, Genesio! Hey, Genesio!" his brothers shouted at him, as if he were ten miles away.

"You didn't do it, huh?" Mariuccio asked tremulously.

"You make me tired," was all Genesio answered. He looked

around in annoyance, darting a swift, ill-tempered glance about him. Then he said, without looking at them, "I told you I was practicing!"

Now that he'd given it a try, he studied the river again, silently estimating the distance. Beyond the far edge of the current, there was another ten-yard stretch to the opposite bank, where the white stripe plunging into the river marked where the flow from the processing plant had cut into the bank. Fido too began to study the situation, seating himself comfortably. He panted open-mouthed, shutting his jaws now and then to swallow, or licking himself. He respected his masters' silence, wearing a slightly dejected expression. He looked as if some son of a bitch had given him one in the eye and swelled it up for him, because it was all white; the left eye had only a bluish ring around it. On that side, his ear hung down limply, while the ear on the other side was pricked up, alert to catch the slightest sound.

Meanwhile the boys sprawled out like hogs in the mud began to show signs of life. Tirillo went and posed, still as a statue, by the water's edge, looking oh so weary, and stretching. Then he was quiet again for a bit, head down, clucking his thick tongue against his palate, looking disgusted. "When's that kid going to take the plunge?" said Caciotta, watching out of the corner of his eye so as not to have to turn around. "Don't you know I was born tired?" said Tirillo resignedly, his eyelids drooping sleepily. Begalone had begun to cough so hard that it looked as if he would be spitting up part of his lungs any minute. "O.k.," Tirillo called. And then, in a sudden burst of energy, "Who's going to jump in with me?" "Jump in yourself, and fuck you too," said Begalone between the spasms of coughing that were skimming off the stuff he had in his lungs. Tirillo lifted his arms with a yell, and did a swan dive, spreading out his legs with all the grace of a duckling. "What a ball-breaker!" Caciotta said, while Tirillo was still beneath the surface.

But just at that moment there was a great rumbling and racket that cut all further comment short. It sounded as if an earthquake were on its way. The noise came from the direction of Tiburtino, swelling along the Via Tiburtina and the shore of the Aniene. From over by the Via Tiburtina came a thunderous noise that sounded as if the roots of the earth were being wrenched loose, a very regular, monotonous thunder, in which now and then could be heard scraping and tearing noises like cries of rage, resounding and then dying away suddenly. It kept on, as if an enormous compressor were pounding away at all the arc of the horizon between the buildings of Tiburtino and the Pecoraro hill, crushing and grinding up everything in its path, like an artillery barrage. Nearer at hand, however, on the river bank, it looked as if a troop of monkeys and parrots had exploded out of the jungle, driven by a forest fire, all screaming at the tops of their lungs, and it wasn't clear whether they were moved to make all that racket by terror or by transports of joy. It was an army of little boys, actually, amounting to half the child-population of Tiburtino, all running like crazy, wearing their good pants and waving the shirts and undershirts that they had stripped off as they ran. You couldn't make out what it was they were shouting in chorus from one group to another, for in their mad dash they had scattered and dispersed all along the bank. But they were rushing forward together with the rumbling noise, and as the source of that uproar began to be identifiable, their shouts became clearer, too. "The *bersaglieri!* The *bersaglieri!*"* they yelled, as the ones in the lead poured into the swimming-place like a landslide, and it could be seen that they didn't give a good goddamn about the *bersaglieri,* but that this was an excuse to raise a little hell. Running like horses with their hair tossing in the wind, Sgarone, Roscietto, and Armandino led all the rest, their faces

* Traditionally, light infantry, trained to maneuver and parade at a run.—*Trans.*

gay and mocking in contrast to their headlong stampede and their wild outcries. It was a show gotten up by the little boys, who felt that they could face up to the older ones because there were so many of them, and they were having a good time cutting up. The human avalanche tore by, raising heavy red dust all along the bare river bank; following the curve of the river and yelling mockingly but with all the steam they had, "The *bersaglieri!*" they turned up toward the Via Tiburtina. The motorized column was already coming up, with dispatch-riders on motorcycles, and armored cars, alternating with trucks full of rows of *bersaglieri* wearing camouflage, their automatic rifles between their legs, and with tanks whose treads kneaded the asphalt pavement as if it were butter. The boys in the lead were already starting to scramble up the bank alongside the road over by the bridge, while the stragglers, a bunch of little pains-in-the-ass including some brats of five or six, had formed ranks and were now marching in step, sarcastically trumpeting the *bersaglieri* march—"Pappappara pappa para, papparappa pappa paara." Swept up by the general enthusiasm, Caciotta too started to run after them, and even Tirillo, who had just emerged from among the oil-streaks and gobs of spit in the river. Borgo Antico and Mariuccio yelled to Genesio, the cords in their necks standing out sharply, "You coming, Genè? There go the tanks!" Genesio shrugged, and as if he hadn't heard them, he sat down abstractedly among the bushes, right where he happened to be at the moment. "You coming, Genè?" the other two went on calling anxiously. Then, seeing that Genesio didn't have the slightest intention of coming, they suddenly started off themselves, trotting after the two big boys toward the bank above the Via Tiburtina, followed by poor Fido, thoroughly confused by now.

The only ones left at the swimming-place were Alfio Lucchetti, off by himself, and looking sullen now that Zinzello had gone; Alduccio, still burying his head in his arms in the dusty earth that was beginning to scorch in earnest; Genesio, lonely as a hermit at the far end of the swimming-place; and Begalone. Begalone was still coughing, letting out scraping and spitting noises that sounded as if they had been made by a ladle knocking about inside a steel drum. His yellow skin was covered with a red flush that hid his freckles; his chest, which looked like the ribs of the crucified Christ, appeared to have boiled meat on its bones instead of ordinary skin. He went to his trousers to pull a handkerchief that was covered with red stains out of a pocket, and, coughing, he pressed it to his mouth. Nobody paid any attention to him. So he went on coughing, cursing and blaspheming. At last the fit passed, and he got up slowly and put the handkerchief back into his pocket, afterward tossing the bundle of clothes away under a bush like so many scraps of rag. Since the coughing spell had made him dizzy and even nauseated—most likely from weakness, since he had scarcely slept the night before—he got the notion that a bath might do him good. He pulled his carcass along the ground, first carefully tying up the bit of string that went around his head like a threadbare ribbon, keeping in place the faded yellow hair that fell down in a long hoodlum cut as far as the first joint in his spine; he moved very slowly because no one was watching him, going up to the foam-covered edge of the water, meaning to slip in and just soak, sort of, like old men when they wash their feet, or Alfio, not far off, who had given up his youthful ambitions and now just used the river as a bathtub. Sticking his feet in the water, he pulled them out again, first one and then the other, with a jerky motion like a chicken, because it felt unexpectedly cold, and he ground his teeth, "Jesus fucking Christ." Then he began to get used to it, and he moved angrily out into the stream, going in slowly until the water was up to his nipples, sticking out of his chest as red as two bits of sealing wax. At last he began to swim, and he paddled around a bit out in the middle of the river. But then he began to feel even worse. His head spun like a stammering woodpecker's, and inside his stomach it felt like dead cats. He thought he was going to faint. He got scared, and began to swim frantically toward the bank. When he set foot on land again, dripping water, he couldn't straighten up. He kneeled down in the mud and began to vomit. Since he had had nothing to eat the day before, the poor bastard had wolfed half a basketful of bread and some spicy sausage this morning. He must have been having trouble digesting it, and now he was heaving his guts out.

That's how the boys who had dashed over to the road to watch the tanks go by, until the very last one had turned up toward Ponte Mammolo, found him. "Begalone's sick!" Caciotta proclaimed loudly when he saw him stretched out on the ground, face-down in the mud. They all ran up then, but he didn't seem to take any notice, lying there with half-shut eyes staring at nothing. Caciotta and Tirillo began to shake him by the shoulders. "Hey, Bègalo, hey, Bègalo, how're you feeling?" He made no answer; his face, covered with filth, was enough to turn your stomach. All around him at least thirty disheveled and sweaty kids pushed and shoved in order to get a better look at him. But Alduccio came up, his face swollen with sleep, and he started to yell, "Give him some room, beat it, you bastards, can't you see he needs air?" He too shook Begalone by the shoulder, and the circle of boys closed again. Begalone said something to himself with a nauseated expression on his face. "What's he saying?" Caciotta asked. "Christ!" said Tirillo, impressed. "Let's wash him," Alduccio decided, and he set about it. Cupping his hands, he got water from the river and dashed it in Begalone's face. Begalone shook his head for a moment like a drunk, and then fell back into his stupor. "Come on!" said Alduccio. The other two helped him, and with a few well-aimed splashes they washed the filth away from Begalone's face and chest. "Now it's up to us," Caciotta mumbled. "We've got to carry him home." Tirillo nodded, with the look of one who's just caught a boot in the head, and a grimace that meant, "Christ, Caciò." They had to make the best of it one way or another. They dragged Begalone bodily a little farther up the bank and left him stretched out while they put their clothes on. Then, surrounded by the audience of excited kids, they dressed him too; he lay limp, and every now and then had a spasm of vomiting. Caciotta grabbed him under the arms, Tirillo took his feet, and that way they began the haul to Tiburtino, stopping every ten yards or so to rest, followed by the train of kids who shoved and jostled to keep as close to the action as they could. Alduccio went with them only a short way along the path, spelling the other two now and then. Just as he was about to turn back, he saw Riccetto coming toward them, obviously in high spirits, all dressed up and walking carefully to keep from getting dust on his perforated white shoes. In his hand he was carrying a new pair of trunks, neatly folded, and his blue shirt flapped over his buttocks.

Then Alduccio ran ahead a little, making up the ground he had lost compared to the procession of kids; he was just in time to hear the first explanations that Riccetto had been sternly demanding. Caciotta and Tirillo were resting and had set Begalone down like Christ brought down from the cross; he began to stir just then, and slowly, assisted by his friends, he stood up. Riccetto looked at him with a pessimistic expression, but when he saw Alduccio, he forgot about Begalone and turned to his cousin with a grin. "Hey, buddy, what's up? Did you fuck up last night?" Alduccio got mad. "Idiot," he said nervously to Riccetto, "you think I'm in the mood for joking? Go make jokes someplace else." His face disfigured with rage, but obviously with a lump in his throat and ready to burst out crying any minute, he turned away and started to walk back toward the swimming-place. "Pissed off, huh?" said Riccetto, following him languidly, full of sarcasm and high spirits. Alduccio turned like a snake. "Go fuck yourself!" he yelled. "Sure, sure," said Riccetto, nodding, "but you know damn well you're going to end up like Lenzetta."

"Just like Lenzetta," he insisted. Lenzetta was in the shit, all right. At the moment he was doing a year in solitary in some prison outside of Rome; he had pulled a thirty-year stretch, no less. One day—maybe he was drunk, or Christ knows what the hell was going on in his head—he had hailed a taxi, driven to a deserted place around the Grotta Rossa, and then, with the pistol he had lifted off Cappellone, he had shot the taxi-driver in order to get the five or six thousand lire the man had in his pocket.

Riccetto fell silent, looking at his cousin, who was walking ahead of him, head down, and then he decided that he'd had his fun, and said, "Come on, it ain't nothing. Buck up, buddy, go on home. It's time, ain't it?" Alduccio looked at him suspiciously, but with an ill-concealed gleam of hope in his eyes. "What do you mean, it ain't nothing?" "It ain't nothing, I tell you," said Riccetto. "I was just kidding. Your mother didn't turn you in. She made up a story about how she hurt herself somehow, some crap like that." Alduccio was silent for a while, still walking toward the swimming-place, thinking. But then he turned, and without saying anything to Riccetto, he went back toward Tiburtino, almost running in order to catch up with the group around Begalone, who was walking by himself now, holding onto Caciotta and Tirillo.

"So long, cousin," said Riccetto tolerantly, waving a hand without turning around.

He went on alone, not hurrying, toward the bend in the river below the processing plant. He started a song, and by the time he had gone through it, there he was on the bank by the swimming-place, where on one side there were the three boys from Ponte Mammolo, out of sight now, and on the other Alfio Lucchetti, who had finished his bath just as if nothing had happened, and was pulling on his old pin-striped trousers.

"Who's that?" Riccetto asked himself, stopping at the edge of the bank. "Hm." He watched him for a bit, and Alfio, his shoulder blades sticking out and his chest bristling with hair, went on dressing, looking mysterious. "Aaaah!" Riccetto said to himself then, remembering that he had seen him at Amerigo's funeral, and he'd been so bothered about him. "Right, I remember now!" And he began calmly to undress, paying no more attention to the man, just throwing a last glance his way when he went off, and thinking, "One of those born losers."

As he was slipping off his trousers, holding the legs high so as to keep them out of the dust, he whistled contentedly and talked to himself, complaining in a low voice about the holes in his socks, or congratulating himself on the fine knit shirt he'd gotten himself. "Just great," he said with conviction, looking at it as he folded it up.

"I'll go to that asshole of a boss," he said when he was in his shorts, "get my money off him, eat, and after that, life with a capital L. Things are looking up, Riccè."

As he drew up that pleasant program, he walked, hands on his hips, to a spot just above the swimming-place, and from there he caught sight of the boss's three sons, over to the left among the bushes. Fido ran over to greet him, mad with affection, jumping up as high as Riccetto's chest and flourishing his forepaws. But Riccetto petted him absently; he was only too pleased to have caught sight of the three boys down there. His good spirits rose even higher. He didn't care all that much for swimming by himself in that quiet and lonely place that was getting even more so as noon came on. But there was another reason for the gaiety that lit up his already good-humored face under the clipped curls. He looked at them. They had noticed him, too, but they said nothing. Riccetto went on watching them. They gave no sign. He stared at them; facing away from him, every now and then they stole a look at him out of the corners of their eyes. Then, when all three had their eyes on him, Riccetto broke the silence, and raised one hand and moved it up and down balled into a fist, as if to threaten them with a beating. The three kids looked at him in a rage, shrugging their shoulders.

"That's right, keep it up," said Riccetto.

"What do you want, anyway?" Genesio burst out, and then withdrew into silence again, like a porcupine curling up.

Riccetto was having the time of his life, and instead of answering right away, he went on staring at them, nodding and twisting his mouth.

At last he exclaimed loudly, "A fine business."

"What business?" Mariuccio asked, speaking for all of them, for since he was the youngest, he felt he was least responsible.

"What business?" Riccetto shouted, his eyes widening. "Jesus, you guys sure got nerve, I'll say that!"

"Yeah, what business?" the boy repeated innocently.

"Why, you little bastard!" Riccetto said harshly, using his most adult tones to suggest paternal reproach. "You mean you've got the nerve to deny it?"

Genesio began to be curious too. Scratching at his foot with a stick, all hunched over, he said, "To deny what?"

"Wha-at?" said Riccetto, and in spite of the well-nigh tragic character of what he was thinking about, a wave of laughter struck him, so that he bubbled like a stewpot.

"You roast people's feet on them, that's what," he yelled, bursting into laughter at the expression he'd just invented on the spot, "and then you say what did we do?" He went on laughing uproariously, almost rolling on the ground over the roasted feet business—even though Piattoletta hadn't been really roasted but just browned a little. The three brothers didn't understand a fucking thing of what he was saying.

"What are you trying to say?" Genesio asked in a hoarse voice.

"You know damn well, you little hood," said Riccetto, calming down a bit.

"We left home, so what?" Genesio admitted without flinching. Riccetto looked at him. He hadn't known about that.

"Oh," he said, "so you left home, did you? That shows you knew that the cops were looking for you all right!"

Genesio was surprised by *that* bit of news, but, hunched over with his chest against his knees, he kept his surprise to himself, and began at once to think things over. But not Borgo Antico and Mariuccio. The smallest one chirped, "It isn't true, the *carabinieri* aren't looking for us!"

"Say it isn't true all you like," said Riccetto teasingly "but you'll see whether it's true or not when they come grab you!"

"Ah, dry up," said Mariuccio.

"And why are the *carabinieri* looking for us?" Genesio asked casually.

"Why?" Riccetto asked sternly. "You got the gall to ask why? What did you do yesterday over by Pecoraro? Hey? Tell me, why don't you?"

"Well, what did we do?" Genesio asked, looking him in the eye almost as if he were daring him.

Riccetto frowned as if he were hurt by all that obstinacy. "Who was it burned Piattoletta at the stake over by Pecoraro?"

At that sally, Genesio was dumbfounded. But then he shrugged, as if putting an end to the discussion, and said in a low voice, "How should I know?"

"You, that's who it was!" said Riccetto, treacherous and triumphant.

"Ah!" said Genesio, shrugging and looking away, his eyes burning under his black forelock.

"No, it wasn't us," said Mariuccio.

"It's no use denying it, you know," said Riccetto, getting a bigger kick out of it every minute. "They got witnesses, if you please."

"What witnesses?" asked Genesio.

"What?" said Riccetto. "Sixty guys seen you yesterday evening, Roscietto, Sgarone, Armandino, all the boys from block 2—what are you trying to pull on me?"

"It wasn't us," said Mariuccio, now almost beside himself.

"We'll see when they put you in jail whether or not you have the nerve to deny it," Riccetto yelled. Mariuccio, outraged, choking with emotion, felt his chin begin to shake, and he repeated, "It wasn't us," already crying.

Seeing that he was crying, Riccetto dropped the game, and still standing above the swimming-place, he began to sing, crushing the three boys down there with his high spirits.

"Go ahead, cry," he said to Mariuccio every once in a while, interrupting his song for a moment. But he began to feel a little uncomfortable about it. He remembered how it used to be when he was like them, how it was when the big boys from the housing projects used to gang up on him, and he used to go around with Marcello and Agnoletto, and everybody ignored him or scorned him. He remembered the time they stole the money off the blind man and went off to go swimming at Ciriola's, and they'd hired the boat, and he'd saved that swallow that was drowning under the Ponte Sisto.

The noon whistles sounded in the distance.

"Let's take our swim," Riccetto told himself out loud. "Or else the boss, and I hope he croaks, will be all tanked up, and I can go whistle for my money. That's all I need, to have to spend the day without a single lira!"

And so saying, he took a header into the river, without paying any attention to Mariuccio, who had already brightened up again, and yelled after him, "Hey, you know Genesio's going to cross the river too?"

Genesio said, "Shut up," and instead of going in himself, he began to think about important things. But then he got interested in what Riccetto was doing out in the river, and he began to watch him intently, as Borgo Antico and Mariuccio were. He went to the water's edge, and half turning toward his brothers, who were absorbed by Riccetto's exhibition, he said quietly, "We'll go home afterward. It's better that way. Otherwise, Mama's going to cry." That decision hurriedly announced, he could watch Riccetto in peace. He was really kicking up a fuss in the water. He worked his arms like flails, beating at the water and raising columns of foam; he put his head under water and raised up his rear end and his legs like a feeding duck; he did the dead man's float on his back, singing at the top of his lungs. Then, turning around suddenly, he swam back to the shore, clambered up it dripping, and putting on a show for the kids, who were watching him open-mouthed, he did a swan-dive into the water.

When his head rose above the surface, he began to swim toward the far shore with long strokes. Without saying anything, Genesio floundered through the mud to a spot below the swimming-place where the water was up to his chest, and took off, dog-paddling swiftly.

"You crossing the river, Genè?" Mariuccio and Borgo Antico called after him excitedly. But he didn't hear them, couldn't hear them, swimming after Riccetto with his mouth shut tight and his head turned to one side so as not to swallow any water.

He passed through the strong current, and was carried downstream a few yards, along with the garbage, and then, still moving his hands swiftly under the water, his head turned to one side, he swam across the far half of the stream. Meanwhile, Riccetto had already reached the other bank, beneath the white stripe made by the acids flowing from the processing plant, and he plunged into the water at once, swimming back as fast as he had come. He reached the shore in a few strokes, doing the dead man's float now and then, and starting to sing once more, he went up the bank above the swimming-place and singing away, began to do gymnastics in order to dry off.

The sun was at its zenith, scorching, and all around below the processing plant it felt as if the air were on fire, and on both the fields and the road, with the tanks rumbling off in the distance, the numbing silence of high noon was descending. In a few minutes, instead of being dry, Riccetto was in a sweat.

Genesio was still on the far bank. He was sitting down in his customary position under the discharge-pipe of the processing plant, on the thick white slime. Above him, like a landslide in hell, the bushy slope crowned by the factory wall rose up, with cylinders and tanks, green or maroon, jutting out, and a bunch of metal boxes on which the sunlight looked almost black, it was so intense.

Mariuccio and Borgo Antico watched their brother squatting over there like a Bedouin. "Aren't you coming back, Genè?" Mariuccio called in his child's voice, still clasping Genesio's rolled-up clothes tightly against his chest.

"I'm coming," Genesio called over, without straining his voice, still sitting in the same position, his head down to his knees. Riccetto was dressing slowly, pulling on his socks and taking care that they weren't inside out. "Now I'll go tell the *carabinieri* you're here," he yelled cheerfully at Genesio when he was nearly ready, "and your father, too!"

As he went off, another wave of well-being swept over him. But this time he contented himself with making the customary menacing gesture with his fist at the boys who were watching him suspiciously from the foot of the bank. As he was starting off, half-turned around toward the boys, he happened to look toward the factory wall, and high up in a small window lost among the great metal cylinders of the tanks, he spotted the face of the watchman's daughter, who had suddenly begun to polish the panes. "Will you look at that!" said Riccetto, who began to get excited on the spot. He went on a few steps, then thought better of it and took another look, then took a few more steps toward the bridge and changed his mind again. She was still up there, polishing away at the glass, which was gleaming in the bright air as if it had turned to liquid. "Fuck it, I'll stick around a while," he said. He stopped, and slipped between two clumps of brush and a patch of nettles, so that he couldn't he seen by the boys down at the river's edge, or by people going by on the Via Tiburtina, though nobody was stirring in the hot sun at that hour. All that could be heard was the sound of cars, and in the distance the rumbling, rending noise of the *bersaglieri* tanks.

When he was hidden behind the bushes, he took his pants off, pretending that he had to wring out his shorts again. He stood there naked, half-concealed, looking at the broad in the window and trying to get her attention.

"Hey, Genè, aren't you coming back over here?" Mariuccio kept calling sadly.

Genesio didn't answer the summons. Then he suddenly jumped into the water, swam as far as the main current, and then turned right back and sat down gloomily once more under the bank and the factory wall.

"Aren't you coming back, Genè?" Mariuccio asked again, disappointed at the turn of events.

"I'm going to stay here a while," Genesio said. "It's nice here."

"Come on, swim back!" Mariuccio insisted, the tendons standing out on his throat with the effort of calling. Borgo Antico began to call him too, and Fido barked, jumping around, but with his muzzle pointing at the far bank, as if he too were calling Genesio.

Then Genesio stood up, stretched a bit—something he never did—and yelled, "I'll count up to thirty and then dive in." He stood silently counting, then stared at the water, his eyes burning below his still neatly-combed black hair. At last he took a belly-whopper into the river. He swam rapidly almost to the middle of the stream just at the level of the factory, where the river turned toward the bridge that carried the Via Tiburtina. But the current was strong there, eddying back toward the bank on which the factory stood. Going over, Genesio had passed through the current easily enough, but coming back was another story. Dog-paddling the way he was doing amounted to treading water in that current, not to making headway. Held in the current, he began to be carried down toward the bridge.

"Come on, Genè!" his brothers yelled from the swimming-place, unable to make out why Genesio wasn't moving toward them. "Come on, let's go home!"

But he couldn't get past the current running like a stream within the yellow river, full of foam, sawdust, and burned oil. He stayed within it, and instead of drawing near the bank, he was carried farther down toward the bridge. Borgo Antico, Mariuccio, and the dog tumbled down the bank and began to scramble downstream, on all fours when they couldn't make it upright through the black mud at the edge of the river, falling and getting up again, following behind Genesio, who was being carried faster and faster toward the bridge. Thus Riccetto, as he was showing off for the girl, who went on polishing the window, dim as a shadow, saw all three boys go by below him—the two little ones tumbling among the bushes and yelling in terror, and Genesio out in the river, still paddling swiftly without gaining an inch. Riccetto got up, took a few steps, naked as he was, down toward the water through the nettles, and stopped to stare at what was happening before his eyes. At first he didn't catch on, and he thought they were fooling. Then he understood, and he tore down the slope, slipping and sliding, but in the same moment he realized that it was useless. To jump in there beneath the bridge would just mean you were tired of living; nobody could get away with it there. He stopped, pale as a corpse. Genesio wasn't fighting it any more, poor kid, just thrashing his arms aimlessly, but still he did not cry out for help. Every now and then he sank below the surface, and came up again farther downstream. At last, when he was quite close to the bridge, where the current split and foamed over the rocks, he went down again, without crying out, and only for an instant did his little black head near the surface again.

His hands shaking, Riccetto slipped on the pants he had been holding under his arm, not looking at the factory window now, and stood here a moment longer, uncertain what to do. He could hear Borgo Antico and Mariuccio screaming and weeping down by the bridge, Mariuccio still clutching Genesio's pants and undershirt to his chest. Already the two boys were starting to climb up the bank, helping themselves along with their hands.

"Be better to beat it out of here," Riccetto said, almost weeping himself, walking hurriedly down the path toward the Via Tiburtina. He went on almost at a run so as to reach the bridge before the two boys did. "I got to look out for Riccetto," he thought. He scrambled upward, slipping and sliding, and grasping at the bushes on the slope that was covered with loose dust and burnt stubble, got to the top, and without looking back, turned onto the bridge. He managed to get away unobserved, for in all the lonely countryside stretching as far as the white jumble of houses in Pietralata and Monte Sacro, and on the Via Tiburtina, there wasn't a soul around at that moment. There wasn't even a car going by, or one of the old buses that ran through that section. In the enormous silence, all you could hear was a tank, lost somewhere beyond the playing fields in Ponte Mammolo, plowing up the horizon with its roar.